Arcane Cube

JJ Michael

To the seekers, the dreamers, and the light-bearers.

"Magic is believing in yourself. If you can do that, you can make anything happen."—Johann Wolfgang von Goethe.

Chapter 1
Tiff

The amber sun dipped below the horizon, its golden light filtering through the slatted wood boards of the Lotterland's farmhouse porch. Tiff leaned against one of the posts, gazing at the wheat field that stretched as far as the eye could see. She couldn't shake the feeling—lately, something out there felt…off.

A series of enormous crop circles had appeared overnight in the past month. Perfect circles, some over twenty feet in diameter, the wheat stalks flattened into swirling geometric patterns. Sheriff Al Benson had come to inspect them each time, but he could find no evidence of vehicles, footprints, or any other clues to point to the pranksters he assumed were responsible.

Tiff knew better, having seen and sensed unearthly things in this valley that defied all logic and reason. There in the quiet, the shadows whispered, echoing memories of the inexplicable sights and sounds haunting these plains—whispers that twisted in the wind, shadows that moved against the grain.

The screen door creaked open behind her. Tiff remained facing forward, feeling the familiar touch of her father's calloused hands on her shoulders. Lincoln Lotterland, a man of imposing stature and keen eyes, stood behind her, embodying years of labor in his firm grip.

"Are there any new ones today?" he asked, his voice gravelly from years of long days and little sleep.

"So far, nothing," Tiff said, leaning into his touch. "I know you're worried about the damage and how it might affect our profits. We're barely scraping by as it is." Her words hung in the air, threatening to choke out hope. "I can get a job after school, and summer break from school will be here," she offered.

Lincoln let out a heavy sigh that carried all the weight of the day's worries. "Tiff, I'm happy that you helped me on the farm, and I don't want you worrying. This land has been in our family for generations, and no one is taking it away from us."

Tiff turned to face him. "Then we do something drastic. Those crop circles could be our ticket out of this mess. Why not follow the example of some farmers in the UK? Charge people to see them and then sell our story to a newspaper or magazine."

Lincoln frowned, shaking his head. "We don't know when the crop circles are going to appear, and I don't hold with all that paranormal nonsense. Besides, I don't want a bunch of strangers tramping through our fields."

"But Dad, what if..."

A loud crash of thunder interrupted her, and within seconds, rain pelted the porch in stinging sheets. Tiff and her dad hurried inside. But Tiff's mind was already racing. Nevertheless, before taking any other action, she had to find the answer to these peculiar events.

Was someone trying to ravage these breathtaking plains that stretch for miles? Her father and others worked hard to grow wheat. Wheat gave them food, money, and pride. The farmers and their families cherished their land and crops, caring for them with fidelity and devotion. The wheat would be sold to mills and bakeries or reserved for personal use. Tiff knew what the damage from the crop circles could mean—the loss of their farm, the only home she'd ever known. But there was more, something her father hadn't said. Something related to her mother, Sarah, who had vanished when she was a toddler.

"Dad, did the crop circles ever happen when Mom was here, or did they have something to do with her disappearance?" The words tumbled out faster than she intended, each one edged with a mix of hope and fear.

Lincoln, his heart heavy with unresolved emotions, turned to her. "Let it go, Tiff. What's done is done. We're not having this conversation about your mother again."

"Dad, please answer this one question."

Lincoln's jaw tightened. He kept his eyes on the window, where wind and rain blurred the view beyond. "I don't know," he said finally, his voice low. "Coffee might help." He left the room, leaving Tiff alone with the sound of the rain and a thousand questions.

The following day, Tiff, with a mix of anticipation and anxiety, snagged one of the few parking spaces in front of Wheatfield High School. Although the school was small, with only three hundred students from grades nine to twelve, it had all the usual features: classrooms on the second floor, the library, gym, and cafeteria on the first, a well-kept lawn where students lounged during lunch hour, and even a football field and track at the back.

As she climbed out of her truck, Tiff noticed that everyone was dressed in blue and white—the school colors—which meant some event was planned for the day. She didn't participate in school activities, except for the mandatory quarterly tornado drills.

Slinging her backpack on, Tiff walked into first-period English with her usual nonchalant stride, masking the quick thud of her heartbeat at the thought of presenting her essay. She slipped into a seat at the back, avoiding eye contact with Mrs. Blavatnik.

Several students gave their oral presentations before her. Tiff slouched lower in her chair, but there was no escaping Hawkeye—the nickname students had given their sharp-eyed teacher.

Tiff's hands trembled as she adjusted the stack of note cards, each crammed with neat, tiny handwriting. When her turn came, she walked to the front of the class, eyes darting across the sea of indifferent faces, and forced herself to begin. Her voice, clear and confident when alone, now barely rose above a whisper. As she stumbled over a complex sentence about censorship and intellectual freedom, a low chuckle rippled through the classroom. A warm flush spread across her cheeks, her stomach knotting up as she concentrated on the next card. The moment the final word left her lips, she rushed back to her desk, knocking into two desks that seemed to loom out of nowhere. She sank into her seat, heart pounding, willing herself to disappear into the floor.

As Mrs. Blavatnik made her way down the aisle between desks, she brushed past Tiff's. "See me after class," she said quietly. Tiff's stomach dropped.

After the bell rang, Tiff dragged herself to Mrs.

Blavatnik's desk. The teacher glanced up from a stack of papers, peering at Tiff over the rims of her reading glasses.

"Tiff, this is one of the best essays I've read in years. Your insights into Bradbury's themes of censorship and intellectual freedom were sophisticated. I'm disappointed you didn't give this essay the presentation it deserved."

Tiff gazed at her shoes, scuffing the floor with her toe. "I didn't think anyone would be interested in it, really," she mumbled.

"Nonsense. You have a first-rate mind; you're passionate about these texts. Don't be afraid to show that." Mrs. Blavatnik gave Tiff her essay, which was decorated with a bold A+ and a B- for presentation.

"Thank you, Mrs. Blavatnik."

As Tiff walked to her second-period class, she vowed to embrace her talents instead of downplaying them. As she entered the classroom, her newfound confidence quickly faltered under the weight of curious stares and whispered comments from her classmates. Many were murmuring about the latest fake crop circle stories linked to her family's farm.

Tiff was feeding the horses that evening when her father came out to join her. "How was school today, kiddo?"

"Fine." As usual, she didn't want to boast about her success in English class—or mention the rumors that seemed to choke the air around her. Earlier, as she moved through the hallways, students had glanced her way, whispering and sharing snatches of conversation about the crop circles. Some of them stared openly.

"Tiff, I apologize for my outburst last night when you

asked me questions about your mother's disappearance. I thought I had told you everything."

"I've been thinking about searching for her again and thought you might remember something else."

"Everyone tried to locate her, including the police and the FBI. But she was never seen again. I still remember the pain of her disappearance; I even became a suspect in the case. And then there was you—a toddler I had to care for. Let it be, Tiff."

She nearly dropped the feed bucket in shock. "Why don't you want me to find her?"

"It's not that I don't want you to find your mother. I don't want anything to happen to you. Your mother, Sarah, was a free spirit and dabbled in things. People in Wheatfield thought she and her family were sinful in the eyes of the Lord because they were supposedly involved in witchcraft."

"Do you believe that?"

"It's complex and confusing. Sarah was a different but good-hearted person who got caught up with the wrong group, and they led her astray."

"I don't remember you mentioning any group. Do you remember who they were?"

"No." His expression darkened with old pain. "As I said, let it go."

Tiff couldn't do that. The ache of loss and longing inside her ran deep.

After a moment, Lincoln put an arm around Tiff's shoulders. "I'm sorry I can't tell you more, but I'm here for you."

She blinked back tears and leaned into her father's embrace.

That night, Tiff lay in bed, staring at the ceiling and thinking of her mother. She couldn't help but wonder if she looked like her mother, or if they had anything in common beyond blood.

Did they share the same crooked smile or a penchant for impulsiveness? Would she ever find out? With a sigh, Tiff sat up and turned on the lamp on her nightstand. She pulled a worn shoebox out from under the bed and lifted the lid.

Inside were the remnants of her search for answers: printouts of unsolved missing persons cases from eighteen years ago, lists of women's shelters and hippie communes within a 200-mile radius, and a map marked with multicolored dots showing the locations she wanted to investigate. There were so many places Sarah could have gone.

She had only been able to contribute a little to the search so far, but she wasn't ready to give up. Tiff picked up a colored pen, her hand hesitating over the next town— not ready to mark it, but not ready to let it go either.

A tear slipped down her cheek, the cool trace of it a stark contrast to the warmth building inside her chest. It was a feeling she couldn't quite understand, a mix of sadness and an inexplicable sense of urgency. Deep down, something whispered to her, a gentle yet persistent voice that refused to be silenced. It told her that her mother was still out there and not dead, somewhere, possibly needing her help. Yawning, Tiff replaced the lid on the box and pushed it beneath her bed. An extended school day loomed before her, yet her thoughts were elsewhere.

The following day, Tiff pulled into the school parking lot and spotted Maddie leaning against her beat-up Honda, staring at her phone. Maddie was the only person who knew about Tiff's search for her mother and had always been supportive of it. They had been friends for as long as Tiff could remember, bonding over their love of sci-fi books and martial arts movies.

Maddie waved as Tiff parked beside her. "Hey, did you finish that History homework last night? I got stuck on the last question."

"Yeah, I can help you with that at lunch." Tiff grabbed her backpack from her truck and slung it over one shoulder, glancing around the parking lot. Most students traveled in packs, laughing and joking on their way to school. But she and Maddie had always been outsiders, and Tiff preferred it that way. She'd no use for fake friends complicating her life.

Maddie fell into step beside her. "Any new leads on the crop circles or your mom?"

"Nothing yet. But I'm not giving up."

They walked through the school's front entrance, going through the security checkpoint. The familiar smell of linoleum filled the air, along with the buzz of early-morning chatter and lockers slamming shut.

"Did you sleep last night? Your eyes have dark circles. I worry about you."

"Some," Tiff said, shrugging it off. "I'm okay; don't worry."

The warning bell rang, and students filtered into their classrooms.

"Come over after school? We can practice some Aikido throws if you want." Aikido was one of her few outlets for her restless energy.

Maddie nodded. "Sorry, Tiff, but I have something else to do." She squeezed Tiff's arm before heading to Calculus, her strawberry-scented blonde ponytail swishing behind her.

Tiff watched her go, and a heavy feeling settled in her

chest. This was the third or fourth time Maddie had put her off. Was she losing her?

Tiff pushed the downcast feeling aside as she hurried to class. She had work to do—a mystery to solve. She would only stop once she found the answers. Her tough exterior hid a fire inside, and it would keep burning until the truth came to light.

Chapter 2
Black Shadow

In a corner of the Red Lion Pub, a conspicuous stranger lingered, his pale skin and stark black suit contrasting sharply with the rustic ambiance. He sat alone, feigning interest in a newspaper while sipping his coffee. Dark sunglasses masked his eyes, adding an air of mystery that didn't quite blend in with the local crowd.

Without warning, a message flickered to life on the glossy surface of the napkin holder—an innovative yet typical display method for Order of the Black Shadow. The words "Code red" pulsed on the screen, followed by a directive that chilled him to the bone. "Portal activity detected in sector 7B. Proceed to the coordinates and investigate. Do not engage. Report back ASAP."

Sector 7B was infamous: a wheat field where, centuries ago, a portal had ripped open the fabric of reality, unleashing a tide of dark agents that devastated the crops and claimed many human lives. The Light agents managed to close it, but not without a fierce battle between the Light and Dark forces. This confrontation had become the stuff of legend among Nephilimbug's fellow agents in the Dark Order. A tale the elders spoke of only in hushed tones.

As Nephilimbug prepared to leave, another message blinked into existence, overlaying the first. The new command was even more secretive and critical: "Priority objective: Locate the artifact known as 'the Cube. Assess whether the target 'Tiff' is an agent of the Order of L.V.X. and confirm possession of the artifact. Surveillance has indicated that her mother may have passed significant assets to her. Proceed with caution."

The Order of Darkness had been monitoring Tiff's family since she was a baby, suspecting that her mother had ties to the Order of L.V.X. Her sudden disappearance years ago had not ended their vigilance; if anything, it had intensified it. Now, with the resurgence of portal activity and the potential involvement of the cube, Nephilimbug's mission carried an urgency that transcended a simple reconnaissance.

Equipped with this new information, Nephilimbug's resolve hardened. This mission was more than a mere check on an old portal; it was a critical investigation into a legacy of light that might be rekindling right under their noses. If Tiff truly possessed the cube, it could shift the balance of power between the Orders. His superiors had made it clear: failure was not an option.

Nephilimbug slid off the worn leather seat, his mind seething over the last command from the Order —a trivial task that did nothing to advance his standing. Ambitious and restless, he yearned not only for a place in the leadership but also to ascend to the position of supreme leader one day. As he tossed a few coins onto the table for his drink, his fingers lingered on the cold metal. Each coin clinked, reinforcing the loneliness of his path—a constant battle to assert his worth in a realm that seemed to undervalue his potential.

He stepped out into the drizzling rain. Outside, the city was a mix of shadow and fog, the streetlamps casting eerie halos in the mist. Nephilimbug turned down a narrow alleyway, his footsteps echoing off the ancient brick walls that loomed on either side. He was headed for a place not marked on any map, a place shrouded in secrecy, known only to those with the right connections-or the right blood-line. Its name whispered in hushed tones, its location a puzzle waiting to be solved.

At the end of the alley, an unassuming black door was tucked beneath the staircase of an old Victorian building, infamous amongst the few who knew of its true nature. Known as The Dwelling, it was rumored to be haunted, a site of numerous unexplained disappearances. To Nephilimbug, it was simply a means to an end.

He drew a small, ornate key from his pocket, its intricate engravings glinting in the dim light, the metal cold and heavy in his hand. Inserting it into the lock, the door gave a soft click, and he pushed it open. The air inside was musty, thick with the scent of mold and something else—something decayed.

The room was small, its walls lined with shelves filled with odd trinkets and dusty books. In the center, a spiral staircase, its steps worn with the weight of countless explorers, descended into darkness. Nephilimbug, his heart pounding with anticipation, made his way down, each step creaking under his weight, the sound amplifying through the chamber until he reached the lower echelon. Here, the air grew colder, and the darkness seemed to swallow the light from his torch, as if the staircase were leading him into the depths of a forgotten world —a world untouched by time and human presence.

At the center of the room stood a stone circle, with runes etched deep into its surface. Nephilimbug stepped into the circle and pulled a vial containing a swirling, luminescent liquid from his coat. Uncorking it, he poured the contents onto the ground, where it sizzled and sparked, illuminating the runes with a ghostly glow.

He spoke an incantation, his voice low and resonating against the stone walls. The air within the circle stirred a wind that seemed to come from nowhere, intensifying until it howled through the chamber like a living thing. Then, with a sound like thunder, a flash of darkness enveloped him, and the stone circle's interior seemed to dissolve into the darkness. When the darkness cleared, Nephilimbug found himself standing in a very different place. The air was hot and dry, carrying the scent of wheat and earth.

Wheatfield, Kansas. He had arrived.

Nephilimbug stepped out of the circle of runes, now a faint outline in the dirt, and looked around at the vast expanse of swaying golden wheat. He donned the Visioscope, a pair of sleek, metallic goggles covering his entire face. Thin wires and circuitry ran along the sides, connecting to a small processing unit on the side of his head. Through these goggles, he could detect and observe the energy waves in the atmosphere that were invisible to the human eye. Nephilimbug scanned the horizon, but everything appeared normal—too normal. Driven by instinct, he ventured deeper into the field, the wheat whispering against his suit as he walked.

Reaching the designated location, he knelt and pressed his ear against the soil. It was inexplicably warm, pulsating faintly like a subdued heartbeat. Nephilimbug's fingers traced the remnants of a crop circle that had once shielded the portal, its protective magic still lingering in the air.

Suddenly, a sharp gust of wind whipped around him,

and he spun to face a crackling rift in the air, its edges shimmering with an ominous white light. Muttering a curse, Nephilimbug realized the gravity of the situation. Lightning—a favored weapon of the Brotherhood of Light—threatened from the glowing fissure. He knew he should retreat, but his resolve hardened. Tired of being underestimated by his superiors and yearning to prove his worth beyond being the son of the slain warrior god Nunanki, he steeled himself for confrontation.

Despite the dramatic crackle of lightning and his braced anticipation, the field remained silent and unchanged. The wheat continued to sway in the breeze, undisturbed by the celestial theatrics. Nephilimbug stood alone, his expectations for a confrontation unmet.

As he retreated, strategizing his next move, Nephilimbug muttered curses against the constraints of his commanders. His heritage demanded respect, yet here he was, scurrying through the wheat like any other operative. The wind carried his words away, echoing his frustration across the empty field.

Nephilimbug's past did not always involve serving the Dark Forces. His name was Lucas, and his mother was of the Earth. She would tell him stories of her life on Earth and how his father captured her and brought her to Nebulore, a planet controlled by the Dark Forces. He had spent his childhood on Nebulore. He hardly ever saw his father, who had often been in battle with the Light Force and was killed in battle.

One day, he was playing with a friend in a nearby cave when they heard the landing of ships. Nephilimbug listened to a voice warning him not to venture out of the cave's safety. He begged his friend not to go, but he ran off to join the others. Nephilimbug hid as the Light agents raided the village with their light weapons, taking his family and others aboard their ships. A part of him wanted to call out to his mother, but another part was fearful of the light agents.

Nephilimbug waited in the cave for weeks until a team from the dark forces arrived to rescue him. From that point on, he became a loyal follower of the Order of the Black Shadow. The elder leader, Ute, renamed him Nephilimbug and warned him never to reveal his physical form to the Earthlings. The people mocked him by calling him a Crossbreed or the ugly one. Nephilimbug set out to prove himself to his new family.

He forfeited his autonomy by swearing loyalty to the Order of Darkness. Once he reached the appropriate age, he was initiated into the role of investigator and spy agent. Because of his ability to transform his body into that of a human, he was mostly assigned to the planet Gaia—a beautiful, seductive, and dangerously unstable world—where he carried out his missions with silent determination. One day, Nephilimbug vowed he would rule not only Gaia, but also Nebulore.

Chapter 3
Hillary Hill

It was night, and Lincoln and Tiff were perched atop Hillary Hill, studying the wheat field below them. Other than the nocturnal sounds of animals and insects, they kept quiet to avoid drawing any attention. Lincoln quietly swigged some coffee out of a thermos and glanced at Tiff, huddled in her blanket to stay warm, with Chip, her mixed-breed dog, at her side.

He was lost in thought as he admired his daughter; her beauty and strength reminded him of his late wife, Sarah. He was worried that the crop circle had something to do with Sarah. She had always been drawn to this field and would often run through the wheat, much like a wild animal, with speed and grace.

Lincoln asked her, "What are you looking for?"

"Answers, my love, answers."

"Answers to what? I don't understand. Spending all your free time in the field is driving me crazy. Will you please tell me what's going on?"

"It's complicated and confusing."

That was all she would say. Sometimes, she would stand in one spot as if waiting for something to happen.

Lincoln's mind drifted back to those early years with Sarah. Things only worsened after they got married. So many nights, she would steal out of the house when she assumed he was asleep and return before he woke. He never asked her where she was or what she was doing. Driven by jealousy, he followed her one evening.

Lincoln froze, his jaw clenched in horror and rage, when he found her. Sarah was in the middle of what used to be a wheat field; it had been transformed into an odd circle. Clad in a flowing white gown, Sarah was a vision of beauty, gently swaying to an unseen melody as she extended her arms toward the luminous full moon. Rachel, her sister, stood beside her, and a guy was next to her. Lincoln tried to step closer, but an invisible barrier had formed. No matter how hard he pushed against it, he couldn't move it. Paralyzed with fear, Lincoln ran away from the field without looking back.

When Sarah told him she was pregnant, he begged her not to go to the field at night for the sake of their unborn child. Sarah complied with his request until Tiff was close to two years old. She left one night and never returned.

Chip let out a low rumble, startling Lincoln. Glancing down the slope, he spotted a crop circle carved into the ground below.

"Damn, right under my eye," Lincoln shouted out.

Tiff bolted up, and Lincoln pointed wordlessly to the sight before them. As Tiff pulled out her phone to snap a few photos, the device refused to turn on. They remained still, their eyes fixed on the field for the slightest sign of movement, yet there was none.

As she gazed in awe at the enigmatic display, a sudden vision appeared in her mind of two distinct groups of beings, easily distinguished by the color of their robes—one wore white and the other black. They were locked in a fierce battle at the entrance of a swirling vortex of rainbow light. The vision disappeared as quickly as it had come, leaving Tiff grasping for more details but finding the memory slipping away.

"Did you see or hear anything?" Lincoln's voice startled her back into reality.

"Nothing," she said. "My phone wouldn't work either."

"I don't understand how they keep getting away with this."

"Dad, Maddie and I can stay up some nights to keep an eye on the area." Though she wasn't sure if Maddie would be available, her friend always seemed to have something to do lately.

"No, I'm calling the sheriff," he said with an anxious sigh.

Sheriff Al Benson, two of his deputies, and a stranger showed up the next day, staring at the space before them.

"Lincoln, this is Lucas Nephilimbug. He's a federal agent investigating the crop circles and other strange phenomena."

The two men shook hands.

"And this is his daughter, Tiff." The sheriff nodded at her, and Tiff gave the sheriff and Nephilimbug a faint grin.

"By the way, Tiff, there's been some talk on social media about mysterious crop circles around your family farm. Can you tell me anything about that?"

"I'm not aware of any posts."

"Stop right there, Sheriff." Lincoln squared off with

him. "If you're implying my daughter's involved, you'd better have more than social media rumors."

"I'm covering all the bases here. Some young people are becoming influencers on social media by using gimmicks to attract attention."

"Before you accuse Tiff of this nonsense, Sheriff, I want Mr. Nephilimbug to know this isn't the first time the crops have been tampered with. During the time of the first settlers here, the wheat was ruined, families abandoned their farms, and rumors swirled among the townspeople about dark shadows spooking the livestock. I hope this isn't starting up again."

"That's an ancient legend. There's no proof about any of those things happening," Sheriff Benson added.

"The circles were here yesterday and thrashed. As you can see, some of the wheat has been damaged." Lincoln glared at the sheriff.

Tiff turned to face Nephilimbug. His pupils matched the darkness of his hair, and his skin was as pale and smooth as alabaster. Nephilimbug's gaze was cold, aggressive, and steady. Tiff attempted to avoid his stare but found herself captivated by his intense, dark eyes. She had never felt so insignificant and exposed.

The warm touch of her father's arm broke her free from the spell.

"Mr. Lotterland, here's my card. If the crop circles appear, please take photos and call me if anything else occurs."

Tiff glanced at Nephilimbug and saw a dark mist emanating as he gave her father the card. Tiff wanted to grab the card and burn it. But Lincoln glanced at it and then shoved it into his pocket.

Nephilimbug smirked at her, which bothered her even more.

Biting her lower lip, an old habit she had shaken, Tiff asked Nephilimbug, "Do you think this has something to do with UFOs or what is happening with the crop circles in the UK?"

"So, you do know about the UK crop circles. The only difference is that in the UK, they appear and stay until the farmers remove them. The wheat here is thrashed, and there's concern about the harvest yield. If you don't mind, Mr. Lotterland, would it be okay if I checked out the fields for a few days and see if I notice any unusual occurrences?"

"Help yourself, because I don't think the sheriff will do anything." Lincoln's tall frame towered over Sheriff Benson. He didn't blink as he glared at the sheriff with his icy gaze.

The sheriff, with his aviator sunglasses askew and his gut protruding over his uniform trousers, glanced at Lincoln. "I don't doubt you, Lincoln," he said. "I'm doing all I can. There's no evidence of how this is being done. Sure, I see the circles, if that's what you call them, and bent wheat. It appears that you have a poor-quality grain. We will keep searching for the culprits."

The sheriff nodded to his men and signaled it was time to leave. Nephilimbug followed them.

Lincoln studied the men as they departed, a bitter taste lingering in his mouth. "This Nephilimbug guy sounds as if he's going to investigate the crop circles," he said to Tiff.

"Um… there's something about him that bothers me. Dad, stay away from him. He gives me the creeps."

"Calm down. I'm not getting tangled up with any government employee whose name I can't pronounce or spell. I want to figure out who's messing with my wheat-field. Then, we can restore some normalcy to our lives. It would help if you checked social media to see what people are saying about the crop circles. My plate is already full, and that information could prove crucial. Sheriff Benson doesn't seem like he's going to do a darn thing."

"Sure, I'll see what I can find out and let you know."

"Thanks, Tiff." He patted her on the shoulder before returning to the small farmhouse, leaving her alone with Chip and thinking about Lucas Nephilimbug. Anxiety gnawed at her, telling her that the stranger's arrival had something to do with more than crop circles.

But right now, she had something more important to do.

Tiff sat in her truck parked outside the tattoo parlor, debating whether to go inside the shop and defy her father by getting inked.

She remembered that on a lazy Sunday afternoon, while they were watching a football game on TV, her father remarked that so many players had tattoos.

"I'm thinking about getting at least one," she said.

"I'll pretend I didn't hear that. There's a difference between thinking about something and doing it, and I know you're not foolish enough to do that."

"It should be a personal decision. Tattoos can be a form of self-expression, a work of art displayed on one's body, or a meaningful symbol that carries personal significance. It's all about individual choice and the freedom to adorn one's body in a way that feels right to them."

"No. I won't allow you to do that while living under my roof. Then you'll want a nose ring and other piercings."

Lincoln ended the conversation, as always, by turning his back on her.

Tears sprang to Tiff's eyes, and she quickly wiped them

away. Besides money, her father's rules kept her from doing it sooner. She'd saved her allowance, gathered courage, and entered the shop. Tiff closed her eyes and tried to concentrate on anything but the needle piercing her chest.

For months, she had been having the same dream: she stood naked in front of a mirror, looking at her body. Above her heart was a tattoo. She drew a picture of it and showed it to the tattoo artist.

As the artist completed her work, she handed Tiff a mirror and explained how to take care of it. Tiff reclined in the chair, eagerly anticipating the final result. She couldn't help but gasp. The design was identical to her sketch of a "T," with the number 369 etched in black. The "T" and numbers were a vibrant mix of yellow, red, and green, neither too large nor too small. The result surpassed her expectations. She felt an instant connection to it. She'd keep it hidden, meant only for her eyes, and not for show.

Sheriff Benson had been watching Tiff since she entered the tattoo shop. Once she left the shop, he decided to pull her over outside of town. He wanted to ask her some questions without having her father look over his shoulder. As he trailed behind her truck, he couldn't help but think about Sarah's disappearance.

After serving in the Marines, he returned home and joined the police force. Sarah's disappearance had caused a stir in their small town. She was well-known to everyone, and he knew Lincoln, Sarah, her sister, and many others from high school who still lived in Wheatfield. The Coleman sisters were alluring, and the guys couldn't help but drool over them, particularly Sarah. Rachel was the youngest of the group and much younger than him.

He'd been quietly obsessed with Sarah, but she never seemed to notice him. The one time their eyes met, it was like she looked straight through him.

Everyone wondered why she chose Lincoln. They were complete opposites. Despite being the main suspect in her disappearance simply because he was her husband, no one truly believed that Lincoln had any involvement. He adored her.

The FBI got involved, but the investigation eventually went cold—not a trace, no leads. He'd revisit the file sometimes, hoping something would jump out, but it never did. Now, with these strange crop circles turning up again, all those old suspicions and unanswered questions had come rushing back. Many speculated that she had chosen to run away with a man she had met due to her eccentric behavior. However, he couldn't fathom how any mother could willingly leave their child behind.

And now Tiff, nearly grown and so much like her mother in presence as well as appearance, was left with nothing but rumors and unanswered questions. That thought gnawed at him more than he liked to admit. He no longer cared about the rumors. He wanted answers—not for himself, but for Tiff. She deserved to know what happened to her mother. He wondered why she was in the tattoo shop; he couldn't picture her conservative father, Lincoln, allowing her to get a tattoo.

He put his siren on and pulled her over.

"Tiff, do you mind stepping out of the truck?"

"Sure. What's going on, Sheriff? I don't think I was speeding, was I?" Tiff got out.

"It has nothing to do with your driving, so don't worry. You and Lincoln don't think I'm following up on this crop circle complaint, but I want to ask you a few more questions."

"Okay."

"Be honest with me. Your dad isn't here, and this conversation is unofficial, between the two of us. You understand?"

"Yeah."

"Are you T-369 on social media?"

"No, what are you talking about?"

"We, I mean my department, have been tracking the social media thread about Wheatfield crop circles, and it seems T-369 has been posting a lot about them and has a substantial following. You can come clean with me."

"It's not me, Sheriff. I have no idea who T-369 is," she gushed out as the tattoo on her chest stabbed her with pain. "I suggest your officers track down the IP address, which may tell you who is behind this. May I go now?"

"Yes, one more thing. When your mom disappeared, the sheriff's office did everything they could to find her. It's a cold case, and I haven't given up on discovering what happened."

"Good luck with that." Tiff slammed the truck's door, thinking, *Who in the hell was T-369?*

Chapter 4
Discovery

Tiff pulled open the attic door, and the rusty hinges let out a long, creaking groan. A puff of dust rushed out, making her sneeze. She waved a hand in front of her face, waiting for the air to clear, then climbed the stairs, each step groaning under her weight.

This was her least favorite room. It was dim and musty, with cobwebs clinging to boxes of forgotten junk. But if there was something valuable hidden up here, she had to find it. The bank had threatened to foreclose on their mortgage. Tiff sighed and flicked on the bare bulb overhead. Somewhere in this mess, there had to be some items worth selling. Even a small amount of cash could make a significant difference. Every little bit helps.

She walked around, looking for anything of interest. Then she saw it, a large trunk hidden behind boxes and furniture. Tiff pulled it out, but it was locked. She searched the area and found a key hanging from a nail on the wall. She grabbed it and inserted it into the lock. It clicked and opened.

Tiff lifted the lid and gasped. Inside the trunk were

clothes, jewelry, and other stuff that belonged to her mother. There was a red dress, a pearl necklace, a leather jacket, a pair of sunglasses, shoes, and more. Her dad never told her about the trunk. He said he had thrown away all her belongings. Did he not want her to learn about her mother? Did he not want to remember her?

She lifted the leather jacket out of the trunk and smelled it, hoping it retained a whiff of her mother's scent. Did she use perfume? If so, what type? As she held onto the jacket, Tiff cried out to the emptiness. "Why did you leave? Didn't you love me? Why didn't you come back for me?" Her words faded into the dusty air, unanswered as tears streamed down her face.

Tiff longed to make sense of the storm of feelings churning inside her. She yearned for her mother, though the anger often crowded out the longing. In this town, she was labeled as the girl abandoned by her mother, a label that filled her with an overwhelming sense of desperation and frustration. What if she never found her? The pain was too much to bear, a hollow ache that would be with her forever.

Tiff tried on the jacket. It fit her perfectly. So excited, she slipped on her mother's heels and paraded around the attic. She took out a few pieces to carry to her room. As she slid the trunk back to its place, a glint of metal caught her eye near the rear side of the trunk. Tiff reached into the shadows and grasped a small box, dragging it into the light. Could this have belonged to her mother as well?

Tiff struggled with the old, rusty lock until it opened. She pulled out a metal cube from the box. Its once shining and vibrant surface was aged and faded. Holding it in the palm of her hand, Tiff gazed at what she thought were tarot cards scattered across the cube, which were glued onto its surface. Despite their worn appearance, she couldn't help but notice a strange symbol in the lower right corner of each card, one that she didn't recognize. As she continued rummaging through the box, she discovered a silver and gold pendant with the letters L.V.X. dangling from a delicate chain.

However, it was the cube that truly captured her attention. Tiff placed the cube gently on her nightstand and clasped the pendant around her neck. As her hands curled around it, a wave of heat pulsed through her skin, subtle yet impossible to ignore. The same thing happened when she reached out and touched the cube. Both objects gave off a slight vibration that seemed to thicken the air around her, as if they were alive in a way she didn't yet understand. *Were they trying to communicate with her?* She wondered. Later, despite her restless sleep, she drifted off, strangely comforted by the presence of the cube and pendant. For the first time in a while, she didn't feel so alone.

Tiff always tried to stay out of the limelight, preferring her own company over the drama that high school often brought. But now she found herself in a predicament where Maddie rarely had time for their friendship. She had no one to confide in about her relentless pursuit of her mother and the unexplainable findings she had recently stumbled upon.

Tiff sat isolated under an old oak tree at the edge of the school's soccer field, her lunch forgotten beside her. In her hands, she carefully turned the mysterious cube, watching as it caught the sunlight, its surfaces gleaming with an almost ethereal light. The cube was small, fitting snugly in her palm, yet it felt weighty, imbued with a significance she could barely understand.

She studied the cube so intently that she didn't notice the new boy from her physics class until he was almost beside her. He stood there quietly, as if careful not to interrupt whatever strange connection she had with the object.

"Hey," Coop said, his voice breaking through Tiff's concentration. He nodded towards the cube. "That's really something. What is it?"

Tiff snapped the cube into her jacket pocket, her movements swift, her expression turning wary. "It's a puzzle cube," she lied, her voice flat, eyes scanning his face for his reaction.

Coop, however, seemed undeterred by her cool response. He sat down beside her, maintaining a respectable distance. His casual demeanor didn't mask his curiosity. "It doesn't look like any puzzle cube I've seen. It seemed like... more than that."

His comment caught her off guard. How did he know? Tiff observed him, noting his earnest expression. Coop's interest seemed genuine.

"Why do you say that?" Tiff asked, her tone a mix of suspicion and curiosity.

"I've read about ancient artifacts and that cube... it looked important," Coop confessed, his eyes brightening with enthusiasm. "There's something about the symbols on it. They look historical or magical or something."

Tiff was taken aback. His guess was uncomfortably close to the truth. "You know about these things?"

"A bit," Coop shrugged, a modest smile playing on his lips. "My mom's an archaeologist. I've picked up things here and there, you know, about artifacts and their energies. That cube pulled at me like it had a story. Does it?"

Now it was Tiff's turn to be intrigued. The cube indeed had a story—one deeply entwined with her family's history and her mother's mysterious disappearance. But how much should she share with someone she barely knew?

Seeing her hesitation, Coop added softly, "I get it if you don't want to talk about it. But if that cube is what I think it is, it could be special. I'd love to know more, only if you're okay with it."

Tiff looked at Coop, weighing her options. His genuine interest, combined with his background, made her reconsider her initial reluctance. *Perhaps he could offer some insights or assistance.*

"It's... it's definitely more than a puzzle," Tiff admitted, pulling the cube back out but holding it close. "It's been in my family for a while. I think it has connections to... things I don't fully understand yet."

"Like what?" Coop leaned in slightly, his voice a whisper of excitement and awe.

"I'm not sure. My mom might have known...but you probably already heard the town gossip that she disappeared or ran off," she said quietly, her voice tightening with emotion.

Coop nodded sympathetically. "Sorry about your mom. I know we don't know each other very well, but I'd really like to help if I can."

Tiff hesitated for a moment longer, then nodded slowly. "I don't even know your name. Let's start there."

"I'm Cooper, but everyone calls me Coop."

"Tiff."

"Can I take a look at the cube?"

"First, swear you'll not tell anyone about the cube or anything we talk about." She stared him in the eye. "If you do, I'll make you regret it."

"I swear to you my lips are sealed." Coop ran his hands across his lips.

Tiff paused again, unsure why she was trusting a

stranger with the cube. "Be careful with it. It gets hot. I think the cube belonged to my mom before she disappeared."

Coop's interest was piqued. "It's not hot or even warm."

Tiff sighed, wondering if she had imagined that the cube was emitting heat the night before.

"Is your mom's disappearance connected to this cube?"

"I don't know. She vanished when I was a baby, but I think the cube and crop circles might have something to do with what happened to her."

"Are you the one with the crop circles in your field?"

Tiff stiffened. "Why?"

"I just meant... You brought them up."

"Forget it. Yeah, the crop circles are showing up again in our field."

Coop turned the cube over, examining each side. "It's a cube with six faces, eight points, and twelve lines." His eyes shone with curiosity. "Where did you say you found this again?"

"In my attic. Inside an old box that belonged to my mom. What do you make of those pictures and the letters on the lower right side of each one? Do you think it could be some code?"

"It's possible," Coop mused, returning the cube. "I can't be sure without further study, but if you want me to help you, I would be happy to take a crack at it."

"That would be amazing. How about we meet at my place?"

"It's a date," Coop said, and then his face flushed. "A study date, I mean. To study the cube."

Tiff hid her smile. Having a nerdy guy around wouldn't be so bad after all. Only later did she realize she'd left out something important: the pendant. Maybe it held clues of its own.

That evening, with her father off at his weekly card game and the house finally quiet, Tiff led Coop up to the attic—the only place she could think of where they wouldn't be interrupted if he came home early. Her room felt too personal, too exposed, but the attic had become something else: a private archive of forgotten things and half-buried questions.

They cleared a space among old boxes and sat cross-legged on the dusty wooden floor. Spread out between them was the cube. The cube shimmered faintly under the attic's overhead bulb, looking out of place in the sea of cardboard and cobwebs.

"These images on the cube are Major Arcana tarot cards, and they're quite rare," Coop said, as he studied them through his magnifying glass. "The art is exceptional."

"What do they mean?"

"Each card has a Hebrew letter in the lower corner," he said, pointing. "And this one—on the west face of the cube—is the Wheel of Fortune. See the alchemical symbols in the circle? Salt, mercury, and sulfur."

"I didn't even see that," Tiff said. "Yeah, I remember those from Chemistry."

"Try looking through the magnifying glass," Coop offered, handing it to her.

Tiff took it and leaned in. "Could they be a clue to help me find my mom?"

"We gather information in the manner of Sherlock Holmes and interpret it effectively," Coop said with a grin.

"Sherlock Holmes?" She stifled a laugh and glanced at the magnifying glass. "That explains the detective gear. I ought to tell you something—I'm not very good with people. So, if you want to be Sherlock, I'm Dr. Watson."

"I get nervous around people, too," Coop said. "It's good we got that out of the way before joining forces."

Tiff smiled. Coop was in for the mission.

She reached behind her neck and unclasped the chain with the pendant. "I forgot to show you this earlier," she said, placing it gently between them. "It was in the same box as the cube."

Coop examined it, turning it over. "This is real gold. Has to be. Twenty-four karats, maybe? And the engraving —L.V.X.—is Latin for light. Why would your mom leave something this expensive behind?"

"I don't know," Tiff said. "Maybe she didn't mean to."

Without saying anything, Coop pulled a small notebook from his hoodie and began jotting notes.

Tiff frowned. "Why are you writing that down?"

"Oh." He looked up, caught. "It's a habit. Helps me think. I won't show it to anyone. Promise."

Tiff hesitated, her eyes on the notebook, then gave a short nod. "Be careful. This isn't a game."

"Understood." He returned to the cube, more careful now.

Tiff searched various sites on her phone, trying to match the tarot cards, but nothing came close. They were both deep in thought when Coop finally said, "I have an idea."

"What is it, Sherlock?"

"Don't go overboard with that," he said.

"Sorry," she smirked.

∿

Coop had left long before Lincoln returned from his poker game. Despite her father's attempts to be quiet, Tiff was wide awake and couldn't stop thinking about Maddie, Coop, the cube, and the alchemical symbols. After researching alchemy, she stumbled upon an article discussing the seven fundamental principles of spiritual alchemy. She learned that spiritual alchemy was attaining spiritual enlightenment. The symbol for water also represents the alchemical principle of dissolution, which frees one from the inauthentic self, or the ego. Tired and weary, Tiff drifted off to sleep, pondering whether this could all be related to her mother. Did these paranormal things belong to her mother? What was her mother involved in? And was she following in her footsteps?

The alarm blared at 5 a.m., but she was already awake, worrying about the day ahead.

While Tiff was in the barn doing her morning chores, Chip barked, alerting her that someone was nearby. When she swung around to face the entrance, she saw Lucas Nephilimbug standing there.

"I wanted to let your father know that I've almost finished my investigation and will send him and the sheriff a report."

"You shouldn't sneak up on people," she said, tightening her grip on the broom handle.

"Sorry if I frightened you." He approached her, stopped, and turned towards the door. "That's an unusual pendant you're wearing," he remarked.

Tiff touched it. She should have remembered to take it off. She didn't want her father to see it.

"May I ask where you purchased it?"

"It was a gift from a relative."

The truth was, she didn't know much about the

pendant—only that it felt protective, as if her mother had left it behind for a reason.

"You can find my father working on the fence on the east side of the property." She returned to doing her chores to end the conversation.

Nephilimbug left as quietly as he had come.

Checking her phone for notifications, she froze, the blood draining from her face. There was a notification from Ancestry. She had a DNA match—a close relative on her maternal side.

Tiff gazed at the name and photo. The eyes staring back mirrored her own. A wave of emotions washed over her: hope, fear, curiosity, and excitement. She clicked on the link to see more details about her relative. Perhaps this was the clue to discovering what had happened to her mom.

Weeks later, at lunch, Tiff managed to lure Maddie over to her table. Maddie had completely changed her look with a short haircut, tattoos, and multiple piercings in her nose and ears.

"I called you several times this morning. Why didn't you answer?" Tiff demanded. "Look at you—new style and new boyfriend."

"Well, I heard you've been spending time with the nerd."

"It's only been a few weeks. But still, I made time for you," Tiff said firmly.

"I'm sorry, Tiff. L.R. always insists on spending time together. Nevertheless, I'm here now—tell me what's going on."

Tiff hesitated before passing her phone to Maddie.

Maddie glanced at the photo of the woman on the screen and said, "She looks a lot like you… but she's black."

"You're forgetting that I'm also a person of color."

"I think of you as Tiff, my B.F.F., who will let me do a do-over one day." She pulled Tiff's long braid.

"I don't think I want blue or green hair with a ring in my nose," Tiff said.

"When you're ready to come out of the dark ages, I'm here for you."

"Are you?"

Before Maddie could answer, Coop approached the table with his lunch tray.

"Hi," Maddie gave him her biggest smile, and her eyes lit up.

Tiff turned to gaze up at Coop as though she was noticing him for the first time. His long, wavy hair highlighted his smooth, tanned complexion. Without his glasses, Coop's eyes were as coppery as his hair.

"Coop, meet Maddie."

He returned her smile and mumbled a greeting before sitting next to Tiff.

When Maddie spotted L.R. and his friends entering the dining area, she jumped up and said, "I've got to go, guys." She was gone before Tiff could even say goodbye.

Tiff watched her join L.R., the football team captain, a real jock. He put his arm around Maddie's waist. Tiff was surprised Maddie chose L.R. as her boyfriend, considering he was a jerk. Tiff didn't like him. He was a bully and an elitist, and she kept her distance from him.

Later that day, they found Mr. Bernstein on his way out. Tiff allowed Coop to do all the talking as she didn't have an amicable relationship with Mr. Bernstein.

Tiff was aware that Mr. Bernstein had differences with her. His frequent neglect of her inquiries, the unsatisfactory marks on her assignments, and his biting remarks about her efforts were clear indicators of his dissatisfaction with her work. It felt as though he was intentionally being hard on her. Puzzled, she pondered what might have led to his apparent aversion.

"Mr. Bernstein," Coop said, urgently, "I've identified the letters as Hebrew, but why are they paired with tarot imagery—and why on a cube? Is there a historical or mystical link between the alphabet and the Major Arcana?"

Mr. Bernstein dropped his briefcase and took it from Coop. "Where did you find this?"

Coop stammered, "I found it amongst some stuff in the attic of my new family home."

"Listen, I only have time to glance at it. Later, I can examine it more in detail," he said as he attempted to put it in his pocket. But Tiff was too quick. She snatched it away and ran in hot pursuit down the hallway, with Coop chasing after her.

Coop caught up with her and asked, "What was all that about?"

"He wanted to take it. I can't let this or any of the pieces we have found out of my sight. They're the connection to my mother and the past. This may be a waste of time, and the cube might belong to someone else. After all, the house has been in my father's family for generations."

"Don't do that."

"Do what?"

He sighed. "You're changing the narrative. I thought you accepted that the cube had something to do with your mom's disappearance and probably belonged to her."

"I do," she said, then hesitated. But I also don't trust Mr. Bernstein. I don't think he even likes me, and I don't know why?"

"Don't worry about him liking you. He's weird anyway." He gave a half-smile. "You're the one who matters in all this."

"You're right. Forget him."

"Cool. I'm good with that."

"For now, anything that has to do with the cube is between you and me."

"Whatever you said." He sniggered.

"Did you notice Mr. Bernstein's reaction? He acted as if it wasn't the first time he'd seen it."

"He was probably interested in its mathematical properties, that's all. We can find other people to help us translate the Hebrew letters, but this might involve a cost. Let me check at the university or one of the temples."

Tiff felt a pang in her chest at the thought of paying for assistance. Her father was in debt, and she didn't want to ask him for more money. She stole a quick look at Coop, who had a broad smile on his face, unaware of her inner thoughts.

Chapter 5
Light vs Darkness

Tiff sat in her truck in Spirits' parking lot. Her heart was hammering in her chest at the thought of meeting Rachel Coleman. She had received an email from her through Ancestry requesting that they meet. It was short and to the point.

Meet me at Spirits tomorrow @ 7 p.m.

Despite her fear, she had come. Rachel Coleman was a close relative in the high centimorgan range, perhaps a grandmother, aunt, or first cousin on her maternal side of the family.

Tiff wiped her sweaty palms on her jeans. *You can do this for Mom.*

She entered the diner with a storm of emotions raging inside of her and surveyed the scene. The café was a quiet hum of subdued conversations and clinking dishes. Nestled in a booth by the window was a woman, her long braids cascading over her face and shoulders. Tiff's breath stopped in astonishment; the reflection before her was akin to her own image.

Rachel glanced up, her eyes widening. She stood. "Tiff?"

Tiff managed a jerky nod, approached the booth, and held out her hand. "It's nice to meet you," she said.

"Likewise. Please, sit."

Tiff slid into the booth and opened her mouth, but no words came out. She sat across from the woman she hoped could tell her about her mother.

She removed the scarf from around her neck, where she hid the pendant from her father.

"That's your mother's. Where did you find that?"

"With some other things of hers in a trunk in the attic."

"I thought she was wearing it the night she left. Your father must have put it there."

"I don't think so, but I really don't know."

Rachel unbuttoned the top two buttons of her blouse and displayed the same L.V.X. pendant.

"Do you know what L.V.X. stands for?"

"These are Latin numbers. The L is fifty, the V is five, and X is ten, which equals 65."

"Well done, but there's more to it."

Remembering what Coop had told her when he first saw the pendant, she said, "The only other thing I can think of is that it represents the Latin noun L.V.X. for light."

"You keep amazing me. In occultism, sixty-five is a compelling number related to the two geometric figures, the pentagram and the hexagram. Always wear it for protection. But enough, you didn't come here for me to teach you esoteric wisdom."

Tiff thought about her encounter with Nephilimbug in

the barn and how he had backed away from her once he saw the pendant. She told Rachel about Nephilimbug and the incident.

"Your light will attract darkness to turn you. The forces are gathering, and you must be ready. Be careful who you surround yourself with."

"Who are you?" Tiff leaned forward, pulse racing.

"I'm your aunt. Sarah is my sister." She responded, letting the words sink in before saying anything else. "Your mother loved you so much."

"You said you loved in the past, as if she was dead," Tiff replied with tears forming in her eyes.

"No, I don't believe that. Wherever Sarah is, she loves you."

Tiff's shoulders sagged. She steeled herself and asked, "My father never mentioned my mother having a sister."

"How is Lincoln?" She laughed.

"He doesn't want me to find out about my mom."

"Lincoln was always very strait-laced, and Sarah was wild. I could never understand why she chose to marry him. I'm only being honest."

"Is he hiding something about Sarah?" Tiff found it odd to say her mother's name.

"Why don't you ask him?"

"He won't tell me anything about her. I was shocked to find out about you. Tell me about her life and what happened to her."

Rachel's eyes darkened. "I'm afraid there isn't much I can tell you. I told the police everything I knew."

Tiff stared out the window at the descending night, disappointment washing over her. The truth continued to be as slippery as a bar of soap, but her determination didn't waver.

She turned back to Rachel with a grim smile. "It's okay. This is only the beginning."

Rachel frowned. "I'm afraid I've told you everything."

"Are you sure?" Tiff insisted and leaned forward. "Did my mother ever mention anything strange happening to or around her? Unexplained events?"

"What do you mean, unexplained events? Does it have something to do with the appearance and disappearance of the crop circles?"

Surprised, Tiff responded, "Yes, you know about that?"

"Yes, it's on the internet. It's garnering a lot of attention. I'm surprised you aren't aware, as a young person. Some of the posts have gone viral."

"I'm ignoring what others might say. Most of them don't know what they're talking about. But what's the urgent message you have for me?"

"Don't mess with the crop circles. This is not child's play, and you're not equipped to handle what could happen."

"What do you mean? Does this have anything to do with why my mom disappeared? Please tell me what happened to her; it's important to me. I want the truth."

"It's very complicated, Tiff. But I will tell you this. Your mother, my beautiful, brilliant sister, was different. She studied alchemy and practiced magic, but was untrained at that time."

"Sarah was an illusionist?"

"No, not that type of magic. I'm speaking of the High Magick of occultism. She reopened a portal in the wheat fields that had been sealed centuries ago after dark forces opened it. They entered this dimension and wreaked havoc."

"Wait, I'm totally lost. What is High Magic of occultism?"

"Occultism means hidden, and the magic, spelled Magick, was used by highly trained priests and occultism in the secret wisdom of the universe. They commanded the elements and time of this universe."

"My mom was a witch?"

"No, Tiff. At a very early age, Sarah was considered an Adept or one who was proficient in occult practices."

"My father talks about that story of someone or something thrashing the fields and people going hungry. Everyone thinks it's just folklore."

Rachel leaned forward, her voice dropping to a whisper. "It's quite real. The portal your mother re-opened wasn't any ordinary doorway. It was something more powerful. The Teachers of the Order of the Light sealed it using sacred geometric patterns made from high-frequency light. It was the only way to stop the dark forces from using the portal as a gateway into this world."

"And who are these Teachers of the Order of L.V.X.?"

"For now, know they're highly evolved beings that are the caretakers of our beautiful planet, Earth."

Tiff felt a shiver run down her spine. "You're talking about the crop circles being high-frequency light used to stop the portal from opening again. If this is true, is it open again?"

"The presence of the crop circle indicates that some paranormal activity is occurring. I was hoping you could shed some light on this."

Tiff sat back against the booth, stunned. "Me?"

Rachel sighed, her expression softening. "I know it's hard to understand, Tiff, and I wish I could share everything. But diving too deep, too quickly, into certain truths can be more overwhelming than enlightening. Your consciousness will adapt gradually."

Tiff's brow furrowed. "But how can I prepare if I don't even know what I'm supposed to be preparing for? You speak of truths and consciousness, but what does that really mean? It's not fair to drop hints about my mother and then leave me hanging!"

"I hear you, and I don't mean to be cryptic. Let's approach this differently. Forget the esoteric for a moment," she suggested. "Let me tell you about Sarah, your mom, in a way that might help bridge the gap between what was and what could be."

Rachel paused, collecting her thoughts. "Sarah and I grew up in Atwood, Kansas, with our adoptive mother. She was a kind woman who took in lost souls, giving us a family when we had none."

"And your biological parents?"

"We don't know anything about them. We were left in a church with a note."

"What did the note say?"

"Take care of these two souls. One day, they will understand why we are doing this. It's their destiny."

"That's crazy."

"As crazy as that sounds, we were adopted by the right person, an astonishing woman and her support group of women."

"Where is she? Can I meet her?" Tiff envisioned having a grandparent in her life. She had faint memories of her father's parents. They cared for her when her father was in the Marines. She was still very young when both died soon after he returned home from duty.

"Habiba was her name. It means beloved or love. I'm afraid she's no longer with us."

Tiff blinked away tears forming in her eyes. "I always thought my mother grew up here and met my dad."

"We did. Habiba believed in communicating with spirits. One day, she packed us up and said that Spirit told her to come to Wheatfield County because our destiny was here."

"What was my mom's favorite color, music, and food?"

"Slow down. We were born on the same day, but two years apart. Sarah was always curious, always exploring, and always asking why. Habiba and the group called her Wild Thing. I was Wild Thing 2," she laughed.

"That curiosity didn't end with the fields here. It grew, as did she, into pursuits that most people would never even dream of. That's the part of her you've inherited—the relentless quest for answers."

"She had me soon after finishing college," Tiff said.

"I was there. Is your room still a beautiful yellow like the sun?"

"Yes."

"Sarah painted your room. As a child, her room was indigo; she wore that color a lot."

Tiff listened, absorbing every word. The simple, human aspects of her story strengthened her sense of connection to her mother. "Thank you, Rachel," she finally said. "Hearing about her like this helps more than you might realize."

They'd talked for hours, Rachel recounting even more details of her and Sarah's childhood without alluding to anything else about Sarah's disappearance.

"One last question," Tiff begged.

"What?"

"Why don't we have other maternal matches on Ancestry? It's the two of us. Don't you find that to be odd?"

"Think about everything I have told you tonight, and

you'll be able to answer your own question." Rachel picked up her purse and stood up.

"If I didn't have my father, I would think we weren't from this world. And you don't have anyone but me."

Rachel winked at Tiff. "You're a quick study. Trust me, you'll need to be."

Tiff pushed opened the café door into the chilly night, her mind spinning. The truth about her mother was strange and sad. Yet, something in Rachel's words had felt real. Grounding. They both vowed to stay in touch.

Tiff drove her usual route on the way home, slowing down when she reached Hillary Hill, when a flash of light caught her eye. Her heart raced as she pulled over, turned on her hazard lights, and exited the car. As she walked through the tall stalks of wheat, a breeze tickled her face. Gazing upward, she looked at the full moon casting its bright luminescence across the night sky. Her smile broadened as she continued on her way, filled with a sense of adventure and excitement. She wondered what she would find in the field.

Tiff reached a clearing and stopped, gasping, as lights swirled around her. They were of different colors and shapes, and they moved with a life of their own. The lights danced in the air, creating patterns and shapes. As she extended her hand to touch one of the lights, it elusively moved away.

She followed it as the wheat field transformed. The stalks of wheat were growing taller and thicker, forming walls and tunnels around her. The ground was becoming softer and wetter, as if it were turning into mud. The air was colder and denser, as if filled with fog.

Tiff's heart raced with fear as she frantically searched for an exit. The darkness had swallowed up the light, leaving her surrounded by inky blackness. Suddenly, a noise behind her made her whirl around. A dark figure loomed before her, tall and strong, dressed in a midnight-colored cloak with a hood obscuring his face. In his hand was a sharp sword that he pointed directly at her.

"Who are you?" Tiff asked, trembling.

"I'm the guardian of this Western gate," he said in a deep voice. "Intone the Name and give the Sign of the Enterer?"

"I don't know them."

"You have trespassed on rare ground, and now you'll pay the price."

He raised his sword and swung it at her. Tiff dodged it by instinct and with the aid of her years of Aikido training. She kicked him in the chest, making him stagger back and drop his sword.

He recovered quickly and attacked her again. He was fast and powerful. Tiff blocked his strikes with her arms and legs, but the pain crushed her. She couldn't keep this up for much longer.

She hunted for an opening to escape, but there was none. The wheat field was still changing, creating more obstacles and barriers around them. The lights were still swirling, but they dimmed and moved farther away.

Panic surged through her as she grasped the reality of her situation; she was losing the battle, and the uncertainty of what would come if he were to defeat her was terrifying. Would she become one of those lights? Would she go to that other world? Would she die?

She tried to fight back harder, but he was too fast. He used a mystic type of defense that she couldn't understand or counteract. He intuited her every move before she made it, and he blocked or dodged them.

He taunted her with words that made her angry and scared.

"You're pathetic," he said. "You're weak. You're nothing."

He slashed his sword at her again, aiming for her neck. Tiff ducked under it, but he followed up with a kick that sent her flying back.

She hit the ground hard, her head striking a rock, and a sharp pain shot through her skull, sending a wave of dizziness and nausea through her.

She tried to stand, but she couldn't move, blood dripping from her head. Through blurry eyes, Tiff watched him stroll in her direction with his sword raised for the final blow. Shutting her eyes and bracing for the finale, she heard him cry out, "It's you."

Forcing her eyes open, she saw a luminous being hovering at the far end of the clearing, obscured by shadows. Through a haze of pain, she saw an ethereal essence approaching, gliding across the ground. *This is surreal*, she thought.

Tiff tried to speak, but no sound came out. Then everything went black.

She woke up in the emergency room of Wheatfield Hospital. Her head and body ached. She heard her father talking to someone before blacking out again.

"What happened to her?" Lincoln asked the doctor.

"She has a mild concussion, nothing for you to worry about. Tiff has minor bruises, and she's dehydrated; all tests returned normal. She's going to be fine. We'll keep her under observation for a few more hours."

"Thanks, doctor."

"Do you know why she was in the wheat field at night, and who might be responsible for what happened to her?"

"We've had some strange phenomena. Tiff went there to check on the fields. I told her not to go alone at night."

"Teenagers don't listen. I've got two of my own. I'll inform the Sheriff's Department."

"I was planning to speak with them, too."

"I'll be back to check on her. The nurse will be in and out."

Lincoln stayed by her side as she slept, holding her hand in prayer.

After a few hours, Tiff's eyes fluttered open. She blinked at the bright lights, confusion etched on her face.

"Dad?" Her voice was hoarse.

He squeezed her hand, relief and joy flooding his eyes with tears. "I'm right here, sweetheart. You're going to be okay. What were you doing in the fields? I thought you were having dinner with Maddie?"

"I... Dad, can we talk tomorrow? Let's go home." Her eyes pleaded with him.

"Tomorrow, I expect you to explain everything. Even if you can defend yourself, the fields aren't safe to be in alone."

"I was looking at the crop circle."

"That crop circle, what's left of it, is a disaster. Another section of the wheat has been destroyed. You were lying next to a bloody rock where you either fell or were pushed and hit your head. Thank God Chip found you."

"Where's my phone?"

He gave it to her. "Please don't use it. It's not suitable for your vision with a concussion."

"Okay."

As Tiff clutched her phone, her thoughts drifted to the cube, hidden safely in the box beneath her bed, where she kept all the clues about Sarah. It had been the first bread-crumb in a trail of secrets: her mother, the crop circles, the strange symbols. Everything had started with that one mysterious object.

"Tomorrow, you'll be taking a break from school to rest up. I'm going to inform the sheriff about the crop circle incident; it's high time he started taking this seriously."

"Please don't tell the sheriff. I don't remember too much of what happened."

"I don't have a choice. The doctor will report it either way. Tell him what you remember. Someone assaulted you. Why don't you want to report it?"

Tiff's cheeks were wet with tears. How could she explain to anyone that she had been attacked by a being from another dimension while swirling lights in the field added to the chaos? She remembered being in worse shape before her father found her. She had a foggy memory of an ethereal female warning off her attacker and soothing her pain with a gentle touch on her injured body. The most hurtful part was believing she was saved, only to be abandoned again when the woman vanished.

Was it possible that the woman was her mother?

Chapter 6
OBS Headquarters

Nephilimbug hovered over the transmission crystal, its dark core pulsing in rhythm with his heartbeat. He hesitated, talons twitching as he debated how best to frame his report. Words carried weight within the ranks of the Black Shadow—especially when sent to the High Council. He was wary of putting his thoughts into writing. Most of it was still speculation, built on fragments and intuition. But his gut told him something was amiss. Deeply amiss. The symbols, the girl, the light—they were connected in a way that defied coincidence. But what? What was the true nature of the Council's plan? He exhaled slowly and continued transmitting his message.

From: Agent Nephilimbug
To: Headquarters of the Black Shadow (B.S.)
Subject: Intelligence Update–Subject: Tiff

Arcane Cube

I'm writing to inform you of the latest developments regarding Tiff, the girl I've been tracking. She's a connection to the crop circles, and I suspect she's part of a larger plan by the Light to use the portal to launch an attack against us. The precision of the symbols and her presence at their center are no coincidence.

Yesterday, I followed her to a local café where she rendezvoused with another agent of the Order of L.V.X. We have clearly underestimated her role. During their exchange, I observed them comparing pendants—each marked with the L.V.X. emblem. These are not trinkets. They signify high status within their Order. This strongly suggests she's a trusted agent and not a passive observer.

Later, I tracked her to Sector 7B—Hillary Hill. There, she appeared to be invoking the crop circle's energy, possibly to activate the portal from the Light's side. I intervened to stop her. She was caught off guard, and I struck her with my shadow blade. Before I could press the advantage, another L.V.X. agent arrived. The situation became too unstable to continue. I withdrew to reassess.

Is Sector 7B being reactivated under your command?

Enlighten me.

The crop circles are clearly deliberate and tactical, not random energy flares. The Order of L.V.X. may be using them as staging grounds for something larger. And the girl—she may be the key.

I have seen no evidence of the cube—yet.

I request your guidance on how to proceed.

Your loyal servant,

Agent Nephilimbug

> From: Headquarters of the B.S.
> To: Agent Nephilimbug
> Subject: Assignment Update
>
> Present yourself to headquarters at once.

After kneeling for several moments in deference to the High Council of the Order of the Black Shadow, Nephilimbug rose. His voice was steady, but beneath the surface simmered frustration.

"The recent surge in portal activity within Sector 7B cannot be dismissed as a mere coincidence," he began. "The crop circle patterns suggest a deliberate containment grid, clearly designed by the Order of L.V.X. They're not only rituals but also are light-based technology used to manipulate the portal's energy."

He paused, eyes narrowing. "These aren't anomalies. They're part of a systematic campaign to thwart our efforts. And I believe the girl is linked to this. Inexplicably, but undeniably."

One of the robed council members interrupted. "We require more than suspicion. Find the cube. Deliver results."

Nephilimbug's gaze darkened. "That raises a question. Is there information being withheld from me? Am I being sent in blind to gauge how far the Light has progressed with the portal? If so, I should've been told. Are we reacting to their strategy—or testing our own vulnerabilities?"

Silence rippled through the chamber. Finally, Ute, the eldest, spoke in a measured tone.

"Your task is to observe and report, not to interpret what lies beyond your station. Continue your surveillance. We'll determine what comes next."

Nephilimbug's posture stiffened. A deeper layer of the mission was unfolding—one he hadn't been briefed on. "Understood. What are your orders, then, given the girl's growing influence?"

"Focus on the girl and her connection to the Order. Do not engage unless necessary."

He inclined his head. "I will remain covert. If she is the key to manipulating the portal, I will uncover how."

"No," Ute cut in. "The cube is knowledge. And through it, power. Find it."

With a final nod, Nephilimbug turned and left the chamber. His mind churning with possibilities—and ambition.

They would never fully trust him. He was not one of them. His mother had been taken during a raid on planet Gaia and forced to marry his father on Nebulore. The other children from their union had died. Only he had survived. And yet, survival had not earned him their respect—only their suspicion.

They were planning something vast. He could feel it. And they didn't want him to be part of it.

But if he found the cube first, they would have no choice but to acknowledge him.

And so, in the shadowed corridors of headquarters, Nephilimbug began to devise a plan—one that could change everything.

Chapter 7
Recovery

The air in Tiff's bedroom was heavy, and the disinfectant and antiseptic scent lingered from her short hospital stay. Her fingers grazed the gauze wrapped around her head, sensing the tight bandages and the faint pulsing of her wound. As she rubbed her eyes, she felt exhaustion sinking into her bones, pulling her toward sleep.

Yesterday's events were too much for her to dismiss. Tiff focused on tiny cracks in the yellowed walls of her bedroom. Her desk lamp dimly lit the room. As she nodded off, her vision blurred, but not before the image of three tarot cards materialized—The Fool, The World, and Death—hovered in the air, glowing with an ethereal light, a silent message from beyond. Tiff rubbed her eyes, and the cards stayed there for several seconds before dissipating. She closed her eyes and slept.

The muted light of the morning sun slipped in through the draperies, casting a soft glow on the furniture in Tiff's room. She opened her eyes, and shadows danced along the walls, creating a whimsical atmosphere. As the aroma of roses wafted through the air, the sweet, floral fragrance was a welcome change from the stench that lingered after her encounter with the otherworldly being. *Where was the scent coming from*, she wondered. It brought a sense of comfort to her troubled mind. She drifted to sleep for a short while.

When she opened her eyes again, bits and pieces flowed back into her consciousness. Tiff reached for her tablet. She noted everything that had occurred the night before, starting with the dinner with Rachel and ending with the fight for her life against a dark being.

Tiff rubbed her eyes, confusion still swirling in her mind. She had to talk to someone about this. She grabbed her phone and dialed Coop's number. After three rings, he answered.

"Tiff? What's going on?" His voice was groggy with sleep.

"I'm sorry for waking you. I thought you were up," she said, relieved Coop had answered. He'd help her make sense of everything that had happened.

Coop was silent for a beat, checking the time on his phone. "No problem. After another thirty minutes of sleep, I'll be halfway to being human. So, be careful what you ask me. Talk while I slap some cold water on this face."

"Something happened in the wheat field last night."

"What?"

"Lights were moving swiftly around the wheat. I wanted to see if they had something to do with the crop circles. I fought with this dark spirit, got my ass kicked, and then this Light Being showed up out of nowhere and saved me. Chip and my dad found me and took me to the ER."

"Whoa, slow down." Coop's voice calmed her frayed nerves. "Start from the beginning. Are you okay?"

"My head and ribs hurt as if someone stomped on them."

"You aren't coming to school today, I guess?"

"No, my dad won't let me, and I don't think I'm up to it."

"Rest, and I'll skip my last class and come over. If something comes up, text me, okay?"

"I don't want you to get in trouble for skipping class."

"Don't worry about it. Gym isn't my favorite class."

Tiff listened to her father's footsteps, then heard a soft knock on her door. He entered carrying a tray with her pain medication, water, a bowl of soup, and a slice of bread.

"I thought you might be hungry, and if you're going to take the painkiller, you should eat something first."

"Thanks, Dad." Tiff sat up in bed as Lincoln placed the tray on her lap and opened the draperies.

"Can we keep them closed? The sun is too bright."

"Sorry. Try to eat something. Sheriff Benson is coming over in a little while. He will want to discuss last night with you. Are you up to it?"

"Not really."

Lincoln pulled out a small yellow envelope with the hospital's logo and placed it on the tray. "The nurse gave this to me. It's your jewelry that they had to take off you."

Tiff gulped down the pill, not looking at her father, thinking about the pendant. Was it in the envelope?

"I'm concerned about you. I don't want you taking on the responsibility of the farm. That's my job. You had no business being in the field at that time of night. I told you it's dangerous."

"Why is everyone saying it's dangerous but won't tell me why?"

"Who is everyone?"

"Coop and Maddie." She was tired of lying to her father, but he wasn't being honest with her.

"Well, that's good to know. Your friends have some sense. The field is off-limits to you and your friends until I can solve this crop circle fiasco."

When Lincoln left, Tiff grabbed the envelope and tore it open. The L.V.X. pendant glimmered inside, along with her earrings and ring. She held it in her hands for several moments before reaching under her bed to retrieve the shoebox where she kept her things about Sarah. An odd sensation came over her as if a voice was calling her to find a new place for the shoebox. With some effort, she managed to secure it behind her desk.

Tiff heard the familiar sound of Chip barking and distant voices downstairs. She slowly descended the stairs and made her way to the living room.

"There you are," Lincoln greeted her, motioning towards the sheriff and Mr. Nephilimbug, who were sitting in armchairs.

"They're here to ask about what happened last night." He helped her into the large, well-worn leather recliner where he usually sat.

"Tiff was shocked to see Nephilimbug and said, "I thought you had finished your report and left."

"I was wrapping it up when the sheriff informed me of your assault. I hope you're all right?"

"I'm fine," Tiff sneered. "You should see the other guy. He ran off."

"So, you did see him?" The sheriff asked.

"Not really. He was dressed in all black and wore a hood."

"How tall was he?"

"Um…about Mr. Nephilimbug's height."

"Was he thin, fat, or muscular?"

"Solid. Yes, he was solid."

"You didn't see his face at all?"

"No."

"Did you see him making the circles?" Nephilimbug interjected.

Tiff paused before answering, "No, I didn't."

"How did this guy come to assault you?"

"I remember seeing a light and going into the field to investigate. I think I came upon him, even startled him. Then he charged me," she said breathily.

Nephilimbug asked, "Did he say anything to you?"

"No."

"I think that's enough for today, gentlemen." Lincoln walked to the archway of the living room and the hallway.

"We might have more questions for you later, Tiff. If you recall anything, please call or text me. Oh, one more thing." The sheriff pulled out a small sheet of paper and showed it to her. "Do you recognize this sketch?"

It was the sketch she had given the tattoo artist. "Yes."

Lincoln's hand shot out, snatching the sketch without a word. "What is this?" he demanded.

Sheriff Benson looked at Tiff and said, "Do you want me to tell him, or do you want to?"

"Tell me what?"

"It's no big deal; it's a sketch of my tattoo," she said.

"And it's also the avatar T-369 used by someone on social media connected to the crop circles," Tiff added.

"May we see yours?" The sheriff stared at her.

"Don't show him anything until you tell me what this is all about, Tiffany."

It didn't escape Tiff that her father had used her full name, something he rarely did.

"I'm not that person on social media. It's a coincidence that we have the same avatar."

"How did you come by yours?" Sheriff Benson asked.

"I dreamt about it."

Nephilimbug watched the exchange with amusement and couldn't resist interjecting cheekily, "So, every time you have a dream, do you rush out to get it inked?"

"That's enough," Lincoln said. "Unless it's a crime and some charges are being brought against Tiff, I think it's best you both leave."

"Lincoln, you may not think so, but I'm doing my job. In the meantime, take care of that bruise, young lady."

After they left, Tiff waited for her father to reprimand her because of the tattoo. He never said anything, but the disgust on his face told her everything she needed to know. Tiff curled up on the sofa, and Chip lay beside her. She could barely eat the soup he had prepared for her lunch. Her mind relived all the events from the night before and the sheriff's questioning. Could something or someone from another dimension penetrate this dimension, and who was T-369? She was happy when Coop showed up. Lincoln, still not talking to her, left them alone.

Coop sat in the chair across from the sofa. He had pulled over Tiff's lunch tray and finished what she hadn't eaten. Even though he had quickly read her notes, he wanted her to hear the story of meeting her aunt and encountering a being from another dimension.

"Bear with me; my head and ribs still hurt."

She recounted the details of her conversation with Rachel, the strange familiarity in Rachel's eyes, and the tales of her and Sarah's early childhood years that only a close friend could know.

"She said my mom was called Wild Thing, and she was Wild Thing 2. Crazy, huh?"

"I like those monikers. They're cool."

Then, with as much enthusiasm as Tiff could muster, she told Coop about the strange occurrence in the wheat field.

By the time she finished, Coop was quiet.

"This is unsettling," he finally said. "That the battle in the wheat field happened the same evening you met up with your aunt. And this flash of light you saw..." He trailed off, then in a careful tone, asked, "Tiff, I don't want to worry you, but there are stories of people who've claimed to experience strange time slips or shifts in reality. What if this flash transported you somehow?"

"That's impossible. It might work in the movies, but not in real life."

"Maybe not in the usual sense," Coop said. "But there are theories about parallel universes and alternate dimensions. What if you caught a glimpse of another reality for a moment?"

Her mind raced with the possibility. "I'm still worried, and you aren't helping me," she said.

"I'm sorry," Coop said. "Look, this is all speculation. But let's look into this further. There may be clues to help explain what's going on."

Tiff nodded, a chill running down her spine. "Rachel said my mother was a Magician who practiced High Magick, that's magic with a k."

"Umm, we have you, the luminous being, battling the attacker while the light swirls around, forming a crop circle. That's magical stuff or something out of a Marvel Movie."

"You think the luminous being was my mother?"

"To be truthful, I don't know what to believe."

"Something about both of them was familiar. I wish I could remember more. And my problems are piling on top of each other now." Tiff told Coop about the sheriff stopping her after she left the tattoo shop, their conversation, and his visit, which included Nephilimbug.

"This guy, Nephilimbug, is creepy. Something about him makes me feel uneasy and scared. It's the way he looks at me."

"He thinks you're sexy." Coop smiled.

"No, it's not that. It's like he's trying to read my mind or worse, plant thoughts in it. Really strange."

"Don't worry about him. He's a low-paid government employee doing his job, that's all."

"I hope he leaves soon, like he said he was going to do," Tiff said, reaching up and touching her tattoo.

"Can I see it?"

Tiff pulled down her sweater as far as she could.

Coop, blushing, came closer and peeped at her chest.

"Cool, I have several, too." He lifted his shirt, and his body was covered with tattoos."

"Wow, I'm impressed. You don't have any on your arms."

"Not yet. I'm saving the arms and legs for special events in my life. I hadn't had many until I met you. I'm going to have a cube inked right here." He pointed to his forearm.

"That sounds great. If you don't mind, I'll have them ink a matching one."

Coop smiled. "Have you checked out this T-369 avatar online?"

"Yes, and the posts weren't extraordinary or strange. They were general information about crop circles."

"Let's look again."

Tiff pulled up the page, and they scrolled through the posts. "I don't remember seeing this one." She read it aloud: *Where shall we meet in 1, 2, 4, 5, 6, 7, 8, or 369?*

"That's code," Coop exclaimed. "I'm not sure what it means, but 369 might have something to do with Nikola Tesla's theory of 369-the Tesla coil. You reduce a compound number to a single digit by adding all the numbers."

"369 adds up to 18 and then 9. What would that number have to do with my mother and the other numbers?"

"Keep reading. It says here that the series of numbers 1, 2, 4, 5, 6, 7, and 8 can represent the material world, and 369 is considered the Divine vibrations—the spirit world."

"The message might mean, where shall we meet in the material world or the Spirit world?"

"And the 'T' could represent Tesla, but I don't see what he has to do with this."

"This search engine states that Nikola Tesla said, "*If you only knew the magnificence of the 3,6, and 9, then you would have the key to the universe.*"

Tiff stretched and shook her head. "None of this makes any sense about my mom. T-369, who are you?"

Coop glanced at his watch and stood up. "I should get going," he said. "My dad is leaving again, and I have no idea when I will see him next."

"At least you don't have someone watching your every move," she said, her voice quiet but full of frustration as she glanced away.

"You don't know how lucky you're to have your father here for you. He's being protective because of what happened to your mother."

"He doesn't even talk to me about her."

"What do you mean?"

"Whenever I bring up my mother, he shuts down. There aren't even photos of her in the house. It's like she never existed."

"Imagine yourself in his position. She has disappeared, leaving him uncertain of what to think or do. Yet, he's always been here for you, raising you alone." Coop paused, then added softly, "And I think he's done a terrific job."

Tiff gave a small nod but avoided eye contact as she shifted the focus to him. "Doesn't your father live with you?"

"Yes and no. My father's job in the military meant we moved around a lot when I was growing up. Once he retired, he started working for a company that required him to travel frequently. As a result, my mother and I have taken on most of the responsibility. Helping my mom care for my younger brother is one of my primary tasks."

"Doesn't your father live with you?"

"Yes and no. My father's job in the military meant we moved around a lot when I was growing up. Once he retired, he started working for a company that required him to travel frequently. As a result, my mother and I have taken on most of the responsibility. Helping my mom care for my younger brother is one of my primary tasks."

"Coop, I didn't know. Am I taking up too much of your time with all of this? You already have so much on your plate."

"Never. You are my refuge. My father has promised to be home for the summer and is considering quitting his current job to find a part-time position in Wheatfield, as I'll be a senior and leaving for college the following year."

"That's cool."

"I hope he follows through with his promises. I can't

help but wonder if he's a spy. We should add my father's name to the list of missing parents," Coop said.

Tiff studied his facial expression and realized he wasn't joking.

That night, Tiff lay awake for hours, her head throbbing with relentless, pulsating pain, each heartbeat echoing like a drumbeat in her ears. The room swam in and out of focus, the walls pulsing with a rhythm that matched her pain, and her mind spun with questions. By the time pale moonlight filtered through her window, she had decided. She had to find answers, no matter the cost.

The following day, she texted Coop:

TIFF

Can you go with me to see the psychic on Friday night?

COOP

Are you up to it?

TIFF

Yes, I'm better. If anyone has insight into strange phenomena, parallel worlds, and tarot cards, it'll be a psychic or medium.

COOP

Possibly. Won't that freak you out more?

TIFF

I'm already freaked out. Truth matters, strange or not. Will you come with me or not?

COOP

I'm in, "Wild Thing 3."

Tiff smiled, gratitude washing over her.

Chapter 8
Lotterland Farm

Nephilimbug activated his shadow cloak, triggering a power surge as he left his physical body behind and soared through the night sky. He had one destination in mind: the Lotterland farm. The girl might possess the cube —and he had to obtain it, no matter what. The allure of its secrets pulled him forward with insatiable urgency.

Arriving at the farm, Nephilimbug slipped silently through the door. Inside, the sound of Lincoln's snoring echoed through the quiet room—he was sprawled across the couch, oblivious. Nephilimbug, harboring a deep disdain for human males, hovered close and whispered with venom, "You're a failure, a bad father, and worthless."

With silent steps, he began his search, methodically scouring every room, drawer, and closet. But the cube remained elusive.

He paused at the threshold of Tiff's room, calculating his next move. Rummaging through her belongings, he found a sleek silver laptop on her desk, the screen dark and waiting.

He tapped his Wrist-Tech Amplifier, powering it up

and breaching its security in seconds. A soft hum filled the air, underscored by a faint metallic scent—the telltale sign of shadow tech in motion. Her recent searches confirmed what he feared: tarot cards, Hebrew letters, sacred geometry, and the cube.

Stunned and infuriated, he searched the room again but still found no trace of the cube. A cold realization struck him: Tiff had anticipated danger and taken it with her.

"Clever girl," he muttered under his breath. Headquarters would not be pleased.

Before leaving, Nephilimbug decided to plant seeds of doubt in her mind. He moved her belongings just enough to be noticed—her teddy bear tossed on the floor, her toothbrush replaced with her hairbrush, a houseplant swapped with her math textbook. Each action was a calculated disruption.

As he retreated into the shadows, a wicked smile curled on his lips. Let her wonder if she was losing her grip. Let the unraveling begin.

Chapter 9
Psychic

DeBora, renowned for her professed psychic talents, successfully established a boutique in the bustling mall, catering to her extensive following. Her services, which included personal readings, attracted a diverse crowd, particularly the affluent professionals of the community. The shop offered an array of mystical items, including esoteric literature, tarot decks, gemstones, and ceremonial candles. The ambiance of her consultation space was set by the soft glow of candles amidst an array of crystals and dream catchers, with the aromatic scent of white sage permeating the air.

DeBora's hair was a mess of curly, bright red strands sticking out at odd angles. Her cat-eyeglasses were perched on the bridge of her nose, giving her an intellectual look about her. Her face was covered in thick white powder. She wore a dress from another era, with a high neck, long sleeves, and elegant white gloves.

"Welcome," she said. "How may I help you?" She glanced at the clock, noting the late hour. The store was quiet, its shelves dimly lit, and no other customers lingered.

With a sweep of her gloved hand, she ushered them to a nearby table surrounded by four velvet-upholstered chairs, their fabric slightly worn from years of use.

Tiff explained the flashes of light in the wheat and the appearance and disappearance of the crop circles but left out her encounter with Rachel and the cube. By the time she finished, DeBora's smile had morphed into a frown.

"This is most unusual," the psychic said. "It seems you may have a lot of psychic energy around you. The good part is that it's awakening your psychic abilities. Still, the energy also brings all the negative demons."

"Did you say demons?"

"Yes, I did, sweetheart. If you don't believe in them, you're wasting your time here."

Tiff said, "It's not that we don't believe. We don't understand how these beings or demons appear in our world. Yet, the concept of demons in our reality is a challenging pill to swallow."

DeBora hesitated, her eyes piercing. "Demons, my dear, aren't only figments from tales. They're real energies drawn to the shadows within us. Your recent experiences might have stirred the veil between worlds, inviting them closer. You called them."

"What do you mean?"

"This is classic mind stuff. Our negative thoughts set up the right energy to attract them. They feed off negativity and constantly cycle this low energy—jealousy, hate, and separatism—in our lives."

DeBora grabbed her stack of cards, shuffled them, cut them, and then laid several out on the table. She stared at them before saying, "Girl, what have you gotten yourself into?"

Tiff saw the cards, and her face twisted with fear. "Those are the cards in my vision." She pointed to the

Fool, and across it lay the World. Below them, the Devil card lay ominous and unyielding.

"Death doesn't mean death, does it?" Coop squinched his brows.

DeBora ignored him and said, "The spirits and angels are trying to contact you," nodding at Tiff. "You're waking up, and it ain't going to be pretty if you keep resisting your destiny."

"What destiny? You're the second person to mention my destiny. Can you please tell me more about it?"

"That's for you to figure out. Why should you believe me? Use your psychic abilities."

"What abilities? This has been a waste of time." She stood up.

DeBora continued staring at the cards. "My guides tell me you're planning to journey beyond this physical plane."

"You mean I'm going to die?"

"No, this inward journey requires you to pass seven tests. DeBora said, her voice distant as she listened inwardly. "They're telling me that the initiation will come first. Then you'll find what you're looking for. She paused, her eyes narrowing. "Wait, what?" DeBora blinked hard, as if trying to understand what the voices were trying to tell her. "Got it! Time to shut this down." She nodded her head. Looking at the two of them, she muttered, "Time for you two to leave. You're leaving. I'm not getting involved with demons, a magical cube, and definitely not the Black Shadow. Who did you piss off in the other world?"

"I don't know what you're talking about," Tiff said, leaning forward slightly in her chair. "What do you know about the cube?"

DeBora picked up the cards and slid them back into the pack. Standing up, she waved a hand dismissively.

"Look, don't worry about the twenty-five dollars. We didn't do a full half-hour. I can't help you. You should leave."

"I don't understand. Can you at least tell us what you mean by the Black Shadow? Who are they?"

Widening her eyes, DeBora uttered gravely, "Trust me, you don't want to know. You might avoid the worst. Now go and let me cleanse this space." With that, she ushered them firmly towards the exit.

"Did you pick up anything about my mother?" Tiff asked, standing up and knocking over the chair.

"Leave, now!"

Coop grabbed Tiff by the arm and pulled her through the door.

They looked back, and DeBora had put the closed sign in the window and shut the blinds.

After their experience with the psychic, Coop and Tiff went to the Wheatfield Center to unwind. The center was a small community gathering spot that hosted music, pool, darts, and card games for teens after school and on weekends. On Friday nights, local students performed live entertainment.

Tiff glanced around and immediately spotted Maddie and L.R. playing pool with a group of friends. As she expected, Maddie's turn came up, and she made her shot with ease. Tiff wasn't surprised—she had taught Maddie how to play years ago on her father's old table. Maddie looked up and locked eyes with her for a moment as Tiff and Coop approached.

"Hey, stranger," Tiff greeted. "How have you been?"

"Oh, the usual," Maddie replied casually.

L.R. hollered, "It's your shot. Are you playing or going down memory lane?"

"Gotta go," Maddie muttered and turned back to the table.

"I have a lot to tell you," Tiff added, wincing at the memory of their last awkward encounter. "Let's talk whenever you have time."

"Sure, whatever," Maddie scoffed and walked away.

Tiff watched with sadness as her childhood friend disappeared into the group. She caught L.R. staring at her —his lingering look made her uneasy, stirring an instinctive distrust she couldn't shake. She returned to Coop, who was waiting with two smoothies in hand.

"Let's stay and play darts," he said.

"Is this a date, Coop?"

"Maybe. Depends on how good you're." He gave her a crooked grin.

They played a couple of games and mingled with the other students. Tiff was surprised by how much fun she had —and how easily she fit in with everyone. Several classmates stopped to talk or ask questions about the crop circles. Every so often, she glanced over at Maddie, who was laughing and holding court like the life of the party. Tiff felt happy for her but couldn't help missing what they once shared.

On the drive home, they were still in an upbeat mood, talking nonstop about all the fun they'd had with the other students. But when they pulled into the driveway, her father was already standing on the front porch with his arms crossed, a storm brewing on his face.

"Where have you been?" he asked as Tiff climbed out of the car. "You were supposed to be home hours ago!"

"I'm sorry, Dad," Tiff replied. "Something came up, and I lost track of time."

It was a weak excuse, and they both knew it.

"What's gotten into you? This stops now. You're grounded for a week."

Tiff opened her mouth to argue but thought better of it. She had pushed her luck too many times already.

"Yes, sir," she said, eyes lowered. Coop lingered a few feet away, looking apologetic on her behalf.

"Look, I'm trying to do what's best for you," Lincoln added, his voice softening. "You can't keep running off without telling me where you're going or when you'll be back."

"I know," Tiff said quietly. "I'm sorry."

He studied her for a moment, gauging her sincerity. "All right then. Get inside."

Tiff obeyed, pausing on the threshold to glance back at Coop.

"See you," she said with a slight wave.

"Bye," he replied. "Hang in there."

She managed a small smile and stepped inside, the screen door creaking shut behind her. Her father stood in the living room beside his favorite chair, lost in thought. She walked over and wrapped her arms around him from behind. He tensed at first, then slowly relaxed into the embrace.

"I'm sorry," she whispered. "Really. I don't mean to worry you."

"I've failed you as a father," he blurted. "I can't seem to do anything right."

"No, Dad! How can you say that? You've been the best father a girl could ask for," Tiff cried.

She knew Lincoln loved her and only wanted to protect her—even from the parts of herself she didn't yet understand. She left him on the couch, his head in his hands, weighed down by despair. She had to find out what was going on—and how to help.

Rushing upstairs, she flung open her bedroom door and froze. The faint smell of metal lingered in the air, like the trace of electricity after a lightning strike. Her teddy bear, Bertie, was lying face down on the floor, far from his usual spot on the bed. Her potted plant had been moved from the desk to a shelf among her math books.

Someone had been in her room, and they wanted her to know it.

Her phone beeped. Coop had texted.

COOP

Is everything okay?

TIFF

Something's not right. My room's been messed with—Bertie was on the floor, my plant moved... it smells awful, like something rotten or burnt.

COOP

What?! That sounds serious. Do you want me to come back over?

TIFF

No, it's late. I can handle it.

COOP

You sure?

TIFF

I'm sure. I'll stay calm and figure this out.

COOP

Okay. Promise you'll call if anything else happens.

TIFF

Promise.

COOP

I've been searching everywhere for info on
the Black Shadow—still nothing legit.

TIFF

I know someone who does know.

COOP

Who?

TIFF

Rachel Coleman. My aunt. She's not telling
me everything. Time for truth or dare.

COOP

Don't go alone. I don't want my girlfriend
ending up with another head injury.

Tiff smiled. He called her his girlfriend. They were officially an item.

Tiff woke as sunlight filtered through her window. She yawned and stretched, then checked the time. It was a little after 8 a.m. Usually, she slept in on the weekends, but after the events of the past few days, she felt restless.

She fixed herself a bowl of cold cereal while her father tended to the animals outside. As she ate, she thought about her conversation with Rachel and the strange vision in the wheat field. The memories stirred something deep inside her. Despite the risks, she felt more certain than ever that she had to uncover the truth about her mother—even if it meant upsetting her father again.

Once she finished eating, Tiff put on her boots and headed out to help with the farm chores. The physical work cleared her mind. For a while, she lost herself in feeding the animals, mucking the stalls, and baling hay.

Around noon, Coop texted her to see if she wanted to meet up, but she told him she was busy with chores and still grounded for the weekend. Though she missed him, she didn't want to cause more trouble.

The rest of the day went by slowly. Tiff made dinner for herself and her father, who seemed less upset with her than before. Afterward, they watched a sports program together, trading a few casual words about farm work and local news.

Before heading to bed, Tiff checked her phone. There were several messages from Coop, all checking in on how she was feeling and whether anything unusual had happened. She smiled and typed back a quick reply.

TIFF

No!

COOP

Cool.

Tiff was looking forward to the final bell of the school year, which would mark the start of summer break. Her father had been pushing her to apply to college, even though money was tight. It weighed on her, but not as much as the mystery that now consumed her thoughts.

That night, her body ached from the long day. The farm work, the tension, and the nonstop swirl of thoughts left her worn out. She fell asleep thinking of the wheat rippling under a cloudless sky and the strange symbol that kept surfacing in her mind. Somewhere in the tangle of dreams, an image formed clearly—a single tarot card, the Wheel of Fortune, spinning endlessly. It turned round and round, revealing glimpses of light, shadow, and fate. Tiff drifted deeper into sleep, the wheel still turning.

Chapter 10
Stand Your Ground

Tiff was overjoyed when Maddie phoned to invite her to her birthday bash. Although they had endured several disagreements, nothing compared to the rift between them now. Tiff couldn't fathom living without her closest friend.

Tiff hesitated. L.R. and his gang would be there. The group made her uneasy, especially L.R. His lingering stare gave her chills, making her feel uncomfortable and distrustful of his intentions.

But this was Maddie's big day. Tiff pushed aside her doubts and agreed to come.

The morning of the party, Tiff's stomach churned with nerves. She glanced at Coop's text, wishing her luck. He had bailed at the last minute, choosing to hang out with his nerdy friends. Tiff frowned, frustration simmering beneath her anxiety. He was turning out to be quite the boyfriend. This was her first outing since being grounded.

Fuming, she made her way into the town. But before heading to the party, she had one last task to complete. An hour passed, and she emerged from the hair salon with a bag containing her chopped locks.

Lincoln wouldn't be back until it was time for her to leave for the party, giving her enough time to gather the courage to face him. Before leaving the parking space, Tiff flipped down the sun visor to look in the mirror. As she gazed at her reflection, something struck her for the first time—she saw herself.

The stylist had treated her to a complimentary makeover, enhancing her striking features. Her almond-shaped eyes, with hints of green in the irises, were accentuated with precise, bold eyeliner and thick mascara that made her long lashes pop. The bright red lipstick the stylist applied added glamour to her petite face. Tiff couldn't help but run her hand over her head, reveling in the feeling of her short hair. She was loving her new look.

Tiff could hear Lincoln's footsteps echoing through the house. He had returned home a while ago and was calling out to her from downstairs, asking if she wanted anything to eat for dinner.

"I already ate. I'm dressing for Maddie's party tonight."

"I think I'll eat these leftovers. Is Coop going with you?"

"No," Tiff said, sighing heavily.

"I don't want you out too late. Let's plan for you to come home by eleven at the latest, but before midnight."

Tiff didn't respond and rushed to her room.

She lost track of time as she admired her outfit in front of the full-length mirror in the bathroom. The cutout jeans and cropped top were far from anything she had ever worn. She had stumbled upon the perfect jean jacket at a thrift store to complete the look. Her mother's silver chain and dangling sterling earrings adorned her neck and ears, adding a personal touch to the ensemble.

With each step she took down the staircase, her pumps —a lucky thrift store find—added a graceful sway to her steps. Tiff reached the archway connecting the dining room and living room and paused. Lincoln was at the table, nursing his fourth cup of coffee for the day, his dinner untouched in front of him. He looked up mid-sip and choked slightly. The room remained silent, weighed down by tension. She waited for him to say something. Instead, he stood abruptly, his expression tight with disapproval, and brushed past her, muttering, "Be home by ten p.m. instead of eleven," without giving her a second glance.

Tiff blinked back tears, not wanting to ruin her makeup.

With a resigned sigh, Tiff headed over to Maddie's house. Unbeknownst to her, a large black crow trailed silently behind, settling on a neighbor's tree as she stepped out of her car. Tiff plastered on a smile, clutching Maddie's present as she walked up the front steps. The muffled sound of laughter and music spilled through the open front door.

Here we go, she thought, stepping into the lion's den. Her gaze immediately landed on L.R., leaning against the wall with a smug grin. Tiff gritted her teeth.

Tonight, she would avoid L.R. at all costs.

Tiff approached Maddie, who let out a high-pitched squeal of joy upon seeing her.

"You came!" Maddie threw her arms around Tiff. "I'm so glad. This is going to be the best birthday ever."

Maddie latched onto her arm. "You look hot!" she exclaimed. "That makeup, your hair—I love the pixie cut on you. The guys are drooling over you. I'm glad you decided to come!"

"Happy birthday," Tiff said, giving Maddie her gift. "Don't wait, open it now."

Maddie tore into the wrapping paper, revealing a new sketchbook and a set of colored pencils. Her eyes lit up. "These are perfect! Thank you so much."

Tiff smiled, relieved she'd chosen something she knew Maddie would enjoy. One of the boys in her English class asked her to dance, and then another guy. Tiff danced and talked to others in her school whom she often avoided.

Maddie grabbed her arm and pulled her into another room. "Aren't you glad you came?"

"Yes, yes. I haven't had this much fun in a long time."

"Where is Coop? I invited him, too."

"Um...he had another commitment but wishes you a happy birthday."

Tiff glanced at the doorway, and L.R. was there with his cronies behind him. He sauntered over to them with a predatory glint in his eyes. Her heart sank -her plan to stay away from him was thwarted.

"Well, well," L.R. said. "If it isn't little Miss Crop Circle," he laughed. "Are you in this dimension or an alternative reality of crazies like your mother?" His friends joined him in laughing at Tiff.

Maddie's eyes widened. "Shut up and go away, L.R. You don't know what you're talking about."

L.R. leaned in close, his breath hot against Tiff's ear, and said, "Next time you play in the field, take me with you. My boys and I will show you a good time." Tiff shoved him away, disgust churning in her gut.

As L.R.'s words sliced through the festive noise, a cold

fury settled in her bones. She waited for Maddie to say something to him, but she was talking to her other guests who had wandered into the room. Tiff's trust was broken, not only by Maddie's recklessness but also by the painful sting of being publicly embarrassed. It was as if each laugh from L.R.'s friends was a reminder of how far she had drifted from her old life. Betrayal and hurt twisted inside her.

With her face burning, Tiff turned and hurried through the crowd of partygoers. She left quickly before she did something she'd regret. The cool night air soothed her frayed nerves. Tiff stood on the patio, staring at the stars as tears pricked her eyes. She'd been so stupid to think this party would be different. Someone grabbed her from behind. She turned. It was L.R. He had followed her out to the patio.

Tiff gritted her teeth, heart pounding, as L.R. leaned in closer. His hand slid around her waist, gripping tight, and panic rose in her chest.

She wasn't going to let him touch her or stand by helplessly while he did what he wanted.

With a snarl, Tiff seized L.R.'s wrist and twisted, flipping him to the ground. He landed hard on his back, the air leaving his lungs in a wheeze of surprise.

Silence fell over the patio. Tiff stood over L.R., chest heaving, as his gang watched her in shock.

L.R. sputtered, face twisting with rage. "You little freak!" he said, struggling to his feet. "I'm going to…"

"What?" Tiff snapped. "You're going to do what? Touch me again?" She shoved him. "Try it."

L.R.'s eyes narrowed, yet he made no move to strike. His gaze shifted to Maddie, and he shrugged his shoulders.

Tiff, overcome with anger, approached Maddie and said, "I can't believe you shared all my deepest secrets with him." She shook her head, the full depth of Maddie's betrayal hitting her. "Some friend you turned out to be."

Maddie's face crumpled. "Tiff, I didn't mean to! Let me explain."

She turned away from the others' gaping faces, the weight of their stares too great to bear. Her heart raced as she hurried to her car, the pounding music fading behind her.

As she drove home, she mulled over everything that had happened. She couldn't believe how awful L.R. had been or how Maddie had betrayed her—some friend. Tiff had wasted so much time trying to repair their friendship, and for what? More heartache and disappointment.

Why did everything keep changing in my life?

She missed the way things used to be, missed having someone she could count on. Maddie had been her best friend for as long as she could remember, but Tiff wasn't sure their friendship could survive this.

She took a shaky breath, wiping her eyes again. It may be time to accept that some things weren't meant to last. As much as it hurt, she had to face the truth: her friendship with Maddie might be over for good.

Tiff sat in the car, not ready to go into the house. Chip had been waiting for her on the front porch. He ran over to the car, and she let him in. Burying her head in his coat, Tiff couldn't hold back the tears. Now that Maddie had shown her true colors, she felt like she had no one to turn to.

Except there was one person. Tiff pulled out her phone and scrolled through her contacts until she found Rachel Coleman's name.

Her fingers trembled over the keypad as she typed out a message.

TIFF

Hi, are you awake?

She kept an eye on her phone, expecting an answer. Silence prevailed, and with each passing moment, the pain of abandonment deepened.

As Tiff exited the car, Chip followed behind her as she walked to the house, hoping her dad didn't wait for her. Then, she glimpsed a light and sensed a cool breeze enveloping her. Chip's ears perked up. He ran towards the field. She called for him to come back, but he kept going. Her father swung open the door.

"Tiff, is everything okay?"

"Yes, Chip ran off chasing something."

Tiff started running after him, but Lincoln stopped her with a stern command. "He will come back when he's ready. Come on in now. I don't want you wandering around the field."

Tiff stood there, torn between following Chip and obeying her father's instructions. She turned to face the vast fields and then made a decision, sprinting towards the golden wheat field in pursuit of Chip. Lincoln followed close behind her, mumbling under his breath. When he caught up with her, she was already gazing into the center of a swirling crop circle where Chip appeared frozen.

Tiff raised her arms, attempting to push through an invisible barrier that prevented her from entering the field.

"Dad, what's happening? I can't go any further."

Lincoln was also immovable, unsure of what to say as Tiff pushed against the barrier with her shoulder. She ended up falling through it as if it were never there. Tiff saw stars, Chip licked her face, and Lincoln helped her.

"What happened?" she asked.

"You tripped trying to reach Chip. Let's go home."

"A moment ago, a crop circle was there, and an invisible barrier was preventing us from reaching Chip. He was stuck over there. Didn't you feel that barrier?" Tiff pleaded.

"What are you talking about? You tripped. There's no barrier, he said, pointing at Chip now sniffing at the ground not far from them. Let's go home and look at your shoulder."

Tiff stood there for several more moments. Her eyes shifted from Chip to her father's face, full of fright and anguish.

She called for Chip as they turned to go home. He came to her side but looked back toward the field, ears perked, a low growl rising deep from his chest. It was all the confirmation Tiff needed.

Chapter 11
Truth Be Told

Lincoln's knuckles turned white as he gripped his coffee mug, the silence between them thick with unsaid words. He glared across the kitchen table at Rachel, his voice icy with restrained anger. "Why are you here after all these years, Rachel? Do you think you can waltz back into our lives?"

Rachel fidgeted, her fingers twisting the frayed edges of her sweater. She avoided his piercing gaze. "Tiff found me. She's asking questions about her mother—about Sarah. I thought it was time she knew more."

"You thought you'd come and disrupt our lives again?" Lincoln's voice rose, the mug in his hand trembling with his fury. "As if you didn't cause enough damage, helping Sarah vanish into thin air?"

"I didn't help her disappear, Lincoln." Rachel's voice was soft but firm. She finally met his gaze, her own eyes filled with a plea for understanding. "Tiff deserves to know about her heritage, about her mother."

"Her mother—who abandoned her," Lincoln snapped.

"And now you want to dredge up the past? You want to fill her head with your delusions?"

Rachel sighed, a mix of frustration and sorrow crossing her features. "It's not a delusion. Sarah did not have a mental illness, Lincoln. She was a gifted metaphysician, exploring realms beyond your understanding."

"And you think that's what Tiff should hear? That her mother was off chasing fantasies?" Lincoln's voice was scornful.

Rachel's demeanor hardened, her resolve clear. "It's not nonsense. It's her legacy. Sarah was special, and I believe Tiff might be, too. She has a right to explore her path, to know where she comes from."

Lincoln slammed his fist down, jolting the table. "And what? End up like Sarah? Disappearing without a trace, leaving her family behind?"

"That's not fair, and you know it," Rachel countered, her voice steady. "Tiff is reaching out, trying to understand her powers. Ignoring this won't protect her."

Lincoln rubbed his temples, the fight slowly draining out of him. "Powers? There you go with that nonsense again. I want to keep her safe from all your craziness. That's all I've ever wanted."

"And I believe understanding her true nature is part of that safety," Rachel insisted. "You can't shield her from who she is. Not forever."

Lincoln looked away, his expression tormented. After a long pause, he muttered, "Tiff is safe here. Sarah had a mental illness, but you and your family didn't want to admit the truth. Instead, you were involved in witchcraft. I saw with my own eyes what you were doing in the fields."

"That's not true. Whatever you saw, you don't understand," she said firmly, disappointed in his response.

"Maybe you're right. Or maybe I'm."

Rachel nodded, her expression sympathetic. "I know this is hard for you. But I think it's time we both faced the truth—for Tiff's sake."

For a few seconds, the conversation tapered off into a heavy silence, each person lost in their tumultuous emotions.

"Go," he said. "Please, leave us alone. I can protect her much better than you protected Sarah."

Rachel hovered for a second. "We'll see about that," she said, then turned on her heel and left without another word.

Lincoln sat motionless at the table, Rachel's parting words echoing in his mind like a fatal blow.

He had known this day would come, eventually. Tiff was too bright and curious to be kept in the dark forever. She would dig until she uncovered the truth, no matter how hard he tried to distract or deter her.

He had to tell Tiff about her mother before she heard Rachel's lies. She deserved the truth, even if it shattered what little peace he had left.

As Rachel drove away from Lotterland Farm, she couldn't help but think about the days and weeks following Sarah's disappearance. Perhaps Lincoln was onto something; maybe it was all her fault.

They were both engrossed in exploring the unknown, delving into quantum physics, alternate realities, and astral projection. Sarah had always been more well-versed in it all. On the night of the full moon, when Sarah disappeared, Habiba and the other women gathered for their customary ritual in the wheatfield. All nine lay down within the crop circle at its center, protected by an invisible force that prevented anyone from entering or leaving. They chanted before closing their eyes to open themselves to divine energy.

Rachel's last memory was waking up to find Sarah missing. Habiba was the only one who wasn't shocked; she explained that Sarah had chosen to move on to the next phase of her spiritual journey. There was nothing they could do but remember her in their hearts. They were sworn to secrecy about it all. But she had told someone—Lincoln. He told her she was insane and to stay away from Tiff and him forever.

She wiped away a flood of tears, remembering first the loss of Sarah and then being banished from Tiff. Rachel reflected on her conversation with Sarah before the ritual.

"Follow Mother's instructions, no matter what," Sarah had advised.

"What do you mean?" Rachel had asked, worried.

"Everything will work out," Sarah reassured her.

"And Tiff?" Rachel pressed.

Sarah's eyes grew misty, but she smiled and said, "Follow Mother's instructions."

"You're scaring me, Sarah. What's going on?"

She kissed her, and the ritual started.

Even after the police investigation ended and Habiba had transitioned, Rachel was determined to find her sister, knowing she wouldn't be found in the physical world—at least not as Sarah. Rachel set off on a quest to Mt. Shasta to find the Ascended Master known as the Teacher. Her goal was to learn advanced practices of quantum leaping, remote viewing, and astral projection, all under the guidance of this mystical sage.

After tirelessly searching for the Teacher for months, Rachel was caught off guard when an older man approached her while she was sitting on a bench in a small park. She initially mistook him for a beggar and kindly offered him some of her lunch. However, to her surprise, she realized he was not a beggar at all, but rather a tall, mystical figure. He said, "Follow me, and your training will begin." Without waiting for a response, the Teacher turned and started walking toward the ancient stone archway at the edge of the clearing in the park. Rachel followed him without hesitation into the unknown.

After years of honing her mind and achieving incredible feats, one morning, while deep in meditation, she heard her Teacher say, "The girl is the answer. She is the one." Rachel knew what it meant. She had been keeping tabs on Tiff's progress through remote viewing but had never interfered—until now. It was time to seek out Tiff and bring her into their plans to find Sarah in the multiverse.

Chapter 12
Pinocchio's Nose

Lincoln waited until after dinner to approach Tiff about Rachel's visit. He helped her clear the table of dishes and put them into the dishwasher. She caught him staring and offered a small smile, but his frown didn't lift.

"Dad? What's going on?"

His throat tightened as a dozen emotions warred inside him. "There's something I want to share with you about your mother."

"What is it?" she asked, tone guarded now.

"Her sister, Rachel, came to see me today."

"Wait, what? Rachel was here?"

"She said you reached out to her."

"I did. I met her through Ancestry. We had dinner once. I was going to tell you, but… you don't like talking about Mom. You've never told me anything about her side of the family. Not one thing. Why not?"

"It's complicated," he said quietly.

"Try me." Her arms crossed, and the softening in her expression disappeared.

Lincoln closed his eyes. The silence stretched long and uncomfortable.

Finally, she slammed a dish into the dishwasher rack.

"What did you want to tell me?" she snapped. "I'm not a child. I deserve to know the truth."

She switched on the machine and left the kitchen without another word, her shoulders tight with frustration. The hum of the dishwasher filled the space behind her.

When it stopped, she returned. Arms crossed. Expression unrelenting.

"I'm still waiting."

He nodded. "Your mother and I met young. Fell for each other fast. She was the prettiest girl I'd ever seen. And… different."

"Different how?"

"She was too sharp for this town. Too curious. Always reading, always asking questions no one wanted to answer. Ministers, teachers, even doctors. She'd debate them all, asking about mysteries—things I didn't understand. We got married. And when she got pregnant with you, we were thrilled. But after you were born, something in her changed."

"Do you mean postpartum depression? Or… she didn't want me?"

"Tiff, don't say that." He looked up sharply. "She loved you. But she was struggling—really struggling. Her mind started turning inward."

He stared at the floor. "She'd sit for hours with her eyes closed, making strange sounds under her breath. Then she'd vanish into the fields for hours."

"And you didn't stop her? You didn't think something was wrong?"

"I asked her. Over and over. She'd say the same thing."

"Which was?"

"That she had a mission. She called it the Great Work. Said she had to fix something she'd broken. But she never explained what. Most days, it was like she wasn't here— like she was somewhere else in her head. She'd say things like, 'Time isn't real,' or 'I've seen what comes after this life.' She said she could move through time. Not her body, but her mind alone."

Tiff didn't respond right away. It felt like the floor beneath her had shifted. She swallowed. Her throat burned. This couldn't be real. Not her mother. Not the woman she dreamed about every night.

"What are you saying?"

"Sarah had schizophrenia."

"No." The word came out fast, too loud. "I don't believe that."

She stepped back, one hand bracing the edge of the counter. Her pulse raced. It couldn't be real. Not her mother.

"A doctor didn't officially diagnose her," Lincoln said. "I told Dr. Broomall about what I'd seen. He begged her to come in, but she wouldn't. He said he couldn't say for sure unless he met with her."

"Dad, Dr. Broomall is your medical doctor, not a psychiatrist."

"I know. I was doing what I could. Sarah wouldn't see anyone except a midwife. She and Habiba delivered you."

"You never told me my grandmother helped deliver me. Why not?"

"Sarah's family was strange. And I wanted to shield you from all of it."

"But you really don't know if Mom had a mental illness?"

"I talked to others. From everything I've heard… she wasn't exactly normal."

"What others?" Tiff narrowed her eyes.

"It doesn't matter. I'm not getting into that now."

"Accept, like I did. Sarah was sick."

She looked away, lips parted but silent. "Do you think I have what Mom had?"

"No. No, you're nothing like her." His voice wavered. He wiped at his eyes with the back of his hand.

"Then what did happen to her?"

"One day, she left. Vanished without a trace. I always assumed her family put her in a facility. Rachel and her mother wouldn't say a word. I checked every hospital I could think of, even in other states. There was no record. Nothing."

He exhaled hard. "I should've told you. I was trying to protect you, but I was wrong. You had a right to know. I'm sorry it took me so long to say this."

Tiff turned away, arms folded tightly across her chest. So that was it. That was the truth he'd hidden for years. It felt like a thousand puzzle pieces had been thrown at her all at once. After a long moment, she turned back to him. Her voice was flat but composed.

"Thanks for telling me. But it doesn't change anything."

She left the kitchen without looking back. Whatever Lincoln believed, she knew deep down that he only saw part of the truth. He thought Sarah was unstable. He probably thought the same about her. But something else was going on—something much deeper. And if she was going to uncover it, Rachel might be able to help her.

Tiff shut her bedroom door and locked it, something she hadn't done since she was a little girl. She leaned against it, her breath shallow. The silence buzzed in her ears, the weight of what she'd heard pressing down like a storm front.

Her phone buzzed, the screen lighting up like a flare in the dark. Two messages. One from Maddie. One from Coop.

She opened Maddie's first.

I didn't reveal your secrets to L.R. I asked him if he or his friends made the crop circle and trashed it. He denied it. I wanted to cover every angle. In the UK, people sometimes make fake crop circles. I broke up with him. He's awful. Please—can we meet?

Tiff exhaled slowly. She wasn't ready for Maddie. Not now. Trust wasn't something she could offer easily at the moment.

She opened Coop's text.

How was the party? I wanted to go with you, but this guy from a language exchange program was visiting my friend, and it was the only time he could meet. I showed him the cube photo—he knows the Hebrew alphabet. I didn't want to say anything until I was sure, but... I think I know who we should see next. Can we meet?

She read it again. Coop wasn't pushing. He was simply there.

She tapped her reply, fingers moving with clarity she hadn't felt all day.

Sure. I'll meet you at the Wheatfield Center in twenty minutes. We need to talk.

When Tiff arrived at the center, Coop was already there, with two bottles of watermelon juice in front of him. He beamed with excitement, his eyes sparkling, as he offered her a bottle of juice. "Do you want something to go with it?" he said, pushing the bottle toward her.

"No, this is perfect, thanks." Tiff sat across from him, comforted by his thoughtfulness but also noticing his eagerness. "What's going on?"

"Are you okay? You look a bit flustered."

"I'm okay. What did you find out?"

"Ari, the guy I met with last night, said it's tied to the Hermetic Qabala and the Tree of Life," Coop said, barely able to sit still. "He says it holds ancient secrets—or mystical codes—for those involved in the Hermetic mysteries."

Tiff pulled out the cube and turned it around, looking at the tarot cards on it and comparing them to the ones on the chart. Her tone shifted, revealing a spark of curiosity as she asked, "Really? By the Kabala, you mean the religion that Madonna and other stars are wrapped up in?"

"No, not that one, but the Hermetic Qabala, spelled with a Q. The Jewish mysticism is spelled with a K, and the Christian with a C. Bizarre, right?"

"What was my mom involved in?" Tiff traced her fingers around each square of the cube.

"I'm not sure, but if that cube were hers, it points that she was involved in or studied Hermeticism."

"Maybe the women who raised her and Rachel were Hermetic Qabalists, and that's how they got involved."

"We are speculating without hard facts. But there's a way to find out. Ask your father."

"I don't think he knows. He mentioned my mom was involved with a group, but he didn't know anything about them."

Coop's eyes still glinted with excitement. "There's more that Ari told me. There are stories about places on Earth that serve as portals to other worlds. They're often marked with a symbol to signify their significance."

"And you think the wheat field is one of these places?"

"Yes," Coop said.

Tiff finished her smoothie, her mind spinning. Coop's theory made sense. Rachel had said Wheat Field was different.

"What do you suppose occurs if we take the cube to the field?"

"I'd stay away from there. Think about what happened to you that evening." Coop fixed her with a worried gaze.

"Come on, Coop. You'll be with me."

"Our next move should be to talk to your aunt and Ari."

"You sure have a knack for practicality, Sherlock Holmes! Where's the thrill-seeking side of you? I doubt anything will come of it anyway," Tiff replied.

Coop pondered her words before stating, "All right, but didn't Rachel and your father tell you to stay away from the field?"

"We won't stay long. I'll look at the field differently this time to determine if I can sense anything."

"Okay, let's go now before the dark sets in."

"Let's do this." Tiff grabbed her bag.

Chapter 13
Crows

Nephilimbug felt powerful as he viewed the humans coming and going near the restaurant. Pathetic Earthlings dazed and asleep in their own skin. They had no idea who they were or the power they carried. Their dull vibrations made them so easy to influence. It only took a few psychic pulses to plant doubt and confusion. He had done it before.

L.R. had been one of his targets. The boy's reaction at the party had amused him, though the performance was clumsy. Still, the potential was there. With proper training, L.R. could be useful for small operations.

But Tiff was another matter. She radiated with something raw and dangerous—boundless potential waiting to crack open. And that worried him.

He took flight, his wings slicing through the thick afternoon air, then gave a high-pitched caw. More crows circled into view, responding to his call. He beckoned them down to the trees flanking the center.

Not to harm the girl—only to unsettle.

As Tiff and Coop stepped out into the waning

daylight, the sky dimmed unnaturally. Clouds clustered where there had been none. In the tree branches above, black wings rustled and settled, eyes gleaming like polished onyx.

They would follow. Watch. Wait.

And when the moment came, he would take the cube.

Chapter 14
Illusions

Tiff and Coop hurried out of the center, clutching their bags and glancing nervously at the sky. It was supposed to be a sunny afternoon, but the clouds had gathered, casting a dark shadow over the city. They could hear the crows cawing from a nearby tree, mocking their escape. They felt a chill run down their spines.

They reached the parking lot, racing toward the car to beat the rain and get away as fast as possible. But before they could reach it, a bright flash of light burst across the pavement. A swirling energy vortex opened in the air. They had no time to react as a powerful suction yanked them off their feet. They screamed as they vanished into the unknown.

Tiff blinked at the sight before her. Jagged rocks jutted into a deep blue sky while a swollen red sun cast an eerie glow over the terrain. Two moons hung overhead, looming with watchful eyes.

Crows were everywhere, flying around them.

"Where are we?" she cried.

"Not where," Coop corrected. «*When*." This could be a distant past or future, an alternate history. There's no way to be sure." He batted a bird away.

Tentatively, Tiff started walking to escape the crows stalking them. Coop followed close behind her. The ground was firm under her feet, yet it crunched with a noise akin to shattering glass. Kneeling for a closer inspection, she scattered some of the fragile crystals and gasped in surprise.

Countless bones lay scattered across the ground, shattered into fragments. Her heart pounding, Tiff stood and surveyed their surroundings.

In the distance, a massive creature lumbered into view. The man towered over them, his muscular frame hidden beneath a long, black cloak. The hood obscured his facial features, making him seem mysterious and dangerous. He held a gleaming sword, its sharp edge catching the light as he pointed it at them.

"I'm the guardian of this Southern gate," he said in a deep voice. "Intone the Divine Name and give the Sign of the Enterer?"

"It's happening again, hooded entity. But not the same one who attacked me. His voice is different and his size," she said. "We must leave before he kicks both our asses."

"Then get us out of here," Coop said, tugging on Tiff's arm.

But it was too late. The creature let out a bone-chilling roar and charged, hunger etched into its hideous features. Tiff's blood turned to ice in her veins. They were intruders here, trespassers in a land ruled by beasts.

And they had nowhere left to run.

Tiff's instincts kicked in as the creature bore down on them. She grabbed Coop's hand and yanked him to the side, dodging the beast's snapping jaws.

"We have to fight it!"

"Are you crazy? That thing will tear us apart!"

"Do you have a better idea?" Tiff shot back. Summoning her courage, she launched herself at the creature, aiming a kick at one of its hind legs.

Her foot connected with a loud crack. The creature shrieked in pain, nearly toppling over, but righted itself and rounded on Tiff in a rage. She backflipped out of the way as it charged again, grabbing a sharp bone fragment from the ground. The creature opened its mouth to roar, and she flung the makeshift weapon with all her might.

It struck the beast in the throat, eliciting an agonized gurgle. The creature stumbled and collapsed, lifeless, in a cloud of dust.

Tiff stood over the creature's body, her chest heaving.

Coop, stunned, asked, "How did you do that?"

The truth was, she didn't understand her abilities. But at that moment, standing in an alien world with Coop at her side, she realized one thing: she no longer had to hide them. She gave him a small, triumphant smile. "I'm still figuring that out, but I feel this won't be the last demon I face."

Coop squeezed her hand, his touch warm and reassuring. "You won't face them alone."

Tiff was grateful they had survived this strange ordeal —and emerged stronger for it.

When they went to step forward to explore this strange land, the gatekeeper appeared before them again, repeating the same statement. "I'm the guardian of this Southern gate," he said in the same deep voice. "Intone the Divine Name and give the Sign of the Enterer?"

"Not again," they both said.

At that moment, Tiff smelled a sweet floral scent. It was comforting and put her at ease. Then, she glimpsed the ethereal woman once more, bathed in a supernatural glow that appeared to invite her into a gateway of light. Without a second thought, Tiff grasped Coop's arm and ran through, ready to follow wherever the mysterious woman may lead them.

Chapter 15
Delusions

The rustling of wheat stalks brushed against Tiff's face, awakening her senses. She blinked open her eyes, squinting at the bright sun peeking over the horizon.

Her head pounded. She lifted a hand to rub her temple, noticing with a start that she was lying in the middle of the wheat field. Memories flooded back—the portal opening and being ripped from Coop's grasp as they tumbled into the abyss.

Panic surged through her. Where was Coop? She pushed herself up too quickly, and the world tilted. "Coop!" She stretched her hoarse voice across the field. Tiff's face was flushed, and her hair was stuck to her forehead with sweat. In the distance, she saw a body lying still in the wheat. Tiff sprinted towards it and fell to her knees next to him. Fear and panic etched deep lines in her features as she shook Coop's still body, sending shivers down her spine. *What if his consciousness didn't make it back?*

Coop's eyelids fluttered open. "Tiff?"

She threw her arms around him, holding back her tears. "You're okay. Thank the Universe."

His arms wrapped around her in return.

Pulling back, Tiff scanned him for injuries. "I don't know how we ended up back here, but I'm glad we made it out of that place in one piece."

Coop nodded, his expression grim. "We have a lot to talk about."

"Yeah," she said softly. "We do." Her throat tightened as she remembered the gatekeeper and the second portal she had believed would return them to their own time and space. Instead, they had been separated. Images flashed in her mind—an alien landscape, twisted creatures, and strange versions of themselves. She shuddered at the memory.

He mumbled out the words, "I'm a little disoriented, but talk to me while my consciousness joins my physical body."

She told Coop about the strange world she had witnessed, the odd terrain, and the unfamiliar constellations in the sky. The creatures she had seen there, both strange and familiar, were twisted reflections of animals she knew.

Coop listened with rapt attention, his brow furrowed. "Could be a parallel universe. One where history diverged from our own at some point, leading to different events and evolution."

"There's more. I saw other versions of us there— different versions, with different lives."

"Other versions of us?" Coop said, his eyes widening behind his glasses. "You mean doppelgangers?"

She nodded. "Their lives were completely different. In that world, I was..." She trailed off, a lump forming in her throat. She had seen herself leading the life her father would have wanted for her: safe, ordinary, and painfully dull. "What did you see?"

"I don't remember anything. You didn't see me there. Perhaps I had already returned to our timeline."

"Really, without me?"

Coop reached over and took her hand. His palm was warm, and she clung to it like a lifeline. "Look, we're back together," he said.

She hesitated to tell him what she had seen—his father living with another family, raising two daughters. Maybe it was an illusion. Or maybe a different timeline. She wasn't sure.

Tiff threw her arms around him. "Thank you."

When she pulled back, her voice was quieter. "You've told me about your father. But what about your mother and brother?"

"Of course," Coop said, a wistful smile tugging at his lips. "I have a twin brother named Caleb. He was born with cerebral palsy, which has always made me feel very protective of him."

Tiff listened as Coop spoke about Caleb, the challenges he faced, and how close they were. Although Coop didn't say it outright, she could tell how much he admired his brother's strength and perseverance in the face of adversity.

When he finished, she said softly, "He sounds amazing."

"He is." Coop glanced away, blinking hard. "I'm sorry. I didn't mean to get all emotional on you."

"Don't apologize. I'm glad you told me about him and your mom."

Coop's eyes shone with gratitude. "She's fantastic. After Caleb was born, she gave up her career as a lawyer. She's been a stay-at-home mom ever since. I can see the sadness in her eyes, as well as love. Bertha Crowley should be the mother of the year."

A comfortable silence settled. Tiff gazed at the rustling sea of wheat, her thoughts drifting to the strange world they had visited and all its strangeness. She shivered, and it had nothing to do with the breeze.

"That place frightened me," she said abruptly. "More than I want to admit. It felt empty. The people didn't have a mind of their own. They were going through the motions, repeating the same routines."

"What you're describing, they sounded robotic," Coop said grimly. "Or people who had lost their sense of self."

Tiff nodded, thinking about the alternate version of herself she had seen drifting through life without purpose or passion. *I never want to end up that way,* she thought. *I want to live—fully and deeply—with all the beauty and pain life has to offer.*

Feeling better, Coop stood and dusted off his jeans. "How did that vortex develop and sweep us up into it?"

"I have no idea. I want to talk to Rachel about this," she said. "About why this gatekeeper keeps showing himself and won't let us pass, and that strange world I saw. She might know something."

"Are you sure that's a good idea? She told you to stay away from the crop circles."

"If anyone will listen with an open mind, it's her."

After a long moment, Coop nodded. "Then I'll go with you," he said. "Whatever happens, we're a team."

Tiff blinked, tears suddenly welling up in her eyes. She didn't know what dangers they might face in the days ahead, but as long as Coop was by her side, she knew she could meet them without fear.

They started walking slowly through the field, the rustling wheat brushing their legs, their thoughts heavy. The normalcy of the field, the setting sun, and the distant sounds of evening traffic were jarring after the intensity of their ordeal. It was Coop who broke the silence.

"I feel as if I'm in my body again. But when we were there…in that place…did it make you think about what matters most and who's important in your life?"

Tiff stopped walking and turned to face him. "Yeah," she said, her voice rough. "It made me realize I've been holding back… not really being me."

"I know what you mean. It's time to be authentic, follow your dreams, and not what others want for you."

A warmth spread through Tiff, not from the sun, which had now dipped below the horizon, but from the connection, the shared experience that had somehow brought them closer.

"Let's do this," she said.

They agreed to meet with Ari first, if he was still in town, and then discuss the matter with Rachel.

Coop pulled the phone from his back pocket to text Ari.

COOP

Hey, are you still in town?

ARI

I had to change my plans and will leave
later this week.

COOP

I want you to meet Tiff and show you the
cube. We had some crazy experiences.

ARI

Are you available tomorrow after school?

COOP

Yes, I'll be home around 6:30 p.m.

ARI

Cool.

Chapter 16
Ari

Ari finished typing his text to Coop, his fingers pausing over the send button. He was about to meet Tiff for the first time in this timeline, to finally see her in physical form and examine the mysterious cube that had quietly shaped both their destinies. The anticipation buzzed beneath his skin, but a shadow of restraint lingered. He had to remain silent about their true connection, about who they really were to each other. With a sigh, he pressed send and leaned back, his gaze drifting out the window.

His thoughts slipped to the past, to a snow-covered day on a Swiss mountain. He had been twelve, eager to keep up with his older brothers as they tore down the slopes. But he was too slow. Soon, their laughter faded, and he found himself alone, rounding a sharp bend into a quiet, untouched section of the mountain. The snow was pristine, thick, and undisturbed. The silence felt otherworldly.

It was there, in the quiet, that he first met the Teacher.

The man had appeared suddenly—an older figure

dressed entirely in white, his presence serene and commanding against the stark landscape. Ari had blinked in surprise. "Why are you out here without skis and proper gear? Are you hurt?"

The man smiled. "Come here, my son. You'll be safe."

"Safe from what?" Ari asked, puzzled.

Then came the distant rumble. The avalanche.

Fear surged. But before he could run, the man embraced him. Snow exploded around them. Ari remembered nothing more.

He woke up in a hospital bed. Miraculously unharmed.

His father had wept, saying they'd thought he was dead. They found him in a hidden cave no one had known existed. Ari told no one about the man in white. Not then. Not until he was fifteen.

By then, Ari had become a discontented teenager, drifting between divorced parents in New York and Florida, invisible among older siblings. He acted out, and his father threatened to send him to military school.

Then she came.

He met September one summer at his mother's and stepfather's country club. She was a waitress. He was a member. But class meant nothing to him when her emerald eyes and fiery red hair lit up his world. She stargazed, walked barefoot in the woods, read esoteric books, and lived with her grandfather in a log cabin tucked deep in the forest. She fascinated him.

Months later, before he left for Florida, September insisted that he meet her grandfather.

They hiked to the cabin on a crisp spring day. The air smelled of pine and promise. The door stood ajar, and a tall man waited at the threshold.

September ran into his arms, then turned. "Papa, this is Ari."

Ari met the man's piercing blue eyes, and time stopped. It was the Teacher.

Memories flooded back: the snow, the embrace, the impossible safety. Ari stood frozen.

"Ari? You, okay?" September nudged him.

He followed them inside, his eyes locked on the Teacher. The cabin was warm, the air humming with invisible knowledge.

They spent summers there. Swimming, fishing, and reading. Stargazing. Exploring the boundaries between matter and mind. The Teacher never left the cabin grounds. He never shared his name. September called him Papa. Ari called him Teacher. He guided them through studies of consciousness, metaphysics, and Hermetic laws. His books were sacred—never to leave the cabin.

Ari fell deeper in love with September, dreaming of attending the same college. Before he could suggest it, she surprised him with a plan: to take a gap year and travel the world. He convinced his reluctant parents, promising to attend college and then pursue a career in law. Eventually, they agreed.

Together, they traveled to Stonehenge, the pyramids of Egypt, and Machu Picchu. Young and in love, they lived for months in Thailand and planned to explore Nepal.

And then the Teacher came.

Ari had been ecstatic to see him—until he saw the solemnity in his eyes.

"She has a mission," the Teacher said.

September said nothing. She simply nodded and began to pack.

That night, under a quilt of stars, they held each other.

"I don't want you to go," Ari whispered.

"I love you. I always will. But my time here is over. My path calls."

"If you love me, you won't go."

She stood and turned away. "Until our souls meet again."

The words shattered him. Words lovers of spirit whispered when separating across lifetimes.

He cried out for the Teacher. He came, descending like starlight.

"What mission could be so important that it keeps us apart?" Ari asked, voice breaking.

The Teacher's eyes held compassion. "You have known love. Now you know sorrow. The choice is yours—dwell in pain or follow the path of unconditional love."

It wasn't what Ari wanted to hear. Rage tore through him. He lashed out in fury and fled down the mountain.

When he returned, both the Teacher and September were gone.

He stayed in Nepal a month longer, grieving. Then returned to honor his bargain.

He enrolled at Harvard, like his father. Studied law. Joined the family firm. And felt utterly hollow.

Until the Teacher returned.

One morning, after a long night of drinking, Ari stumbled home and collapsed on the couch. The next day, groggy and disoriented, he found a package on his table. Inside was a book titled "Hermetic Qabalah." A note lay atop it:

You have a mission.

He never forgot those words. That was so many years ago—but it felt like yesterday. Ari blinked several times, his chest tight. The path he had walked since then had been another kind of avalanche—one filled with dark forces, secret orders, and shifting realities. The memory of her still pulsed through him, raw and unresolved. She was never far from his mind.

Everyone he met, he tested. His heart would know if it were her soul.

And now there was a girl named Tiff, supposedly connected to a magic cube. Soon, he would meet her.

And most likely, discard her like the rest.

Chapter 17
Soul Recognition

Tiff's breath hitched as Coop introduced Ari Aleister to her. His warm, firm handshake met hers, and she was struck by the intensity in his dark eyes. A single unruly curl fell across his forehead, daring her to reach out and tuck it back. She resisted—but barely. A strange wave of familiarity passed over her. Not mere attraction, but something deeper, something she couldn't name.

Tiff took the plush lounge chair opposite Coop and Ari. The warm scent of cookies and freshly sliced fruit floated from the kitchen, drawing Tiff's attention briefly. Coop's mom had left the snacks in the family room—a cozy space with off-grey walls, a crackling fireplace, and an inviting sense of comfort.

She forced herself to speak, trying to shatter the haze. "So, how are you finding the States and the language program?" she asked, her tone a careful balance of interest and nonchalance.

Ari's eyes crinkled slightly. "It's everything I hoped for," he said, as if they were the only two people in the room.

Coop interjected, "Ari lived here once when his dad's job brought them to the States."

"I was a toddler, so I don't remember much," Ari added.

Without preamble, Ari's expression turned serious. "There's something important I need to tell you—about the cube and what it really means."

Tiff sat up straighter. Coop leaned in.

Ari began, "First, it's called the Cube of Space and is a map—a spiritual blueprint for soul travel. The cards show the stages of awakening. The struggles. The growth. The Universe isn't limited to the physical realm. It's dual—material and spiritual. There's a vast dimension beyond what our senses can grasp. We access it through meditation, dreams, and out-of-body experiences. When we do, it offers a more complete understanding of reality."

Tiff blinked, processing.

"There are two opposing forces in this dual realm," Ari continued. "The White Light and the Black Shadow—or Qliphoth. One seeks to awaken us. The other seeks to enslave us."

Tiff leaned forward. "What do you mean by that?"

The White Light is the source of all creation. It seeks to remind humanity of who we are, multidimensional beings of consciousness and power, capable of shaping reality. It invites us to connect with the divine and transcend limitations. It communicates through our consciousness, offering wisdom for those who listen.

"And the Black Shadow?" Coop asked.

"It's the mirror opposite," Ari said quietly. "It hides the truth. It wants humanity asleep and afraid. It spreads fear, hatred, and distraction. It uses agents—spirits, corrupted humans, even false systems—to keep us from waking up. It tells us we are powerless. It thrives when we forget who we are."

Tiff shivered. Ari's words made even abstract ideas feel real. Heavy.

"But there's hope," he continued. "Masters have learned to resist. They've found tools to help others awaken."

"Tools? Like what?" Coop asked, curiosity sparking in his voice.

"Tools like the Cube of Space," Ari replied. "Along with the forces of nature—sound, light, and symbolic weapons of consciousness. The cube is one of the most powerful. It's constructed using twenty-two Major Arcana cards, each placed according to the eight cardinal directions and the inner planes."

Tiff frowned slightly, trying to grasp the concept.

"It's more than a box of tarot symbols," Ari continued. "Each card on the cube is a pictorial key. These symbols speak the language of the subconscious mind. They awaken parts of us we don't access with logic alone."

"So why is that important?" Tiff asked.

"Because the Universe—the breath of God, or what some call Superconsciousness—moves through two aspects: the self-conscious and the subconscious. They correspond to the masculine and feminine principles. Or, if it's easier, think of them as the brain's left and right hemispheres— logic and intuition."

Coop nodded slowly, while Tiff still looked uncertain.

"Okay... but how does that connect to my mother?" she asked.

Ari's expression softened. "If this cube belonged to your mother, she may have been using it as a map, seeking to evolve her consciousness and unlock her inner power."

Tiff reached into her purse and retrieved the cube.

Ari took it reverently. "May I?"

She nodded.

He turned it slowly in his hands, examining the surface. "It contains all twenty-two cards. Each one is placed exactly where it should be—aligned to the cosmic directions. There's something powerful about this one. I can feel an energy field radiating from it—heat, almost. It's more than symbolic. This feels like an active Cube of Space."

Tiff hesitated. She wanted to say, *You felt the heat too?* — but instead asked, "Do you have any idea how she came into possession of such a powerful tool?"

"It's possible she was studying esoteric teachings—maybe even involved in what is called the Great Work. Guard it carefully."

He handed it back.

Tiff didn't speak right away. Instead, she studied the cube as if she were seeing it for the first time.

Her mind flashed to what her father had said—Sarah's obsession with fixing a mess. "Tell me more about the Great Work," she said.

Ari hesitated. "I've already told you more than I should without proper training."

"Then teach us."

"Soon, I return to Safed—the City of Kabbalah."

"I have one more question."

"Ask."

Tiff told him about the dream—the triangle, the numbers 3-6-9, the strange avatar online, and their research into Tesla's theories.

"What tarot cards correspond to those numbers?" she asked. "And what do they mean?"

Without even looking, Ari answered, "The Empress. The Lovers. The Hermit."

"And where are they on the cube?" she pressed.

"It's complicated, and even if I told you, you wouldn't understand. You're not ready yet," he said gently. "But trust me, your time is coming."

She wanted to ask him: *If her mother's soul was traveling in another dimension, did that mean she had died in this one?* But a strange heaviness settled over Tiff as Ari began to pack to leave. She didn't understand why she suddenly felt hollow, as if something vital were slipping through her fingers.

Before stepping out the door, Ari turned to her.

"Until our souls meet again."

Her breath caught. *Why did those words sound so familiar?*

Ari, cloaked in quiet mystery, had held her attention in an unshakable grip. Ari's quiet intensity lingered even after he walked away. It wasn't only the things he said, but something about him remained with her. She couldn't shake it off.

After Ari left, Tiff stayed with Coop's family a little longer. His father, Thomas, had returned from work, and the easy warmth of their home helped her come back to Earth.

Later, Coop walked her to her truck.

"Promise me you'll go straight home. Don't go to the field. No matter what."

"Not you, too," she teased. "I promise."

"Good." He smiled. "Wasn't Ari... something else?"

"I took notes. It's a lot to absorb." She hesitated. "Let's meet with Rachel next?"

She sent a text and received a fast reply:

RACHEL

Tomorrow evening, 7 p.m. Same café. I'm addicted to their sweet potato pie.

Tiff shared the message, and Coop nodded in response. Then his eyes shifted, almost nervously.

"This might not be the right time, but... will you be my girl?"

Tiff laughed softly. "I thought I already claimed that title. Who else would leap through portals with me?"

Coop grinned, leaning in to kiss her goodnight.

From above, a pair of crows watched silently.

Chapter 18
Supernatural Espionage

Across from Coop's house, Nephilimbug observed from the shadows as Tiff and an unfamiliar figure joined Coop. Was this newcomer another agent of the Light? Were they assembling a team to mount an offensive against the Order of the Black Shadow? His mind buzzed with urgent questions, each one heightening his concern and fueling his resolve to uncover their intentions.

Nephilimbug adjusted the settings of his Wrist-Tech Amplifier with a swift movement of his hand, and the air around him charged with dark energy. He was ready to summon one of his most skilled agents, Titanu, whose unique heritage and abilities made her invaluable for the complex missions ahead.

With a decisive flick of his wrist, the screen shifted, and Titanu's image materialized. Today, she appeared as a young Asian woman, her features perfectly aligned with the Earthling aesthetic of delicate beauty. Her appearance was one of her many disguises, each crafted meticulously to blend seamlessly into the human world. Tomorrow, she might adopt the guise of a Native American or any other persona required for her mission.

"Titanu," Nephilimbug's voice resonated with authority, "I have an assignment for you."

Titanu nodded, her expression composed. She wore a simple, elegant outfit that complemented her current form, her posture relaxed yet attentive. As a crossbreed like Nephilimbug—a Nebulorean father and an Earthling mother—she had been under his tutelage since her recruitment. He had honed her abilities, teaching her to switch between her human and Nebulorean forms with flawless precision, a skill that gave her a significant and crucial edge in their covert operations.

"Your assignment is to track and monitor a person who might be a light agent. He has connections that could be problematic for us, and recent intelligence suggests he's involved in something that could expose us," Nephilimbug explained, his gaze intense as he assessed her reaction.

Titanu's face showed no surprise; she was used to the high stakes of their work. "Understood. Do we have a location on him?"

"He was last seen in the downtown area, heading towards a local bar known to be a hotspot for various undercurrents of activity," he continued, uploading the coordinates and recent surveillance images of him to the screen. "Your ability to blend in will be crucial. We believe he may be more than he appears, possibly a key player in a larger scheme orchestrated by the Order of Light."

Titanu absorbed the information, her mind racing through potential scenarios and strategies. "I'll infiltrate the area tonight. Do you require direct engagement?"

"Observe and report back. If an opportunity arises to gather more detailed information discreetly, seize it.

However, do not compromise your cover. We can't afford to alert the Light to our awareness," he instructed sternly.

"Understood. I'll maintain a low profile and gather as much intelligence as I can, and learn his name," Titanu confirmed, her tone resolute.

The screen flickered slightly as she prepared to disconnect. "I won't let you down."

With that, her image faded.

In the dimly lit streets of downtown, Titanu discreetly followed Ari, her senses attuned to his every move. She blended seamlessly with the evening crowd, her gaze fixed on the tall figure navigating through the bustling cityscape. Nephilimbug's instructions were clear: determine if Ari was a threat, if he carried an L.V.X. pendant, and identify any vulnerabilities that could be exploited.

Ari, unaware of the silent observer shadowing his steps, made his way into a popular local bar known for its lively atmosphere and eclectic patrons. Titanu followed, slipping inside the bar a few steps behind him. Inside, the air was thick with the scent of spirits and the sound of casual conversation. She found a secluded spot at the far end of the bar, where the shadows enveloped her, providing a perfect vantage point to watch Ari.

As Ari settled at the bar, his demeanor relaxed noticeably after a few drinks. He struck up a conversation with the bartender, his laughter ringing out occasionally over the hum of the crowd. It was clear from his interactions that he was letting his guard down, becoming more open and unreserved as the night wore on.

Seizing the opportunity, the dark agent known as

Titanu slipped out of her initial hiding spot and approached the bartender under the guise of ordering a drink. With a few whispered words and a subtle gesture, she initiated the dark magic of possession, her essence merging with the bartender's, taking control with practiced ease.

Now in the bartender's body, Titanu engaged Ari in light conversation, her questions casual but pointed, probing for information that might be useful. "So, you seem like you've got a lot on your mind tonight," she remarked, pouring him another drink.

Ari, loosened by alcohol and the anonymity that a bar offered, opened up more than he might have otherwise. "Yeah, just thinking about someone special. She's... It's complicated," he confessed, his eyes distant and wistful.

"Oh? Sounds like a story. Care to share more?" Titanu pressed, her tone encouraging.

Ari chuckled, a wistful sound. "It's this woman I love. She's... not really part of this world anymore, but she's still here in a way. Loving her feels like loving a phantom. But she's everything to me."

Titanu noted this carefully, recognizing the information was a valuable key to Ari's emotional defenses. She continued to coax more from him, but it became clear that Ari's heart was wholly devoted to this absent woman, his loyalty and affection deep-seated and unshakeable.

As the night wound down and Ari departed, Titanu disengaged from the bartender. With this critical intelligence, Titanu disappeared into the darkness, her mission completed, leaving behind a bar where no one was the wiser about the supernatural espionage that had taken place.

She reported back to Nephilimbug with her findings.

She couldn't confirm whether Ari wore the L.V.X. pendant, but he did have a gold chain around his neck; Ari's greatest weakness was his love for a woman who was no longer in his life. This emotional vulnerability could prove to be a crucial leverage point should they need to manipulate or distract Ari in the future.

Chapter 19
Betrayal

The last day of school was warm and sunny, promising what was to come for the next several months. Students milled around the courtyard, chatting and laughing, relieved that summer break had begun.

Tiff spotted Maddie sitting at one of the picnic tables with L.R.'s arm draped around her shoulders. Her stomach tightened into knots as anger and hurt washed over her. She hadn't expected to see her with L.R.

Maddie met Tiff's gaze, a trace of guilt flashing across her expression. L.R. noticed the interaction and traced Maddie's line of sight, his lips twisting into a self-satisfied smirk.

Tiff stiffened, heat flooding her cheeks. Despite the sting, a strange relief washed over her. She was finally seeing Maddie for who she really was—and she was glad she hadn't fallen for more lies.

Barely twenty minutes later, Maddie entered the cafeteria alone. When she spotted Tiff at a table, she walked over and gave her a hug. "Hey, Tiff, how are you?"

Tiff wasn't sure what surprised her more—Maddie's hug or the casual way she acted like nothing had happened. She forced herself to stay calm and stifled the sting of resentment. "I'm good. How about you?"

Maddie nodded and sat down next to Tiff's backpack. They chatted about submitting college applications and the upcoming summer break.

"I want something to drink. Walk with me? We can leave our books and stuff here. No one's going to bother them."

"Sure."

As Maddie rose to her feet, she slyly tipped over Tiff's backpack. While Tiff walked ahead, oblivious, Maddie reached in and swiftly pocketed the cube. Unknown to her, she wasn't unnoticed.

From his spot in the food line, Coop watched in disbelief. Realizing the gravity of the situation, he dropped his tray with a clatter and dashed toward them, calling out urgently, "Tiff! Maddie! Wait!"

Tiff saw Coop running toward them, confusion rising. Maddie saw him too—and bolted, panic flooding her.

"What's going on? What happened?" Tiff asked as Coop reached her.

"Tiff, Maddie stole the cube!"

"What? No way! She knows nothing about the cube."

"I saw her take it from your bag when you were distracted. Believe me, Tiff, she doesn't have your best interests at heart."

Tiff's emotions were a jumbled mess of fury and sorrow. She growled, "How did she find out about the cube, and what does she plan to do with it?"

"I don't know. We can't let her get away. Come on, let's go."

"How could she do this to me?"

"That's a conversation for later."

"You're right. Let's go."

They ran out of the cafeteria and spotted Maddie slipping out the back door, moving quickly toward the stadium.

Maddie stopped at the gate, and L.R. emerged from beneath a bench. Tiff's anger bubbled up. She suspected L.R. was behind this, using Maddie to exact revenge for his humiliation at the party.

She screamed, "Maddie! L.R.! Give me back my cube!"

Maddie froze, the cube in her hand. She didn't understand how or why any of this was happening. She stood in a daze, as if sleepwalking.

L.R. looked at Tiff with contempt and amusement. "Well, well, well. Look who's here. The little girl who thinks she can play with fire. You thought the cube was yours? That you could keep it from me. You're so naïve."

There was a flicker in his voice—a cold, calculating edge that chilled her. She'd only ever heard it in one other person: Nephilimbug.

And then she knew. This wasn't L.R. at all. Nephilimbug was possessing his body and mind.

He cackled and sneered. "The cube belongs to the Black Shadow, as do your best friend Maddie and her jock boyfriend. They've been useful puppets."

He turned to Maddie. "Good job, Maddie. You've done well. Now give me the cube."

Maddie extended her arm. As she was about to hand it over, Coop darted in and snatched the cube, tucking it away.

Tiff moved like lightning. Using a swift Aikido throw, she sent L.R. flying into the open field.

He tumbled onto the turf and sat up, stunned, rubbing his head. He blinked at them, confused.

Tiff turned to Maddie. "Please, snap out of it. Block the voice out. Don't listen to him. He's lying. He's using you. You're not one of them—you're one of us."

Maddie's face twisted. Her eyes looked strange, unfocused, as if she were battling something inside. Her fingers twitched. She took an unsteady step toward them.

Tiff touched Coop's arm, urging him to step back as Maddie glared at them, her eyes bloodshot.

"Give me the cube, Coop," Maddie demanded.

Tiff stepped forward. "You're my best friend, Maddie. We've been a team since elementary school. Don't listen to that voice. Remember what we promised? We made a blood pact to always be here for each other. I love you."

Maddie jolted, like something cracked open inside her. Her voice trembled. "Tiff, I don't understand. What's happening?"

Nephilimbug—still controlling L.R.—stood and moved toward them, fists clenched, eyes locked on Coop.

Tiff screamed, "Run!"

Coop took off toward the school. A swirling black cloud engulfed him. Nephilimbug had left L.R.'s body—but L.R., still confused, continued chasing Coop.

Maddie sprang forward, tackled L.R. to the ground, and pinned him. "Help Coop! I got this!"

L.R.'s body went limp. Disoriented, he asked, "What happened? Why are you on top of me, Maddie?"

"I have no idea. Something about a cube," she replied.

Tiff leapt into the air and grabbed Coop's leg as the dark mass tried to lift him. She yanked him back down. They both crashed to the ground.

A sharp breeze swept by, and something slashed her forehead. Blood poured down her face.

The crow lifted the bag and flew off with it.

"No, no," Tiff cried as blood and tears spotted her clothes.

Maddie and L.R. ran over to Tiff and Coop, now standing and staring up at the sky as the crow and the pack disappeared into the cloud.

"What was that?" Maddie asked, wiping Tiff's face with tissues. "A crow? Or a vulture?"

Tiff couldn't stop crying. Maddie handed her more tissues.

They all jumped as the pack dropped from the sky.

"I guess he didn't find what he wanted," Coop said, pulling the cube out from under his shirt.

"You had it all along? While I'm over here crying?" Tiff swatted his arm playfully.

"I never put it in the backpack. I had it under my shirt, next to my body."

"What's so important about this cube? Does it have something to do with your mom's disappearance?" Maddie asked.

Tiff hugged her. "Don't worry. I'll explain everything later. Girl, watch who you hang out with." She glanced at L.R.

A crow flew overhead, and Tiff shivered.

Nephilimbug, with his crow's eyes, gawked at the small group as they walked back toward the school. He was furious and frustrated that he failed to obtain the cube again.

Days earlier, during his surveillance of Tiff, Nephilimbug discovered that her best friend had once been Maddie. Maddie was disposable, but useful—she would carry out his bidding without question. Her craving for attention made her ripe for exploitation, he thought. He observed the disintegration of Tiff and Maddie's friendship as Maddie fell under the sway of that vain, thoughtless boy, L.R. Nephilimbug followed her to the beeches, where she waited for L.R., who smoked and kissed her indifferently. After a while, Nephilimbug hovered over her, unseen, and planted the seed of his plan.

Chapter 20
Complicated

Maddie and Tiff stepped into the school's ladies' room. Maddie's skill with makeup disguised the small slash on Tiff's forehead, and she managed to re-style her hair enough to soften the evidence of what had happened. Her top had been scrubbed clean, though a faint stain remained where the blood had soaked through.

"Hey, are you ready to go?" Coop called from outside the bathroom. He'd been pacing for the last few minutes.

"Yeah, coming now," Tiff replied, her voice lighter than she expected. She caught her reflection in the mirror—different, a little bruised, but still her—and smiled.

When she stepped into the hallway, Coop looked her up and down, a mixture of concern and surprise in his eyes.

"Wow, it looks as if nothing happened to you."

She felt warmth rush to her cheeks. "Thanks. Maddie worked her magic."

Maddie gave Tiff a quick hug. "I'm going to meet up with L.R.. He stayed back to check on something near the field."

Tiff nodded, watching her friend disappear down the hallway.

As she and Coop crossed the parking lot, a familiar figure caught her eye. Mr. Bernstein was standing beside his car, watching them.

"It's Mr. Bernstein! Hide behind that car," she whispered to Coop.

But it was too late. Mr. Bernstein glanced up and, upon seeing them, frowned. He walked over, gaze sharp behind his wire-rimmed glasses. Tiff's mouth went dry. This couldn't end well.

"Ms. Lotterland. Mr. Crawley," Mr. Bernstein began, his voice casual. "Can we have a word?"

Tiff exchanged a nervous glance with Coop. The conflict was unavoidable. She tried to muster a smile, but it faltered under Mr. Bernstein's scrutinizing gaze.

"Of course, Mr. Bernstein, what's up?"

Bernstein didn't return the smile. He took a step closer, lowering his voice to ensure no one else could overhear. "I'm not going to beat around the bush, so I'll jump right to the point. Where did you really find that cube?"

Tiff didn't want to lie to a teacher but couldn't tell the truth either. She opened her mouth, but no words came out.

Coop tensed beside her, his eyes widening. "Uh, like we told you before, sir—we found it while cleaning out my attic. Why do you ask?"

Mr. Bernstein's frown deepened. "I have reason to believe that's not entirely accurate. You see, I'm familiar with objects of that… uniqueness. And I'm quite certain it didn't appear in your attic out of nowhere."

"We no longer have it. I've thrown it away," Coop said, raising his chin in defiance.

Mr. Bernstein's eyes narrowed, his gaze piercing. "I

don't appreciate being lied to. If you don't tell me the truth right now, I'll report to the sheriff and the school administration that you might have stolen it."

Tiff didn't want trouble, but she couldn't give up the cube either. They had come so far in understanding its mysteries. They were out of time, and she didn't know what to do. The conflict had escalated, and there seemed to be no easy way out. She hoped Coop had a solution. Tiff's cheeks burned. She didn't want to share anything about the cube with Mr. Bernstein—not now, not until she knew more herself. Panic rose in her chest. She glanced at Coop again, pleading for help. His eyes were shadowed, brow furrowed in concentration. She could tell he was scrambling for a solution.

"Right. And how exactly are you supposed to prove there was a cube to steal?" Coop asked, squaring his shoulders.

Mr. Bernstein crossed his arms, eyebrows drawing together. "This is not the end. You don't know what you're getting yourselves into. Watch your step." He walked away with his head hanging down.

Chapter 21
The Past

Seeing the cube that day filled Harvey Bernstein with memories of his past—adventurous days filled with love and fear. The cube symbolized a secret world he knew well, and those who owned it: Sarah and her younger sister Rachel. They were a striking pair: tan skin, long brown hair cascading down their backs, and hazel eyes that made them stand out from the rest of Harvey's classmates. Their intelligence and bravery set them apart even more than their looks. In Spanish class, Rachel could often be seen having full-fledged conversations with the teacher in fluent Spanish, to everyone else's dismay.

While he studied alongside Rachel, it was with Sarah that he'd get lost in long talks about quantum physics and the mysteries of the universe. Rachel challenged his logic; Sarah opened his imagination.

Sarah kept a tiny diary and was always jotting down her thoughts in it.

"These insights and knowledge come to me, and I write them down," she once told him after he asked why she was always scribbling.

"Where do they come from?"

"If you promise not to laugh or think I'm crazy, I'll tell you."

"Never, I swear. You and Rachel are the smartest girls I know."

"Okay then—the Teachers tell me things."

"What teachers?" He knew it couldn't be the schoolteachers; she was more intelligent than they were.

"Oh, Harvey, forget it."

But he couldn't forget it. Sarah would tell Rachel and him fascinating things about creation, life on other planets, and black holes. He inquired with Sarah about her Teachers, whom she always spoke so much about. Harvey wanted to meet them.

"They are Masters of the Cosmos, having gone through eons of lifetimes and initiations. I began communicating with them when I was a toddler, and now I engage with them seamlessly."

"Teach me how to talk to the Teachers."

"You and my sister are so alike. She keeps asking me to teach her, too. But I don't know how. It's something that happened to me."

"You're different."

"No, Harvey. I'm conscious."

The summer before Sarah was to leave for college, she displayed even more odd occurrences. She showed Rachel and Harvey a diagram of a cube with peculiar symbols placed on precise areas.

"It's called the Cube of Space," Sarah said, holding up a worn book she'd been studying. "The Teachers showed it to me first, then I found it here—in this diagram."

"Harvey, can you and Rachel help me create this. We need plenty of plain cardboard paper, paint, silver wrapping paper, and glue. Don't forget a ruler and scissors!"

Harvey became her faithful assistant, while Rachel was her mirror and confidante.

It took a few weeks to finish the project. Sarah drew and colored twenty-two tarot cards, Rachel cut them out, and Harvey stuck them on the precise spots Sarah told him to. Sarah was adamant that it had to be perfect, or the Teachers wouldn't accept it. After thirteen attempts, she felt they had done something the Teachers would approve of. Sitting around the kitchen table in their house, they gazed at the cube.

The three sat motionless, their eyes closed, not speaking a single word. Sarah had told them to visualize the cube as being real. Harvey opened his eyes and jumped up, knocking over the chair in shock. The cube had transformed from cardboard to a solid silver metal cube adorned with stunning pictures.

"We did it." Sarah picked up the new cube and examined it.

"How did that happen?" Harvey asked.

"You witnessed the process of the philosopher's stone—the transformation of base into brilliance." She spoke softly and left, taking the cube with her.

Rachel grabbed Harvey by the arm to hold him back as he tried to follow Sarah with more questions. "When she's ready to share with you, she will. Be patient. It was big for her to show you how to change a cardboard cube to a stunning metal cube."

"How did she do it?"

"Using her mind to change the cube's energy to a higher vibratory frequency."

"Do you know how to do that?"

"No. Remember earlier, she asked us to visualize the metal cube with the tarot card images."

"How did visualizing a metal cube change one from cardboard to metal? That's impossible."

"It's about learning how to work with the universal principles and believe in them and your gifts. Energy is very potent when more people are involved in a group creation. That's what Sarah always tells me when I have doubts."

Harvey had no idea these extraordinary happenings were only the beginning of a string of summers unlike anything he'd known before.

During the year, he oscillated between being a typical college student and witnessing and learning about the mystical teachings alongside Sarah and Rachel.

Before graduating, Harvey was offered a top job with a technology company in New York, which would have required him to stay on the East Coast. Would Rachel marry him and move to New York?

"I'm going with Sarah to travel the world, Harvey. I'm not ready to settle down."

Her words stung him. He wanted to go with them but wasn't asked, which hurt him even more.

Harvey trailed behind Tiff and Coop at a slow pace, watching as they turned into the local café. He dreaded going home to his small apartment—no wife, no children, not even a pet.

One night, years ago, a voice he believed to be his spirit guide had whispered in his ear as he lay on the couch, intoxicated and wallowing in self-pity. It told him not to accept the job in New York, but to return home.

In Kansas, there were no high-paying jobs available for

an MIT graduate. So, he settled for teaching high school physics.

Harvey avoided Tiff. She reminded him too much of Sarah and Rachel. He knew who she was—and felt sorry that they had deserted her, too.

As he neared the stop sign, a car passed in front of him. He glanced at the other driver, who appeared unaware of his gaze. Harvey's eyes widened in astonishment.

A car behind him honked. Snapping out of his daze, he made a quick U-turn to follow the vehicle.

He watched the old SUV pull into the same parking lot Tiff and Coop had entered earlier.

His heart pounded as Rachel stepped out of the car and walked into the café.

Chapter 22
Rendezvous

Coop and Tiff sat in the café, waiting. Right when Tiff began to worry that Rachel might not show, she rushed in.

"Sorry, I'm late," she said.

"This is my friend, Coop. And Coop, this is my mother's sister, Rachel."

"I thought we were meeting alone."

"It's nice meeting you too, Aunt Rachel," Coop said through clenched teeth.

Rachel, without responding, glanced at Coop before turning back to Tiff.

"Coop's been helping me figure things out—especially about my mom and the cube."

"Did you say… cube?" Rachel's expression sharpened.

"Yes."

"Can you describe it?"

Coop showed her a photo of the cube on his phone. Rachel took it and studied the image from various angles.

"Where did you find this?"

"In the attic. Did it belong to my mother?"

"I haven't seen this in so long. Yes, this cube was your mom's prized possession. Sarah would never have left it unless..."

Her words trailed off as the waitress approached. After taking their orders, Rachel remained quiet for a moment, but Tiff pressed on.

"Please, finish what you were saying."

"We should start from the beginning. Your mission is tied to Sarah's vision. Habiba and the other women encouraged and nurtured the unfolding of her intuitive abilities. At that young age in my life, I never had visions or received messages from the unseen like she did." Rachel paused for a sip of tea. "One vision was about you."

"Me?"

"Yes. She told me she could see a small child in her auric field. The child clung to her dress and kept saying, *'I'll find you.'*"

They ate in silence for a moment before Rachel continued. "She didn't know what it meant at the time, only that the vision lingered with her. It felt prophetic."

Tiff clung to every word, picturing her mother as a young girl experiencing mystical visions.

She took a breath and decided to be honest with Rachel. "Something... strange has been happening to us. Weird things. And we were hoping you could help us understand."

Rachel set down her mug, her expression sharpening with curiosity. "Go on."

Tiff didn't hold back. "It started a few weeks ago, in the wheat field...."

She explained everything: the portal, the parallel world, and the strange beings they encountered. Coop added the parts she missed, their story weaving into a bizarre but cohesive narrative.

When they finished, Rachel exhaled slowly, her eyes fixed on the tabletop as if piecing together a puzzle she'd long expected to see completed. Then she looked up, a spark of recognition in her gaze.

"So, the wheat field portal has opened once more."

"All this time, you knew?"

"Of course. Your mother activated it. That's how she traveled through the cosmos."

"Why did she shut it down?"

"She didn't. The Order of L.V.X. closed it. Your mother was reprimanded for opening it."

"Why?"

"She reactivated a portal the dark forces had once used to enter this reality."

"Then where is she now?"

"In another dimension."

"Meaning she's dead?"

Rachel shook her head gently. "Lesson number one— we don't die. Our consciousness lives on. The body is temporary."

Tiff frowned. "Another dimension?"

Rachel set her cup down. "There's a difference. A dimension is a separate plane of existence, with its own laws and structures. A timeline is a variation of this world —a different sequence of events. Your mother crossed into something deeper."

Coop leaned forward. "Tiff, it's like those robotic doppelgängers you saw. They were interpenetrating our world from a different timeline."

"Yes," Rachel said, nodding. "But Sarah had advanced to the point where she could materialize and dematerialize her astral body."

Tiff shook her head. "How is that possible?"

"It was one of her spiritual gifts as an alchemist and

magician. She was close to reaching a higher level of knowledge—what we call a Master Magician. But something went wrong. I don't know what exactly—only that she never intended to leave you."

Rachel paused, then added, "Sarah was worried that the dimensions and Earth's timelines were being compromised. She said she had to act fast. She was afraid something was coming—something dark."

"It sounds like she feared something might happen," Tiff whispered.

"I agree," added Coop.

Rachel glanced at Coop again, smiling. "I had a friend like you when I was in school, too."

Tiff's fingers tightened around her mug. "There's someone—or something—trying to take the cube. Can he also materialize and dematerialize?"

"Do you know about the Order of the Black Shadow?" Rachel asked.

They both nodded.

"As one of their agents, he can take over other bodies as a walk-in. The host's consciousness is paused—whether human or animal—and he operates as them. Or he influences others by vibrating at a low frequency, filling their minds with dark thoughts until they act on his behalf."

"So... he could be anyone?" Tiff asked.

"Yes. He feeds on power and fear, and those under his influence have sometimes risen so high, people mistook them for gods. And yes, some of their female agents are incredibly cunning."

Tiff's eyes widened. "That explains it. The man who came with the Sheriff—Lucas Nephilimbug—he claimed to work for a paranormal research group."

"There may actually be such a man. But the one you

met? That was him. The dark agent. And he's not done yet." At that moment, the café lights flickered.

Rachel's eyes scanned the room. She lowered her voice. "He's here. And he's not alone. He's after the cube. Do you have it with you?"

"Yes."

"Give it to me. Then leave. I'll contact you."

Tiff pulled the cube from her pocket. As she passed it to Rachel, the object jerked in midair. They both reached for it, but it was too late.

Nephilimbug materialized from the shadows and grabbed for the cube. It slipped from his grasp as Rachel encircled it in a field of light. She seized it and ran for the door, Nephilimbug right behind her.

Coop and Tiff leapt from their seats and rushed after them, but Rachel was already in her car, peeling out of the lot.

Across the street, Harvey sat watching the café. When Rachel burst out the door, running full speed with something clutched in her hands, he blinked in disbelief. Her car roared past, a flock of crows chasing close behind.

Adrenaline surged. He stomped the gas pedal.

Like old times, chasing one of the Coleman girls.

Chapter 23
The Cube

Tiff paced the parking lot, clutching her phone. Rachel wasn't answering; it went straight to voicemail. Anger and fear surged through her. How could she have handed over the cube? It held the universe's secrets—the very thing the Black Shadow wanted to destroy.

She had trusted Rachel. After all, she'd saved them from the agents and revealed glimpses of her magic. But now Tiff wondered if it had all been a trick.

"Hey, calm down, okay?" Coop said, leaning against the car, watching her. "We'll get it back. Rachel is one of us. She wouldn't betray us."

Tiff stopped pacing and glared at him. "How do you know that? She talked about death like it meant nothing, as if people don't really die. It's like their consciousness floats off into another dimension. What kind of nonsense is that?"

"Have you forgotten what we went through earlier in those portals? I believe her—but it's always good to have healthy doubt."

"It's possible she's not telling the truth. Maybe she's an

agent of the Black Shadow. Maybe she's using the cube for something dark." Tiff bit her lip. "We don't even know where she lives. How are we supposed to find her?"

Coop thought for a moment. Then he smiled and pulled out his laptop. "I can find her through her car tags."

"How are you going to do that, Sherlock?"

"Easy. When she sped off, I got her tag number."

"That still doesn't explain how you'll find her address."

Coop popped open his laptop, fingers flying across the keyboard. "I can access Wheatfield's vehicle records. Their system isn't exactly state-of-the-art. I have her tag number. The missing data is her birthday."

He typed in Rachel's name and the tag number, then paused. "Do you have any idea what her birthday might be?"

"She graduated two years after my parents. I remember her telling me people thought she and Sarah were twins. They were born in the same month and on the same day, but two years apart."

"What is it?"

"I'm calculating. My mom is thirty-seven, and Rachel is thirty-five. Her birthday is November 17, 1989."

A few keystrokes later, Coop grinned. "Got it!" He turned the screen toward her. "This is Rachel's address."

Tiff stared at the screen, hope rising in her chest. She wanted to believe Rachel hadn't betrayed them—but doubt still clung to her like a shadow.

"How did you learn to do that?" she asked.

Coop shrugged. "Long hours of being alone and bored. And honestly? Their system was a joke. The password was *'310'*—the building's street number. Took me less than five minutes to figure it out. I wouldn't have done it for anyone else but you."

Tiff let out a breathy laugh, despite the tension.

"Let's go then. Let's get our cube back."

Chapter 24
Wild Thing Two

Rachel raced into the dimly lit house, her breath quick with urgency. With deft movements, she placed the cube atop the fireplace mantel, securing it within a shimmering case of protective light. This barrier, visible and penetrable only to those attuned to a higher frequency and knowledgeable of the sacred God Code, was her first line of defense.

She then steeled herself for the confrontation she knew was coming, her focus sharpened, unwavering in the face of what was approaching. Closing her eyes, Rachel summoned her light armor, which cloaked her in a radiant, impenetrable sheath. Raising her hand, she conjured a gleaming sword of pure light, grasping it firmly as it materialized from the ether.

She stepped out the back door into the woods, positioning herself near a sturdy oak. From there, she became a silent sentinel, her senses heightened. It wasn't long before she detected a presence—a dark silhouette peering through the back window, a dark agent. She intuited that it was the one Tiff had spoken about-Nephilimbug. He had already shifted from his crow form into his Nebulorean body, his menacing wings now fully unfurled. His voice echoed through the trees, a sinister blend of threat and negotiation: "Show yourself, give me what I want—the cube—and I will spare the life of Tiff and her friend."

At the sound of Tiff's name, her grip on the sword tightened.

With a calm, deliberate stride, Rachel emerged from her hiding spot. With a sudden burst of speed, Nephilimbug lunged toward her, his own dark blade materializing from the shadows. Rachel parried his attack with precision, the clash of their weapons sending sparks flying into the night air. She countered swiftly, her blade tracing arcs of light as she drove Nephilimbug back.

The forest around them seemed to hold its breath as the battle reached its peak, the air crackling with the energy of their clash. Rachel maneuvered with agility, her years of training evident in her every move. She dodged a vicious swipe from Nephilimbug and responded with a series of rapid thrusts, each aimed at critical junctures in his defenses.

Nephilimbug growled in frustration, his attacks becoming more aggressive, more desperate. He managed to clip Rachel's side with a shadowy tendril, the impact sending a jolt of pain through her. Rachel staggered but quickly regained her composure, her resolve hardening.

She channeled her energy, her light armor glowing more intensely. With a powerful shout, she unleashed a torrent of light from her sword, a radiant beam aimed directly at Nephilimbug. He barely managed to deflect it with his wing, the force of the blast pushing him back several feet.

Seizing the moment, Rachel advanced. She moved like a force of nature, her every strike precise and powerful.

Nephilimbug was forced to retreat, his usual confidence waning under her relentless assault.

The battle reached a critical moment. Rachel's eyes were steely, her stance unwavering. "This ends now, Nephilimbug," she declared, her voice echoing through the woods.

Rachel skillfully maneuvered Nephilimbug into a vulnerable position, pinning him to the ground. However, the sudden blaze of car headlights distracted her, allowing Nephilimbug a moment to strike. He slashed at Rachel's neck, shattering her protective L.V.X. pendant and shoving her aside.

As she tumbled to the forest floor, the rustle of his wings signaled his departure. Rachel knew her physical form was fading fast, and she scrambled to retrieve the broken pieces of her pendant. With the remnants in her palm, she traced a sacred circle and whispered ancient incantations. Pressing the reassembled pendant against her wounded neck, the magical energies wove together, staunching the flow of etheric life force.

Weak yet determined, Rachel dragged herself to a nearby clearing to recover and keep watch. From her vantage point, she saw Tiff and Coop exiting the car. She enveloped them in a protective light shield, her instincts telling her that Nephilimbug might still be nearby. Her mission was to protect her niece, the young light warrior, and deliver her safely to the Teachers with the cube.

Drawing a deep, revitalizing breath, Rachel's energy slowly returned. She touched her neck, relieved to find no trace of blood. She had failed to destroy the dark agent, but she would not fail to protect Tiff.

With a faint smile, she readied herself for the next phase of her mission. The real work was about to begin.

Chapter 25
Wild Thing Three

Tiff and Coop drove along a narrow, winding road cloaked in mist. This part of town was unfamiliar, and they couldn't understand why Rachel lived so far from civilization. They followed the GPS directions carefully, but there were no signs of other houses or people nearby. In the distance, they finally spotted Rachel's car and a weathered house that they assumed was hers.

Coop parked beside her vehicle and left the headlights on as they surveyed the house. The quaint structure bore the marks of time—faded paint peeled from the siding, and the roof sagged slightly with age. It looked like a forgotten relic, untouched for many seasons.

There was no sign of anyone, no movement in the air —only silence and mist pressing close around them.

They walked up the steps and knocked. No answer. Coop tried the knob—it was unlocked. They exchanged a wary glance, then nodded to each other and stepped inside.

"Rachel?" Tiff called out repeatedly, but no one answered.

The interior was sparsely decorated, with modest furnishings and woven rugs on the timber floors. Mystical symbols and fantastical creatures adorned the walls through posters and artwork. Crystals in various shapes and colors glittered on a low table, surrounded by smoking incense, flickering candles, and an array of curious artifacts. An uncanny aura filled the air, as if they'd stepped into another realm.

Tiff wandered toward the fireplace and waved her hand slowly across the mantel's edge. After a moment, she rejoined Coop in the center of the room.

"What was that about?" he asked, nodding toward the mantel.

"Oh, nothing. I felt drawn to it."

When Tiff turned to speak again, a soft glow shimmered near the hallway, and Rachel appeared as if from nowhere. She was dressed in a flowing white gown, an amethyst pendant resting on her chest.

She led them to a space lit by white candles, scented with the aroma of burning incense.

"Sweet potato pie and tea?" she offered warmly. "We can finish our conversation at the café."

Tiff's emotions boiled over. "Where is the cube?" she demanded.

"Sit, and let's talk," Rachel said calmly. "The cube is safe, don't worry. If I hadn't intervened, the Black Shadow agent would have taken it from you. That would've been disastrous."

"Why do they want the cube?"

"It's a powerful tool—and a weapon, in the wrong hands. For those who know how to activate it, it can shift realities. The cube is part of your mission."

"Whatever that is."

"You already know. What's the one thing you've always been searching for?"

"Finding my mother."

"What else?" Rachel pressed.

"To know the truth. Something inside me has always whispered that there's more to life than what we see. I want knowledge, but not only from books. I want to feel it. Live it."

Rachel smiled. "You got it."

"My mission is to find my mother and become a Wild Thing Three."

All three of them laughed.

"If only we had Sarah's diary. She once told me she had to marry your father so you could be born. It's all part of your destiny."

"Mom had a diary? It's not in the attic."

"Yes, and too bad. That diary holds the key to the mysteries of the cube, where Sarah might be, and your role in it all."

"I'll try to find it."

A sharp cawing outside made Tiff jump. Crows slammed into the house.

Rachel didn't blink.

"Recheck your house for the diary. Ask your father again if he has it. And more importantly, it's time to start your spiritual quest."

"You said it's time. So, what's the first step?"

"Where do we start?" Coop added, finally joining the conversation.

"A spiritual journey begins here." Rachel pointed to her heart. "Before anything else, you learn to listen to yourself, to the silence, to what's real beyond the surface. Meditation helps open that door. It's the first step to remembering who you are. Have either of you ever meditated?"

"My martial arts practice included it, but I didn't keep it up."

"I've tried a few times," Coop said. "But my brother Caleb is dedicated. He says it sharpens his mind and helps him do things that defy logic."

"Coop, in this lifetime—and probably in others—you're Tiff's spare. I was Sarah's. That's a good thing. You're meant to undergo the same training. But your path will veer."

"Veer good or bad?" Coop asked.

Rachel smiled. "Let me explain it this way. Sarah had her path, and I have mine, but we are both on the Path of Return to the Higher Source. The steps we take depend on the growth of our souls. Trust the universe. That's what I'm doing."

Tiff and Coop sat cross-legged on the vibrant rugs that covered Rachel's living room floor. Candlelight danced on the walls as Rachel continued.

"Once, I was part of a caravan traveling with fellow seekers," she began, her voice threading memory and wonder. "And there, in the depths of the Moroccan desert beneath a sky littered with countless stars, I was engulfed in light and lost to time," she said, eyes glinting with the memory. "But the spirits whispered their secrets to me. As I chanted the old words, a vortex of wind rose around me, revealing truths and powers no book could teach."

Tiff and Coop sat, captivated. The world outside—the danger, the cube, even the urgency—faded. Magic filled the room.

Rachel paused, her gaze distant. "The power I felt that night... it was as if I could touch the essence of the universe. And for a moment, I held the threads of fate in my hands."

A sudden chill snapped Tiff back to herself. She blinked and looked at Coop, who seemed as mesmerized as she was.

Realizing how late it had gotten, she thought of her father. He'd be worried.

As if reading her mind, Rachel said, "It's okay to leave now. You'll be fine. I've cleared a path for you. Stay on that path, no matter what you encounter. And, Tiff, are you ready to search for your mother?"

"What do you mean?"

"Come with me this summer. There's a place I believe holds answers."

"Wait, you can't go without me," Coop said quickly.

"I don't know if I can leave. My dad needs help on the farm."

"Think about it," Rachel said. "You said you wanted to experience life and find your mother. That door is opening now, if you're brave enough to walk through it."

Tiff hesitated. "Why haven't you found her with all your powers and travels?"

"I tried. But I realized it's not my mission. It's yours. I'm here to help you."

Coop waved his hands. "If Tiff goes, I'm going too."

"Of course," Rachel said, smiling. "I wouldn't have it any other way."

Halfway down the road, Tiff suddenly exclaimed, "Stop the car!" Her face was etched with realization. "We forgot to get the cube," she said, turning to Coop with a look of concern. "Her magical stories totally ensnared us."

Coop pressed the accelerator gently, continuing their drive. "We'll come back tomorrow. Let's trust the Universe to keep it safe."

"I'll try," Tiff responded, her voice tinged with reluctance but also a trace of awe. The evening's enchantment still lingered, helping to soften the sting of forgetting the cube.

As they hurried along the dirt road, they saw a faint glow in the distance. Someone cried out for help, but they couldn't see anyone. Coop slowed the car down. "Should we stop to help?"

"No, we can't. It could be a trap. Remember that Rachel said to stay on the path."

"But what if it's not a trap? What if someone is hurt? We can't leave them there."

"We can't take the risk. We'll tell the sheriff, and he can send someone to check it out."

Coop hesitated, torn between his compassion and his fear. He stepped on the gas pedal. He hoped they were making the right decision but couldn't shake the feeling that they had abandoned someone.

A short distance back, Harvey stood beside his car, stranded in a ditch. The mist had thickened since he'd swerved to avoid something—a creature, a shadow, he couldn't be sure. One moment, he'd been following Rachel. Next, he was off the road, and his tires sank deep into the soft earth.

He had tried everything to free the car—rocking it, flooring it, even pushing it. Nothing worked. There was no phone signal out here, and the cold was beginning to seep through his jacket.

When headlights finally appeared in the distance, he felt a wave of relief.

He shouted, waving his arms. "Over here!"

The car slowed. It was the second one to pass him by. The first had come earlier, on their way in. He hadn't managed to flag them down in time. Now they'd missed him again. Harvey's shoulders slumped. His heart sank. There was only one thing left to do.

He started walking.

Chapter 26
Forever Young

Tiff climbed into the attic, her heart pounding with anticipation. Rachel had said the diary held secrets—her mother's hidden truths, her occult experiences. If the diary existed, it could be the missing piece.

But after searching every box and crate, she found nothing. Dust, old photos, forgotten clothes—but no diary.

Maybe her father had thrown it out.

She descended the ladder, brushed dust off her jeans, and entered the living room. Lincoln sat watching a basketball game, half-immersed in the screen's glow.

"Dad, do you know anything about Mom's diary?"

He glanced at her, brow furrowed. "What diary?"

"The one she used to write in all the time."

He scratched his beard. "I remember she always had a notebook, or something like it. She'd go up to Hillary Hill with it—sit there for hours, writing. I figured she must've taken it with her."

Tiff felt a wave of disappointment.

"Or did you get rid of it?"

He frowned. "No. Of course not. Why would I do that?" His voice dipped, touched with hurt.

"Sorry, is there anywhere she could've hidden it?"

"Not that I know of. Sarah always said that the hill was her sanctuary—where she felt connected to something bigger than herself. Whatever that meant."

"Do you remember what it looked like? The color or shape?"

"I don't know. I didn't pay attention to those kinds of details. I think it was black or green, with lined pages."

"What size?"

He rubbed his face, thinking. "Maybe it wasn't a school notebook. It was small, and I think it had a lock."

As she turned to go with Chip padding after her, Lincoln called out, "Wait. How'd you even know about this diary? Why are you looking for it?"

"I found some of Mom's stuff in the attic. Rachel mentioned the diary. I want to know more about her."

Lincoln's jaw tightened. "Stay away from Rachel. She's trouble. I wouldn't be surprised if she's behind those crop circles."

"Why are you accusing her?"

"Just a hunch. She shows up, and suddenly we've got supernatural graffiti all over our wheat fields."

Tiff didn't bother responding. She muttered something under her breath and raced up the stairs. Pulling out her phone, she texted Coop.

TIFF

Do you have a metal detector?

COOP

No, what do you need it for?

TIFF

My dad said my mom spent a lot of time on the hill writing. Maybe she buried the diary there.

COOP

I checked Google. There's a store in town where we can rent one for twenty dollars an hour. How long are we renting it?

TIFF

Umm, at least an hour or maybe two.

COOP

Okay, I'll pick it up. What time do you want me to meet you?

TIFF

In an hour.

COOP

I'll be there.

Tiff inserted a smiley emoji.

It was a perfect day for treasure hunting. The sun beamed overhead, and the sky stretched out in a brilliant blue. Tiff met Coop at the foot of the hill. As they climbed, they carried a metal detector and a backpack filled with snacks and water. Chip tagged along, tail wagging, nose to the ground. At the top, a wide view of the golden wheat fields unfolded beneath them. Tiff thought of her mother sitting here on Hillary Hill. A pang of nostalgia and sadness hit her—she wished they could've shared those moments.

Tiff turned on the metal detector and began sweeping it over the ground. Coop followed her, holding the backpack and watching Chip chase butterflies. Forgetting about the time, they searched for close to two hours, covering every inch of the hilltop, but found nothing.

Frustrated and tired, Tiff was about to give up when she heard a faint beep from the metal detector. She stopped. Something metallic was nearby. Dropping to her knees, Tiff began digging with her hands, feeling both excited and nervous.

Coop grabbed the shovel and dug deeper until he hit something hard. Tiff fell to her knees and searched the area until she felt something. She pulled out a mason jar with a rusty metal lid and brushed off the dirt. She frowned, disappointed that it wasn't what she was looking for, but something was inside it. She opened the jar and pulled out a photo that was fading with age, along with a note folded in half.

Coop sat next to her as she took out the photo. It showed three children smiling at the camera in front of an old brick school building. Two of them were girls, and one was a boy. They appeared happy and carefree. Tiff recognized the girls as her mother, Sarah, and her sister Rachel. They were wearing matching dresses and ribbons in their hair.

But who was the boy? He had dark hair and brown eyes, and he was holding Rachel's hand. They were a trinity. The boy wasn't her father. Her father had blond hair when he was young.

She flipped over the photo. There was something written in faded ink:

The three-time travelers
We will live forever.

A shiver ran down Tiff's spine. Time travelers? What

could that possibly mean? She unfolded the note and read its contents:

> *To whoever finds this,*
>
> *We buried this jar as a time capsule to tell you that you are not from here, but a visitor for a short time. Your mission is to explore this reality, learn everything you can, and ascend to a higher level. We invite you to join us in our pursuit of truth and freedom. Tread carefully!*

Tiff held the note, feeling shocked and confused.

Sarah was young, but her eyes were old. The kind that could look clear through you. Even now, she felt a strange sensation, as if that were happening now. She felt a surge of emotions: curiosity, anger, fear, sadness, longing. Looking at the wheat field below her, Tiff screamed to herself, *Where are you, Mom?*

Suddenly, a breeze stirred around them, gently brushing against her skin. Tears slid down her cheeks, glistening in the sunlight. Their trails shimmered on her flushed face as they fell. Her features were contorted with emotion. Engrossed in her reverie, she barely noticed as Chip tenderly licked her face while Coop's eyes reflected quiet concern.

"Hey, are you okay?"

"I wanted her diary, and I got this crazy note about time travel. Sounds like sci-fi." She handed him the note and the photo.

Coop read in silence, his brow furrowed.

"Wow," he said at last. "Tiff... this is wild. Your mom and aunt were doing something big. But who's the little dude?"

"I didn't interpret the note that way, but you're right.

Sarah and Rachel are some extraordinary women. And the dude isn't my father."

They sat, holding the jar, the photo, and the note, unsure of what to do next.

Scouring the hill with the rented metal detector had taken them longer than anticipated. To compensate, Coop handed over an extra twenty dollars. She looped her arms through his, and they both gazed out into the vast wheat field.

They didn't care about time right now.

They only cared about the photo and the note.

They only cared about the three kids in the photo and what lay ahead of them.

They only cared about living forever.

Chapter 27
Compromise

That night, Tiff lay in bed, staring at the photo and reading the letter. She wanted to ask her father about the photo, but thought better of it, not wanting to stir up old grief or suspicion. If he saw her mother and aunt with the mystery boy, he wouldn't react very well.

Before turning in, she received a text from Rachel.

Tiff pondered her message for a while before responding. She had planned to work this summer and help her father with the farm bills. But the desire to find her mother was overwhelming. She replied.

TIFF

Could you give me a couple of days, please?

RACHEL

Meet me at my house before noon, two days from now.

Tiff answered with an okay emoji.

Excited but scared, she wondered how she'd tell her dad she was running off for the summer with her aunt to find her mother. *This will not go well*, she thought.

She texted Coop and told him about the plan.

COOP

I'm in too.

TIFF

What about your parents?

COOP

They agreed to give me a break. Besides, next year, I'll be going away to college anyway.

Tiff hadn't decided on college. She was more focused on finding out what happened to her mother. She still had time to apply, but first, she wanted to figure out the details of this spiritual quest before asking her father for money.

Anxiety swirled in her mind as she lay awake, trying to decide whether to leave the farm. What if she regretted it? Would she miss the life she left behind? After tossing and turning, she eventually fell asleep.

Tiff saw herself walking up a glass staircase that seemed to go on forever. The space around her looked like a night sky—dark and full of stars—but quiet, like a place meant for learning.

At the top of the stairs was a plain wooden door. She didn't know why, but she felt nervous opening it. Still, something told her to go inside.

A woman was sitting on the floor in a room that resembled a classroom, but without walls. She had long silver hair and calm eyes. In front of her were three items: a mirror, a feather, and a black stone.

The woman pointed to each one as she spoke.

"The mirror shows what you avoid seeing. The feather reminds you to move even when you're afraid. The stone helps you stay steady when everything else feels unreal."

Tiff looked at the mirror and saw herself—stronger, more confident. As she reached toward the feather, a loud crack echoed above her, like thunder. Suddenly, stars formed the shape of the cube and exploded in light. Everything went white.

She woke with a jolt, heart pounding. But the dream faded fast, like mist, and she couldn't remember much of it.

Tiff snoozed a few more moments, hoping to hold onto the dream, but its details slipped further away. Once up, she rushed through her morning routine. Chip trailed her from room to room as she scoured the house again for Sarah's diary. Despite checking every likely and unlikely spot, it was nowhere to be found.

Chip tilted his head from side to side. She petted him and pulled him to her, burying her into his coat. Part of her longed to stay here, to continue the familiar rhythms of farm life with her father and Chip. But another part yearned to discover the truth about her mother. Before she could dwell on it, Coop knocked at the door.

"I had some errands to do and thought I'd stop by for a few minutes."

Tiff hugged him quickly and offered lunch.

"No, I'm good, but thanks. I told my parents about the trip, and they're on board. My father quit that job and will be home. Are you ready?" His voice was gentle, his eyes full of understanding.

Once again, she was struck by how easily he read her, how well he understood her inner conflict.

"What should I do? My father needs me here, but I can't ignore this chance to learn about my mother. I'm see-sawing back and forth. Rachel gave me until tomorrow to decide."

Coop's voice remained calm. "I know how much this means to you, and I have your back. You won't be alone. What's there to decide?"

Tiff opened her mouth but stopped. As they sat quietly in the kitchen, her eyes drifted to the window where midday light poured in. That's when the dream came rushing back, clearer now. The stairs. The room. The woman. The mirror, feather, and stone.

"I had a dream last night," she said slowly. "I didn't remember it at first, but it's coming back to me now."

She told Coop about the symbols in the dream and what the woman had said. "It felt like a message. Like I'm supposed to stop hesitating and go."

Coop listened, his gaze steady.

"I think that's my answer," she said quietly. "The dream helped me decide. And knowing Sherlock will be with me."

"Then let's do it," he said. "Together, Watson."

Tiff smiled. "Okay. We leave tomorrow."

Lincoln was in the back pasture, repairing an old section of the fence. As Tiff approached the area, the rhythmic sound of his hammer striking nails provided a steady backdrop to her turbulent thoughts.

"Dad," Tiff called out, her voice stronger than she felt.

Lincoln paused, wiping the sweat from his brow with

the back of his handkerchief as he turned to face her. His expression was weary, lined with the years of sun, wind, and the weight of keeping the farm running. "What is it, Tiff?" he asked, his tone guarded.

The words she had practiced that morning vanished from her mind. It reminded her of childhood, when she struggled to tell him about a bad day at school.

"It's about this summer," she began, her voice wavering.

Lincoln set down his tools, concern etched across his face. "You sound serious. What's on your mind?"

"I've decided to go on a trip with Rachel," she said, forcing herself to meet his gaze.

The words hung in the air. Lincoln's face hardened. "No," he said flatly, the single word like a door slamming shut.

"Dad, please," Tiff pleaded, stepping closer. "It's important to me. It's about Mom."

"Enough about your aunt and her crazy ideas," he snapped, his voice rising. "I won't let you get dragged into her mess. The farm is our livelihood, Tiff. You belong here."

"But I want to do this," she said, frustration mounting. "There's so much about Mom I don't understand, things I've got to figure out with or without your approval."

Lincoln clenched his jaw. "And what about our little family?"

"I love you, Dad," she said. "You know I do. But I can't keep pretending Mom didn't exist, and neither should you. We need closure. Besides, it's only for the summer. I'll come back. And Coop is going with me."

"His family approved?"

"Yes."

Lincoln turned to her, his eyes glistening. "You're

chasing ghosts, Tiff. What if you go out there and something happens? What if you decide not to come back?"

"Nothing is going to happen to me. I'll come back, I promise," she said, reaching for his rough hands. "Don't you want me to be happy?"

His resistance softened as he looked down at their joined hands. "Of course I do," he said, his voice lower. "But I'm scared, Tiff. I already lost your mother. I can't lose you, too."

"You won't," she said firmly. "I'll be careful, and Rachel won't let anything happen to me. I'll be back before you know it."

At the mention of Rachel, Lincoln pulled away, anger flashing in his eyes. "I don't trust her. She's trying to take you away from me."

Tiff flinched as if struck. "Dad, don't say that. It's not true. No one can take me away from you."

"It seems you've already gone."

"I'm coming back. I promise."

He turned away, gripping the fence post so tightly his knuckles turned white. Then he sagged. The fight left him. When he looked at her again, his eyes were red.

"You remind me of your mother," he said softly. "Headstrong. Once you've made up your mind, there's no changing it."

He pulled her into a hug, holding on so tightly she could barely breathe. She clung to him, matching his grip, hoping he could feel her love and promise in the embrace.

"Go on, then. Visit your aunt. But don't make me wait too long for your return."

Joy and relief washed over Tiff. Through her tears, she smiled. "I won't," she whispered. "I promise."

She wiped her eyes and let out a shaky breath. The

hardest part was done. Deep down, she should have known her father would understand. He always did.

Yet a knot of anxiety still churned in her stomach, a mix of guilt and fear she couldn't quite name. She hadn't told him the whole truth about the journey. She could only imagine the look on his face if he knew about the supernatural forces pulling her in. Some truths, for now, were better left buried.

They walked back to the farmhouse together, her father's arm draped over her shoulders. She took comfort in his warmth and the steady presence beside her.

There was still the rest of the day, and she intended to make the most of it before everything changed.

Chapter 28
Goodbyes

Tiff was up early the next day and enjoyed a bittersweet breakfast with her father and Chip. Afterward, she packed her bags for the trip. Coop was picking her up in a few hours.

As Tiff folded clothes and tucked essential toiletries into her duffel, her mind drifted to Sarah. An image rose unbidden to her mind: a woman with laughing eyes and wild curly hair, smiling and telling her she was the most precious thing in the world.

Tiff rubbed her eyes. She couldn't let hope get ahead of truth—not yet. There were too many unanswered questions and too much uncertainty ahead.

A knock sounded at the door, startling Tiff out of her reverie. Coop poked his head into the room, his eyes questioning. "How's the packing going?"

Tiff folded another shirt. "All right, I guess. Rachel said we shouldn't take much. So, I'm packing the essentials and a few extras. This is exciting, but scary."

"It's going to be okay," he murmured. "This is a good

thing. You will finally learn more about your mother and your family's origins. Remember to trust the universe."

"I know. I'm trying..." She trailed off.

"Scary, exciting, and terrifying all at once, Wild Thing Number Three."

Tiff huffed out a laugh. "Cool. Thank you. For always knowing the right thing to say."

Coop ducked his head, a faint blush staining his cheeks. "What are friends for?"

With renewed determination, Tiff zipped up her bags and headed downstairs, ready to face the uncertainty of the road ahead. Her father stood at the bottom, a weathered Stetson twisting between his hands. His eyes were shadowed with grief, and Tiff understood all too well.

She paused halfway down, throat tightening. "Dad, I..."

"Don't," he said, his voice rough with emotion. "If you say anything more, I will change my mind and lock you in your room to keep you here forever."

Tiff blinked back the sting of tears and launched herself into his arms. "I love you," she said. "You know that. This won't change anything between us."

"I love you, too." He squeezed her close before setting her back with a heavy, sad sigh. "Best get going before I lose my nerve and change my mind."

Tiff nodded, dashing the back of her hand across her eyes. "Yeah," she summoned a shy smile. "See you soon."

"You can count on it." Her father's answering smile wavered only slightly as he bent to brush a kiss against her forehead. "Godspeed, Tiff. I hope you find what you're looking for."

Then she reached down and hugged Chip. "Sorry, boy, you can't go on this one. I want you to protect Dad and watch over the farm. Can you do that for me?" Tiff gave him another hug and turned away before she could lose the tenuous hold she had on her emotions. She crossed the porch to where Coop waited by the car.

The engine purred as Tiff tossed her bags in the trunk. She glanced back at the farmhouse that had always been her anchor. Somehow, she knew then that things would never be quite the same. The life she'd always known was slipping away behind her, a new and uncertain path unfurling ahead.

Tiff steadied her nerves as she waved to her father and slid into the passenger seat next to Coop. "Let's go," she said quietly.

Coop nodded and put the car in drive, guiding them down the dusty road toward whatever awaited them in the world beyond.

Chapter 29

Quest

As Tiff and Coop drew nearer to Rachel's house, their nervousness grew. Excitement simmered beneath the surface. When they arrived, they dumped their packs into the back of Rachel's car with her at the wheel.

Once more, a dense mist enveloped the area. Rachel remained unfazed as she steered the car along the short distance of the dirt road. Finally, they reached the highway, and the fog began to lift. Tiff stared out of the car window, taking in the sweeping scenery that stretched in every direction.

After a few hours, Rachel veered off the highway and onto winding rural roads, the kind that twisted through open fields and forgotten towns. They'd discussed everything except why they were on this trip; Tiff was hoping they would find her mother. Rachel hadn't revealed anything about it other than that it was a spiritual journey. She mustered up the courage to ask Rachel for more information.

"You haven't told us where we're going," Tiff said now

that she was sitting in the front passenger seat. Coop was in the back, snoozing.

"Tiff, you've got every right to ask questions. I'm asking you to trust me anyway," Rachel said, keeping her eyes trained on the road.

"You told us it's a sacred journey. What does that mean?"

Rachel glanced in the rearview mirror, scanning the traffic with a flicker of focus that suggested she was checking for more than just cars.

"This journey goes beyond a trip across the country. It's a passage through the inner landscapes of our souls using our spiritual bodies."

Tiff shifted. "What do you mean by our spiritual bodies? And you keep talking about 'The Teachers.' Can you explain more about who these Teachers are?"

"Okay, first, the spiritual body is your etheric energy field that surrounds the physical body. The Teachers are not of this physical realm. They are advanced beings, ascended masters who have transcended the limitations of the earthly realm. They guide and assist those of us on the path to higher consciousness. Think of them as mentors in the grand school of the Cosmos."

Tiff frowned slightly. It sounded noble, even beautiful, but also unreal. If they were so powerful, why hadn't they helped her mother already?

Coop stirred awake in the backseat, catching the tail end of the exchange. He rubbed his eyes and asked, "That's a lot. How do we change into this energy body?"

"You will transform through specific practices," Rachel replied. "Meditation, visualization, sound, and sometimes direct assistance from the Teachers themselves. Each of you will shift in the way that suits your energy body best."

Coop blinked. "So... we've already done that by going through the wheatfield portal?"

"Exactly. You're composed of energy not only physically but across etheric, emotional, mental, and spiritual layers," Rachel continued. "These layers intermingle, often perceived as a spectrum of colors by those with the gift of sight beyond the ordinary. When you transition from the physical realm, it's your astral body that you inhabit. The body you engage with reflects the vibrational energy field you are in. Crossing through the wheatfield portals, you may have felt physical, but in truth, you were vibrating at an elevated frequency, perfectly attuned to your energetic form."

Tiff glanced at Coop. He seemed to be absorbing this easily. Why was it harder for her? Maybe she needed to see proof, something undeniable. Maybe she still didn't want to believe her mother was no longer fully human, or fully here.

"Got it," Coop said.

"How do you communicate with these Teachers? How do you know you're not imagining things?" Tiff asked.

"A fair question, Tiff. At first, I also doubted my experiences. Communication is not like a phone call or an email. It's more... intuitive. It comes through deep meditation, through dreams, and sometimes through signs. Over time, you learn to differentiate between what's on your mind and what's a true message."

Tiff bit the inside of her cheek. That sounded a lot like what she was already doing—guessing. And still coming up short.

"And what mission do they need us for?" Tiff asked, her voice tinged with skepticism and curiosity.

"The details will unfold as we proceed," Rachel replied. "Know this: it involves aligning with cosmic energy to heal ourselves and the planet. Every generation has its healers, warriors, and teachers. You, Tiff, and you, Coop, are part of this generation's call. But most importantly, it involves finding Sarah because she will play a major role in implementing the plan."

Tiff's chest tightened at the mention of her mother. If Sarah truly had a role to play, maybe she wasn't gone. Maybe she hadn't abandoned them after all.

Tiff exhaled slowly, trying to absorb the weight of Rachel's words. "And this place we're going to is in the state of Washington. What's there?"

"It's a nexus point," Rachel explained. "A place where the veil between dimensions is thin. The Teachers have informed me that something crucial to our quest awaits us there. Believe me. It's all part of the plan."

A nexus point. Another mystery inside a mystery. Tiff's pulse quickened, but she wasn't sure if it was fear or anticipation.

The car fell silent as Tiff and Coop digested her words, each lost in their thoughts about the journey ahead and the roles they were destined to play. The road stretched on, each mile bringing them closer to answers and more questions. Tiff would often view the landscape as they drove. She wanted to remember every detail of the trip.

"We'll stop here for tonight," Rachel said as she pulled into a motel. "And Coop, you can share a room with us. I want us all to stay together. We are being followed."

Tiff and Coop immediately turned to look back at the road. Several cars followed behind, but none stood out. Several crows flew overhead and landed on a nearby tree.

"Don't worry about it. I got this." Rachel parked the car and smiled at her young riders.

Chapter 30
Trapped

As they approached the warehouse, the air thickened with an almost palpable tension, and a knot of anxiety tightened in Tiff's stomach. The frail structure loomed before them, its doors hanging ajar like a dark mouth ready to swallow them whole.

Rachel reached for the rusty handle, pulling the door with an echoing creak. They stepped inside, their flashlights cutting through the darkness, revealing nothing but old crates and dust.

Tiff's disappointment surged into tears. "We came all this way for this?"

Rachel didn't respond as she led them deeper into the shadows. Suddenly, the faint sound of fluttering wings filled the air. Crows—dozens of them—burst forth from the rafters, their cries deafening in the enclosed space. Tiff recoiled, her back hitting the cold wall. She slid down to the floor, covering her ears, trying to block out the noise. The birds swooped down, their wings brushing against her, each touch a feathered caress that sent shivers down her spine.

"Rachel, what's happening?"

Rachel stood unshaken, her expression stern against the swirling chaos above. "This is an assault by the dark forces," she yelled over the din of circling birds. "They're trying to stop us from getting to where we need to be."

Tiff, struggling to be heard, called out, "How did they even know about this place?"

"They have their ways of gathering information," Rachel replied, her voice tense.

Coop grabbed Tiff's hand and pulled her up. "Stay close to me," he said, his voice steady despite the chaos.

They huddled close, watching as Rachel chanted in a low, rhythmic tone. The crows hesitated, their circling slowing as the sound of her voice rose over their cries.

Tiff clung to Coop's hand, her fingers cold and clammy. "Can she stop them?"

Coop's expression was blank.

"We can't stay here; follow me." Rachel ran for the door. When she opened it, the sky was dark, and crows covered every inch of the area.

"I thought crows were supposed to be angelic messengers, but they look menacing. What are we going to do?" Coop asked.

At that point, they heard the screech of a car's tires that pulled up on the sidewalk close to the door.

Harvey cracked the window and said, "Jump in," to the trio.

"Mr. Bernstein, what are you doing here?" Tiff asked.

"Get in the car. We can discuss that later." Harvey yelled again.

The crows swooped down on them, but they managed to get into the vehicle safely.

"Harvey," Rachel smiled widely. "What took you so long?"

"Woman, I have been waiting for you for years," he was bursting with joy.

"I hate to break this reunion up, but our things are in the SUV," Coop said.

"We can't go anywhere near that car," Harvey said in his teacher's voice.

"I'm not going anywhere without my computer."

"Neither am I. All my possessions are in my bag," Tiff said.

"Once it's clear, Coop, you go for it. Tiff, you stay here," Rachel said.

Harvey moved a few feet closer to the SUV. The four of them huddled in the cramped car, their breaths creating a humid fog on the windows as they anxiously watched the menacing crows circling outside. After a few hours, their stomachs growled with hunger; their only source of sustenance was a few meager bottles of water in Harvey's car. Along with the bags, all their snacks and water were in the SUV.

Harvey and Rachel delved into a conversation that spanned over seventeen years. They shared the twists and turns their lives had taken, reconnecting the threads of their pasts.

Tiff listened half-heartedly to their stories. For the first time, she glimpsed a part of Mr. Bernstein's life she didn't know about. Perhaps his aversion to her was linked to his sadness about Rachel leaving. She turned to Coop, who was busy on his phone, and asked, "What are you doing?"

"Trying to figure out who T-369 is."

"I'm glad you're still following that clue. I have no idea who that could be."

Rachel looked at Harvey and smiled.

"T-369, umm," Harvey chimed in. "Can I take a crack at it?"

"You're the physics teacher. What do you think it stands for?" Tiff asked.

"From a mathematical perspective, I would say a triangle, but not all the lines connect."

"That doesn't tell us much about this person. And there were these other numbers on their website."

"What numbers?" Rachel added to the discussion.

"1,2,4,5,7 and 8," Tiff said.

Coop continued staring at his phone. Then he yelled out. "I got it."

"You found out who T-369 is?" Tiff looked at him.

"No, but 1,2,4,5,7, and 8 are the vibrations of the 3rd dimension, and 3,6, and 9 are the Divine vibrations of God. Nine is said to be God's fingerprint."

Tiff said, "But that doesn't tell us who T-369 is or about the code."

"Shall I tell them, or you?" Harvey asked Rachel.

"Go for it."

"Wait." Tiff thought of the photo of the three children in the jar. "It's you. You're the boy in the photo."

"Yes, and I'm also T-369." He chuckled. "I was sending a message to Rachel to let her know about the crop circles forming again in Wheatfield. I knew that your mother or Rachel would come to the rescue."

"So, T doesn't stand for Tesla?"

"No, Triangle. The 369 forms a perfect equilateral triangle, but the 3 and 6 aren't connecting. Rachel would know this and see it as a sign of stress."

"Why haven't you reached out to her before?"

"I did to both of them, but I never received a response." Harvey stole a glance at Rachel.

"It's complicated, Harvey. Let the past go and deal with what's happening in the present."

They all became distracted for a while. Tiff and

Coop sat silently again, as the two adults continued their intense conversation in lowered voices. Coop looked from front to back and the sides. With caution, he lowered the window and scanned the area outside the car.

"I can go now," Coop interrupted them. "Rachel, can you unlock the SUV?"

She clicked her remote key and nodded at him.

"Wait," Tiff grabbed his arm. "This is way too dangerous. Look at those things."

"They're huge. I don't think they're real crows. Please, Coop, don't do it." She begged him.

Coop jumped out of the car and ran to the SUV, fighting off several crows before creeping into it.

Tiff monitored the crows with fright as they appeared out of nowhere, circling and pecking at the windows of both cars. Coop, stuck in the other vehicle, packed as much as he could into two bags. Then he held up a sheet of paper. They all read it.

"Let's wait."

Tiff nodded okay, but every few minutes, she stared out the window.

"Where are we? This neighborhood is deserted. I haven't seen anyone since we arrived. Let's call for help. The police?"

"I don't have a phone. Does anyone have a phone?" Rachel asked.

"My phone is in my backpack," Tiff replied.

Harvey pulled out a phone. "I haven't charged it. It only has a few bars. I'll try to call for help." He dialed the emergency number. No one answered.

Tiff asked, "What is going on here?"

"I think we're in a different timeline or dimension, which is why the phone won't work," Rachel answered.

Harvey laid the phone aside. "What do we do? We can't stay here much longer."

"This is where we trust our guides."

Tiff and Harvey stared at Rachel with skepticism and concern.

Coop panicked upon noticing additional dark silhouettes of crows circling overhead. He hoped the crows would leave them alone. But they didn't. They attacked with ferocity, pecking and clawing at the windows and doors, trying whatever they could to get inside. Coop heard Tiff's scream from the other car and wished he could assist her. Perhaps separating from the group had been a mistake. He pondered whether they would survive this ordeal.

Then the noise ceased again. Coop peered outside and noticed the crows dispersing. He exhaled in relief because they needed to leave. He grabbed the backpack and opened the door, ready to run to the other car. However, the moment he stepped outside, a sharp pain shot through his arm. Glancing down, he noticed blood oozing from a gash where a crow had torn through his sleeve and pecked him. He felt a burning sensation spreading through his veins. He ignored it and ran to the other car, where his friends were waiting for him.

"Coop, are you okay?" Tiff asked, her eyes wide with fear.

Coop declared, "I'm good. Let's go!" He tossed the bags onto the back seat, causing several warm water bottles and snacks to spill out onto the floor.

Tiff swiftly picked up two bottles and gave them to Rachel and Harvey.

Harvey started the engine and drove away from the

scene, hoping they had escaped the crows for good. He was wrong. Glancing in the rearview mirror, he saw them following behind. A dark cloud hung around the car.

"Guys, they're still after us!" He sped up and tried to zigzag on the road, but the crows kept their pace.

Coop, feeling nauseous, took off his jacket and examined his arm. It was swollen and turning purple as his body raged with fever. "I don't feel so good," he croaked.

"What's wrong?" Tiff asked, turning to him.

He showed her his arm, and she gasped.

"Oh my God, Coop, what happened?"

"One of those damn crows bit me."

"Is there anything we can do?"

"I need an antidote."

Coop remembered that his backpack had a survival kit with basic medical supplies. He reached for his bag and opened it, hoping to find something useful. But as he did so, he felt a sudden jolt of pain in his chest. He dropped the backpack and clutched his heart. He felt it beating faster and faster, like a bomb getting ready to explode. He wanted to tell her he loved her, but he couldn't speak. Coop felt his consciousness slipping away from him. He closed his eyes and fell into darkness.

"Coop!" Tiff grabbed him. Her face cringed with fear. "What are we going to do?" she asked her other two companions.

With a voice strained by urgency, Harvey commanded, "Find the directions to the nearest hospital. He must receive help immediately." He pressed the accelerator to the floor.

Tiff tried Coop's phone, but there was no service.

Inwardly, Rachel heard the voice of her Teacher, a presence she knew well and had relied on more times than she could count: *"Beloved One, a portal is opening on Mount Shasta. You know the place. Go there now with your companions."*

She inhaled deeply and turned to the others. "We're going to a sacred spot on Mount Shasta," she said, her voice steady with quiet conviction.

Harvey looked at her, startled. "What? Not a hospital?"

"There's more going on than we understand," Rachel replied. "On that mountain is a place of power—a place where help might reach us in ways a hospital can't."

Tiff blinked at her, unsure whether to believe, but Rachel's gaze remained fixed and certain.

"Trust me," she said. "We're not out of time yet."

Tiff wiped away her tears. There was nothing more she could do for Coop. She leaned close to his ear and whispered, "Hold on, my Sherlock. Watson is on the job."

Coop remained motionless, and when she touched his arm, it was burning.

The drive felt endless. Tiff longed to stop for more water or ice, but the crows were relentless, diving and clawing at the car whenever they slowed. She moistened Coop's forehead and lips with the last drops left in the bottle.

Frustration boiled up. "Why did we go to that warehouse, anyway?" she muttered.

"Because it's the route your mother took. The journey starts in the northwest," Harvey replied calmly.

Her voice rose, edged with disbelief. "Mr. Bernstein, how could you possibly know my mom took this route?"

"I read it in her diary," Harvey said.

"You have my mom's diary?" Tiff gasped.

"Yes. She left it with me."

"Why?"

"I think she knew how much I wanted to learn about what she could do. I was always asking her questions. It's all in the diary. I've been able to decipher parts of it. But some pages are for your eyes only." He glanced at Rachel. "It's in the glove compartment."

Rachel reached into the dashboard. As her fingers brushed the worn leather cover, memories stirred. Sarah's laughter. Her secrecy. Her brilliance. She held the diary for a moment, then handed it and the cube to Tiff.

"I think this belongs to you."

Tiff took them reverently. "I'm not going to read it until you can read it with me. Please don't give up on me now." She tucked the cube and diary inside her jacket and zipped it up tight.

Harvey slammed on the brakes. Up ahead, shimmering in the air like heat off asphalt, was a glowing circle. The portal. Their only way out.

He grabbed his large umbrella, ready to fend off the crows. "Come on, guys. We can do this."

Rachel pulled Coop's limp body from the back seat. Tiff jumped out to grab his other side. Together, they lifted him and staggered toward the shrinking portal while Harvey circled them, swinging wildly at the swarming crows. Black feathers flew. Some birds fell to the ground. Others screamed and dove again.

Tiff kicked one off her leg, heart pounding. The portal was only meters away, but it was closing fast. Through it, she glimpsed a realm bathed in golden light. A place that radiated peace.

"We're almost there," Harvey shouted.

With one desperate motion, Tiff hurled Coop's body through the portal, then flung his pack in after him. Rachel and Harvey leapt next, vanishing into the light as the circle narrowed.

Tiff was last.

She sprinted forward, her hand outstretched. The portal was nearly gone. She lunged, hoping someone would reach back.

But no one did.

With a sharp snap, the portal sealed shut, leaving Tiff behind.

Alone.

Surrounded by crows.

Chapter 31
Rabbit Hole

The crows circled overhead, their shadows dancing across the car's windshield. Tiff shivered, though not from the cold, remembering the disappearance of her friends into the portal and being left alone. She had raced back to the car, fighting off the treacherous birds with Harvey's umbrella. She dared not look out the window as the feeling of being trapped engulfed her. Tiff thought about Lincoln and what he would do in this situation. She searched the car for anything that might be useful for her escape. She found a small flashlight in the car's glove compartment and nothing else.

Despondent, Tiff crawled into the car's back seat and hunched on the floor. She turned on the flashlight and pulled her mother's diary from her jacket with trembling fingers. She had promised Coop she wouldn't read it until he felt better, and they could read it together. But everything was falling apart. *Sorry, Coop. I couldn't wait. I need help —and the answer might be in here.* She ducked under her jacket and opened the book, shielding herself from the endless screeching of the birds outside. The diary wasn't quite as her father had described it. Its purple cover was tattered, adorned with a spiral design that stretched across the entire front. The pattern reminded her of the crop circle in the wheat field. Holding it somehow brought a strange, unexpected comfort.

As Tiff gently opened the weathered pages of the diary with a small key taped to the back of it, a vivid memory flashed through her mind—Sarah, sitting on Hillary Hill, illuminated by the radiance of the morning sun. Sarah's fingers danced over the pages of the very diary Tiff now held.

"Where are you, Mom?" Tiff asked as she stared at her mother's neat penmanship.

If you're reading these words, my darling girl, Harvey has given you my precious possession—the diary with esoteric wisdom and instructions. I wrote this for you. My Holy Guardian Angel informed me about your birth and that you would someday need this practical guide. It is not only a collection of thoughts or a record of days. It is a vessel of knowledge, a map of the spiritual and cosmic journeys I've embarked on. Each entry, each symbol here, connects to a greater truth, one that you might one day seek. And perhaps, when the time is right, it will guide you as it has guided me.

I know you don't understand why I left. The Spirit called, and I answered. I had to sacrifice all that I desired and loved. One day, you'll understand. Please forgive me. I love you.

It would be best if you also had the cube in your possession. I was about your age, or a little younger, when my Holy Guardian Angel gave me instructions to create this cube. She told me it wasn't for me, but for you. It's a type of Arcane Cube, a spiritual initiation map. In many ways, it resembles the sacred cube, but this one has been imbued with magical powers to aid you on your journey.

Arcane Cube

With it, the veil between worlds can be lifted. The Arcane Cube, an object of profound mystique and power, serves two primary purposes. It acts as an essential key to one's soul's evolution, guiding the bearer through the intricate processes of spiritual awakening and self-discovery. Each facet of the cube offers a unique lesson, challenge, or insight, deepening the user's understanding of their inner self and their place in the cosmos. The cube also functions as a sophisticated navigational device for traversing different dimensions and parallel worlds. By manipulating its structure, the user can open portals to alternate realities, exploring diverse existential planes and uncovering the vast, interconnected multiverse's secrets. This dual capability makes the Arcane Cube not only a tool but a gateway to profound transformation and exploration. To access it, you must have the code. I discovered it has a power like no other, and when you least expect it, "freaky things" can occur.

A note of caution: Use it with discretion for the betterment of humanity, not for selfish gain. One day, if you follow the road map for the soul, you'll be granted access to the Divine Cube. For now, please wake up, my little sleeper, and step lightly along the Path of Return.

Tiff pulled the cube out of her jacket. Despite the cramped space, she stretched her legs out on the car floor, carefully balancing the magical cube and the diary on her lap. She turned the cube until she found the side with the Hangman. She studied it and thought it was mystifying. She doubted if it would be much help in helping her to escape. The illustration showed a man hanging upside down from a tree branch by one leg, with a branch on each side for support. Tiff sighed in frustration. She didn't have the password to access its power. After reading her mother's cryptic notes about the cube, she couldn't find a password.

"I don't understand any of this occult stuff," Tiff muttered. She preferred facts and logic, not hazy spirituality. But the cube was her only clue to finding her mother. She wished Coop were with her. Sadness pierced her heart. Did he make it? The thought of Coop and others made her even more determined to find them. She peeked from under her jacket at the darkness that was now everywhere. Tiff hugged her knees as tears ran down her face. "Guide me, please," she whispered to the space, hoping her mother heard her cries for help. With a heavy moan, her eyes closed.

Tiff didn't know how long she had been asleep, but a light woke her up. The cube was suspended in the air, spinning with a brilliant light radiating from it. She reached out to touch it, and as her fingers entered the light's force field, it cast small rainbows across her hands. She smiled. She may not understand the cube's power, but she would try to unlock its secrets to find the truth for her mother's sake and her own.

Tiff opened the diary, flipping through the worn pages covered in familiar handwriting until she found the entry on the Arcane Cube and reread what her mother had written. She needed the passcode *to* activate the cube's power. How would Coop approach this problem? She wondered. Her mind raced through all the facts they had gathered and landed on the number 369. Tiff stared at the cube and whispered 369, and the cube continued to spin without anything else happening. She tried 639, and the cube remained suspended but without any other changes. Despondent, Tiff gave it one last tried and said, "Okay, cube, is it 693?"

Heart pounding, Tiff kept her mind fixed on the cube, trying to ignore the buzzing in her ears. Then, a tugging within her began and intensified, as if she felt herself being separated from her body.

With a sudden wrench, the scene before Tiff blurred and melted away. Dazzling colors swirled around her in a tunnel of light like the ones she encountered in the wheat field. She thought she was being turned inside out.

A gentle wind whipped around her as she realized she was no longer in the car. She stood in a strange new landscape, utterly alien from the mountainside she had left behind.

"It worked," Tiff said in awe. She had crossed into another world. And somewhere in this mystical realm, she hoped to find Coop and the others, and then they would find Sarah.

Tiff stood in awe of the alien terrain. Jagged cliffs loomed above, their surfaces shimmering with iridescent crystals. Strange fungi sprouted from the rocky ground, glowing in shades of purple and green.

In the distance stood a dense forest of gnarled trees, their bark black as ink. Leaves rustled eerily, though there was no wind.

Creatures scuttled and slithered at the edges of her vision, keeping their distance but watching with unblinking eyes. Tiff clutched the cube and diary tighter.

"Trust the Universe," Sarah had written.

Somehow, amidst the strangeness, Tiff knew she had to keep moving. She stepped into the unknown.

Tiff moved carefully, guided by instinct. Echoes of cries and screeches bounced across the terrain, sending chills down her spine. She climbed over jagged rocks and glowing crystal formations until a cave appeared in the distance, partially hidden by twisted black trees. She froze, heart pounding.

In her mother's diary, a sketch depicted a cave entrance that resembled this one.

"The Cave of Mysteries," Sarah had scrawled beside the drawing. "Within lies the portal home."

Tiff's pulse quickened. This was the clue she had been seeking.

At the cave's mouth, she paused and peered into the pitch-black entrance. Whispering a quick prayer, she stepped inside.

The temperature dropped instantly, wrapping her in a heavy, damp chill. She fumbled in her bag for the flashlight and switched it on. A narrow, winding passage stretched ahead.

Tiff's senses were on high alert. The walls pressed in, forcing her to turn sideways in spots. After several twists and turns, the passage opened into an enormous cavern. She swept the flashlight beam across the walls. Strange symbols, like those in her mother's diary, were etched into the stone.

"I'm on the right path," she whispered.

A large, ornate mirror framed in stone stood at the back of the cavern. As she approached it, her reflection shimmered. Coop was staring back at her.

"Coop!" Tiff reached out, but her fingers met cold glass.

Tiff steeled herself. She raised the cube and said firmly, "Six-nine-three."

The cube responded instantly, glowing brighter as a low hum filled the chamber.

"Another portal," she realized.

Light burst from the mirror, pulling her in. A kaleidoscope of color and sound enveloped her as she crossed to the other side.

The terrain had changed. The colors were brilliant,

almost unreal. In the distance, three snowcapped mountains rose above a deep blue ocean. Tiff had never seen anything so beautiful.

Her heart leapt when she saw Coop lying ahead. She ran toward him without thinking—only to be slammed backward by an invisible force. She hit the ground hard and groaned in frustration.

Coop lay completely still on a bed of leaves. Harvey stood nearby, silent and watchful. Nine barefoot women in white circled Coop. One of them knelt at his side, her dark hair loose around her shoulders.

Tiff squinted. She didn't recognize the woman.

Is that Habiba, she wondered, *Sarah and Rachel's mother?*

The woman's movements were smooth and deliberate. Tiff watched as she placed her hands over Coop's wound and seemed to draw something dark and writhing from it. She repeated the action several times, then laid both hands gently over his chest.

In desperation, Tiff yelled out, knowing her voice couldn't reach them through the barrier. The women began moving in a slow circle around Coop, each laying a flower upon him. Rachel—or the woman she thought might be Rachel—remained in place.

Tiff's voice cracked as she screamed, pounding the barrier with both fists. She leaped forward and pushed against it with all her strength, but it held firm. Seconds later, it began to shimmer and fade.

"No, please don't leave!" she cried, but her words only echoed back at her in silence.

Chapter 32
Nephilimbug

Hours earlier, Nephilimbug's gaze hardened as he watched Tiff retreat into the car, her sneers still echoing in his mind. Through the rain-streaked window, he saw her huddle under her jacket, a faint light glowing from beneath it. A part of him imagined being in the car with her, watching her beg for mercy. But then the rain fell harder, sudden and cold, dousing the fantasy and dragging him back to reality. He needed her. She was crucial to his plans.

Looking skyward as the rain washed over him, Nephilimbug vanished within a blazing circle that appeared above. His conflicting emotions swirled as tumultuously as the storm around him.

The door to the Order's chamber slid open with a hiss, and Nephilimbug stepped inside. His footsteps echoed across the obsidian floor as he approached the raised dais where the Elders sat cloaked in shadow.

He dropped to one knee; fist pressed to his heart in a salute. "Masters, I bring grave news. The girl has eluded me again."

"This is most disappointing," the elder leader, Ute, rumbled.

Nephilimbug clenched his jaw. He had failed too many times now, and he could feel the members of the Order losing patience.

"You keep losing her and the cube. Why?" Ute demanded.

"I don't understand how she keeps slipping through my grasp," he said. "It's as if she knows my every move before I make it."

The Elders murmured. Nephilimbug glanced up at their faces. What weren't they telling him?

"You doubt our purpose?" Ute accused.

Nephilimbug lowered his gaze. "No, Master. But to succeed, I need to know everything about the girl and her capabilities."

Silence followed. His boldness carried dangerous implications, but he needed answers.

Ute leaned forward, his claws gripping the arms of his seat. "Do not forget your place, Nephilimbug. Your father was a god, but your mother was an Earthling. You are a crossbreed. The girl is a pawn in a much larger game."

A flicker of resentment rose in his chest, but he buried it quickly. "Yes, Master," he forced out. "I will not fail you again."

But his mind was churning with discontent. There were secrets here, dangerous ones, and he intended to uncover them.

Nephilimbug left the chamber, frustration boiling in his veins. He had been trained since boyhood to obey every command. Yet now, something inside him resisted. An unfamiliar feeling stirred within him, something he couldn't quite define. The girl evoked both anger and compassion, which made it harder to complete the mission.

As he walked down the dark corridor, he considered his options. The archives. If knowledge were power, that was where he would find it.

Nephilimbug slipped into the shadowed library, eyes scanning the dim room. He found the ancient scrolls and began rifling through them.

There, on a crumbling parchment, were details about the Arcane Cube the girl possessed. It could open portals between worlds, but only with the code. There were other, deeper powers within the cube, abilities few could comprehend, but one had to unlock it first through that code.

His eyes widened. No wonder the Elders wanted it. The cube could grant access to realms meant only for beings of great light.

Other texts referenced the girl's mother, a powerful light agent who had once defied the Order of the Black Shadow. She had evaded them for years, but they had finally stopped her before she reached the threshold of ascension.

Nephilimbug leaned back, his mind racing. The pieces were starting to come together, though the full picture was still unclear. He tucked the scrolls into his cloak and stepped away from the shelves. His thoughts burned with urgency and suspicion. He would no longer be their pawn. He would find the truth about the cube, the girl, and the plan behind it all. Then he would decide for himself what came next.

Chapter 33
The Lodge

A faint knocking grew louder, pulling Tiff from sleep. She lowered her jacket from her eyes, and a bright, blinding light greeted her. Everything that had happened hours earlier floated back into her awareness.

A man in uniform stood outside the car window, shining a flashlight. He knocked again and motioned for her to roll the window down.

"Hey, kid, what's going on?"

Tiff saw the park ranger's name—Officer Porter—on his tag. She rolled down the window slowly.

"I-I'm waiting for my friends to come back from their hike. I couldn't go because I didn't feel well," she stammered, squinting.

He lowered the flashlight. "They said they'd be back soon?"

Tiff nodded. "I know it sounds ridiculous, but it's the truth. They aren't ordinary hikers. I'm okay. I can wait for them here."

"Hiking? In the middle of the night? In these woods?"

"Yes, I know how it sounds. But I'm fine."

"Well, kid, you can't stay here. It's not safe. There are wild animals—and worse—around here. Come on. I'll take you to a nearby lodge where you can wait for your friends. We'll leave a note on the car," he said.

"Where is this lodge, Officer Porter?" she asked.

"It's west of here. I'll attach a map to your note."

"No, I'm fine. I'll wait for them here," she repeated.

"Do you have water or food?"

"No," she admitted.

"I can't leave you here. I'll get the map." He turned and walked to his patrol car.

Officer Porter returned a few minutes later and circled a location on a folded map. Tiff wrote on a piece of paper he had given her. "Guys, I'm being taken to a lodge by Officer Porter. Find me there."

He pressed the map and note against the windshield before tucking them under the wiper.

Tiff climbed into the patrol car reluctantly, clutching her backpack. As he got into the driver's seat, she glanced back at the woods one last time.

A single tear ran down her cheek.

The lodge was about forty kilometers from the sacred spot in the woods, but with the winding roads and quiet darkness, the trip felt longer. Tiff tried to memorize each turn, but exhaustion blurred everything into shadows.

By the time they arrived, dawn was breaking. Pale light spilled over the rooftops of three clustered lodges. Two were three stories tall, and one had four levels surrounded by manicured shrubs and blooming flowers. Each was breathtaking.

The main structure blended Gothic arches with rustic cabin charm. Wooden balconies were carved with celestial symbols and mythical creatures. A clear stream flowed nearby, catching the early light and scattering it like a million diamonds. The air smelled of pine and morning dew.

Tiff noticed seven cube-shaped stools arranged near the deep blue stream, each carved with faint markings.

A man and a woman stood on the front steps of the largest lodge. The name ASSIAH was engraved across the entrance in bold capital letters.

Porter parked and waved them over. "Mary and Paul, this is the guest I mentioned."

"What's your name?" the woman asked gently.

"Tiffany, but everyone calls me Tiff."

"Welcome. We've been expecting you. Thank you, Officer Porter. We'll take care of her now."

He tipped his hat and returned to his patrol car before Tiff could thank him.

Who were these people? Tiff's mind raced as Mary and Paul led her up the steps.

Before entering, she thought she saw someone who looked like Ari walking into the next lodge.

Inside, the entrance hall was elegant yet warm: marble floors, cedarwood furniture, a fireplace flanked by simple leather armchairs, and morning light streaming in through tall windows.

"Sign in here, and I'll assign you a room," Mary said.

"Oh, I'm only staying a few hours. I'm waiting for my friends. This place looks too expensive for me," Tiff said, glancing around.

"Mary smiled. "Didn't Officer Porter tell you? There's no charge. We're a nonprofit organization that supports individuals on their life journeys. You may stay as long as you need."

"I don't understand," Tiff said, confused.

"Once you're settled, Paul or I'll give you a quick tour. You're welcome to rest in your room."

"You have room twenty-two. Let me show you."

Tiff followed her through quiet hallways. When she entered the room, a wave of nostalgia washed over her. It reminded her of her bedroom back in Lotterland. She missed her dad and Chip more than ever.

She dropped her backpack on the floor and walked toward the bed. A small tray sat on the nightstand with a bowl of fresh fruit, a plate of buttered toast with jam, and a glass of juice and water. A folded note lay beside it:

Welcome. Rest as long as you like. The bells will signal when it's time to gather for the midday meal.

Tiff sat on the edge of the bed and slowly ate a slice of toast, washing it down with sips of juice, the simple food grounding her after the chaos of the last twenty-four hours.

Tiff pinched her arm. No, she wasn't dreaming. But now that she was safe, the fatigue hit her all at once. She told herself she'd lie down for a few minutes.

Chapter 34
Strike

After leaving Headquarters, Nephilimbug wasted no time in setting his plan into motion against the light agents to seize the cube. He swiftly contacted Titanu.

"Are you in position?" he asked.

"Yes," came the prompt reply.

"Then initiate the strike."

In the shadowy silhouette of the evening, Titanu, a crow with sleek feathers, perched atop a tree. Her keen eyes followed Officer Porter as he escorted Tiff toward a secretive location. With the precision of a seasoned spy, Titanu tracked every turn they took, memorizing their path and the subtle signals they exchanged. The mission was clear—discover and infiltrate the training ground of the light agents.

Once her prey arrived at the lodge, Titanu shifted form. She now embodied a young woman with striking features, an identity she had usurped from a traveler destined for the same secretive facility. With this new guise, she merged seamlessly into a group of initiates, her presence unquestioned, her motives cloaked in a carefully constructed mask of innocence.

Inside the lodge, she quickly adapted, her senses attuned to the ebb and flow of magical energies. She noted the invisible barriers shimmering faintly at the edges of the compound, a fortress of light designed to ward off darkness. Each observation was meticulously recorded in her mind, a report forming for her commander, Nephilimbug.

Meanwhile, Nephilimbug, in crow form, trailed Ari, observing his interactions and the fluctuations in his emotional aura. Ari's vulnerability was apparent—his mind preoccupied with thoughts of Tiff. His psychic defenses were down, presenting a perfect opportunity.

The night before Ari was to arrive at the lodge, he sought solace in the dim corner of a local club, trying to drown his apprehensions in the numbing effects of alcohol. His guard lowered further with each drink, his aura dimming, making him susceptible to influence.

Seizing the moment, Nephilimbug, master of shadows, slipped into the club. Under the cloak of darkness and the pulsing lights, he approached Ari, their energies aligning briefly. With a subtle, dark whisper, Nephilimbug merged his consciousness with Ari's, taking control with a precision borne of centuries of manipulation.

Now, as Ari, Nephilimbug entered the lodge. The invisible barriers, analyzed and understood by Titanu, posed no threat to him. He walked through the hallways with Ari's face, greeted by nods and smiles from unsuspecting light agents.

Titanu, positioned strategically within the gathering of guests, felt a surge of satisfaction as she sensed Nephilimbug's successful infiltration. They met covertly under the guise of a casual encounter.

"Everything is in place," Titanu whispered, her voice a

blend of excitement and caution. "The barriers are, as you predicted, vulnerable at the energy nodes. I've mapped them for you."

Nephilimbug, maintaining Ari's pleasant demeanor, nodded. "Excellent work. Continue gathering intelligence on the interior defenses. I'll handle things from here, pushing our advantage while I can."

As they parted, each slipped back into their roles—agents of the shadow moving undetected within a bastion of light. Titanu resumed her guise as a diligent guest, while Nephilimbug, as Ari, navigated the complexities of the lodge's social and magical structures, his mind plotting further disruptions.

His first strike was Tiff.

Chapter 35
The Offer

Hours later, while the sun still hovered high above the lodge, the guest room where Tiff slept remained cloaked in a false twilight. Enchanted draperies shimmered faintly, casting an illusion of night, complete with pinpricks of starlight glinting across the ceiling. In this hushed and dreamlike space, the mirror on the wall began to shimmer.

Tiff tried to open her eyes, but a kaleidoscope of colors swirling in the mirror blinded her. She blinked several times, and the colors dissolved into darkness. As her vision cleared, indistinct figures shifted within the glass, and the Lotterland farm slowly emerged in its reflection.

Tiff clutched the blanket, dread rising in her chest. The wheat fields were decimated, stalks flattened and shriveled. Her father wandered among them, his shoulders slumped in defeat. Chip lay motionless in the dirt.

"Dad!" Tiff cried out. "Chip! Can you hear me?"

Her father didn't react, consumed by the devastation around him. Guilt twisted in her stomach. She should never have gotten involved with the crop circles. Because of her, the farm was ruined. If only she could reach out and help. The portal remained impassable, taunting her with what she had lost.

Tiff hugged her knees, alone again in the darkened room. She had to find her way back before it was too late.

The mirror shimmered and shifted again, revealing a different scene.

Maddie sat on the curb in front of the rundown diner, its windows boarded and its sign hanging crooked. Her makeup was smudged, and her hair disheveled. L.R. had his arm around her shoulders.

"Maddie, I'm here!"

As before, they couldn't see or hear her.

"This is all her fault," Maddie said bitterly. "Ever since Tiff got obsessed with those crop circles, everything has gone wrong."

L.R. rubbed her back. "I told you she was a nut job and to stay away from her."

"I should have listened," Maddie said. "She abandoned me to chase her stupid crop circle theories, and now the whole town is cursed."

Tiff's eyes brimmed with tears. She had never meant for any of this. She only wanted to understand what was happening at the farm. But her actions had shattered everything she held dear.

"I'm so sorry," she whispered, even though they couldn't hear her.

The scene faded. Tiff buried her face in her arms, racked with guilt. She had to make this right.

A cold laugh cut through the darkness.

Tiff's head jerked up. Nephilimbug appeared in the mirror, standing before her with his black, shining eyes.

"My poor Tiff," he purred. "You only wanted to help, and look what happened."

Tiff shuddered at his mocking sympathy. "What do you want?"

He hissed before answering, "To offer my assistance, of course. Give me the cube, pledge your loyalty, and I will undo all of this."

The mirror transformed again, showing visions of a prosperous farm, the diner restored, and her friends laughing as if nothing had ever gone wrong.

"I will restore the farm, your friends, the whole wretched town," Nephilimbug crooned. "You need only serve me, and all will be as it was."

Tiff wavered. It was tempting, so tempting, to erase all her mistakes. But at what cost? Her freedom? Her soul? Nephilimbug could not be trusted.

She faced him with unwavering calm. "I'll find a way to fix this. Without you."

"You'll regret refusing me, girl."

He vanished. The mirror returned to its normal reflection.

Tiff steadied her breathing. She would fight for her father, her friends, and herself. It wasn't too late. It couldn't be.

How had he gotten into her head? The question lingered as light streamed through the enchanted draperies and the illusion of night dissolved.

And so did Tiff's fear.

Tiff blinked against the sunlight filling the unfamiliar room. For a moment, she was disoriented, unsure of where she was or how she had gotten there.

Then it came back to her—the portal, the strange visions, Officer Porter bringing her to the lodge. She was in one of the guest rooms. But had it all been a dream? Nephilimbug's offer and threats had felt so real.

She shook her head, trying to clear the cobwebs. She

couldn't afford to doubt herself now. The visions held truth. She knew it in her gut: her home was in danger.

Swinging her legs off the bed, Tiff stood on shaky feet. She had to return to the portal.

First, she needed to get out of the lodge without being noticed.

Creeping to the door, Tiff cracked it open and peered into the hallway. Now was her chance.

As she slipped out, she steeled her nerves. She was ready to face whatever came next.

The darkness wouldn't claim her that easily.

Chapter 36
Close Encounter

Tiff snuck out the lodge's back door with her backpack, the cool air brushing against her cheeks. Though sunlight filtered through the trees, the woods felt oddly hushed, a stillness that made every rustling leaf and snapping twig seem louder than it should. She crept along the tree line, pine needles crunching beneath her feet. A shadow shifted between the trunks. Tiff froze, her heart pounding.

"Tiff?"

She let out a breath of relief. "Ari?"

They hurried toward each other and embraced tightly.

"What are you doing here?" she asked.

"It's a long story," Ari said. "What about you? Why are you sneaking through the woods?"

Tiff pulled back, worry etched across her face. "It's Coop. He's hurt, and we got separated."

The words spilled out. "That agent, Nephilimbug, followed us to Mount Shasta and sent crows after us. Coop was badly hurt, and I didn't know if he was going to make it." Her voice caught in her throat. The helplessness had been overwhelming.

She looked into Ari's eyes, afraid she'd see judgment or disbelief, but found only calm concern. A flicker of hope stirred in her chest.

"It's okay," he said gently, placing a hand on her shoulder. "You can tell me everything."

Tiff drew a shaky breath. "We found a portal in the woods. I got separated from the others after they went through it, but I managed to follow. I saw them. Coop was alive, and someone was helping him. But I don't know where that place is or how to get back to it. I need to open another portal, the right one this time, to reach them and then get us home."

Ari looked at her thoughtfully. "You know how to open portals?"

"Yes. I'm still learning a lot about the cube," she admitted. "What should I do? I can't leave them out there."

"For now, rest." He gave her shoulder a reassuring squeeze. "Have faith. We'll figure this out."

"I hope so, because Nephilimbug is in my head."

"What do you mean?"

"He was talking to me. Showing me visions of Lotterland, my family, my friends, all being destroyed. He wants me to give him the cube."

Ari's jaw tightened, but his voice stayed calm. "You're safe here. I promise. I won't let that bug get near you again." He smiled slightly and wrapped an arm around her shoulders.

Tiff managed a small, grateful smile. With Ari by her side, her panic eased just enough to breathe. She nodded, thinking through his words. As much as she wanted to run back out there, she knew he was right.

"Okay," she whispered. "I'll stay for today. But first

thing tomorrow, I need to return to the car. Will you help me?"

"Of course," Ari said, hugging her again. "I'll make sure you find your way back."

Relief swept over her. She hadn't realized how heavy the burden of being lost and alone had been until now.

"Thank you," she said, her voice trembling. "I really appreciate it."

He's right. I need to regain my strength.

For the first time since arriving at the mountain, she felt a seed of hope take root. With Ari's help, she would find her way back to the car, back to Coop and the others, and back to her mission.

As they walked side by side toward the lodge, she let herself lean into Ari's presence. For a moment, she allowed his strength to chase away the shadows, both seen and unseen.

Chapter 37
Switch

Once he had parted from Tiff, Nephilimbug—still zipped into Ari's flesh wrapper—hurried back to the lodge. He didn't want to risk running into too many people who might recognize inconsistencies in his behavior. The moment he returned to his room at Yetzirah Lodge, he sat in silence, savoring the memory of his deception. Everything had unfolded perfectly.

Titanu had performed flawlessly. She had homed in on Ari's weakness, his aching desire for human connection, and seeded it with memories of love and longing. Once Ari was distracted and emotionally unguarded, Nephilimbug struck. With precise timing, he pushed Ari's consciousness into the ethers and stepped into his body with practiced ease.

He had walked in Ari's skin, spoken with his voice, and gazed through his eyes. Earthlings had always fascinated him, and he had spent years studying their behaviors and beliefs. It had seemed only a curiosity at the time, but now that knowledge served him well.

His final test came when he encountered Tiff in the

woods. She had spoken to him openly, confided in him, even leaned into him. She hadn't suspected a thing. Her vulnerability had been striking—so raw, so human.

He slumped back on the cold, hard bed in his room at Yetzirah Lodge. The walls were white and sterile, the furniture sparse. Even the blanket felt too thin to hold warmth. It suited him. The lack of comfort echoed the truth of his existence.

Still, his thoughts drifted to Tiff. Her honesty lingered in his mind. She had spoken of Coop's injury and the portal she'd entered. She had trusted him enough to reveal the cube and admit she now knew how to use it.

That had been the breakthrough.

She didn't realize what she'd given him—confirmation that the cube was in her possession and that she could open portals. The plan was working. Soon, he would retrieve the cube and use it to rise above his mixed blood-line and those who had always looked down on him. The Order would then recognize his superiority.

His mind wandered back to Coop. The boy had suffered from the crow attack. Nephilimbug wished it had been the woman instead. He still longed to tangle with her again, to watch her fall. But there was time.

For now, the mask of Ari must remain intact.

A sudden burn in his throat brought him back to the present. He coughed once, then again, harder, choking as a strange fire built in his lungs. His body convulsed, and he collapsed onto the floor, wheezing.

Panic set in.

His eyes stung and bulged. He couldn't breathe. He tried to hold on to the physical form, but something inside was rising, pushing back against him. In an instant, he was expelled. Nephilimbug shot out of Ari's body, retreating into his grotesque form.

He hovered, dazed, and looked back at the body he had left.

It stood tall, alive, and fully aware.

Ari's eyes were sharp and burning with purpose. His gaze locked onto Nephilimbug with searing intensity. Then he raised his hands.

Flames burst from Ari's fingertips. Nephilimbug barely dodged the blast. The heat was fierce, singeing the air and filling the room with the acrid stench of fire.

With a screech, Nephilimbug shifted into the form of a crow and escaped through the open window. Now perched high on the roof of the lodge, he sat in silence, wings trembling, and pride bruised. Being forced out of a human body was unlike anything he'd ever experienced. The violation of it gnawed at him.

He would make Ari pay for this.

The girl still had the cube.

The plan could still work.

Chapter 38
Oblivious

Ari rushed to the window to follow Nephilimbug, but he was already gone. He sank to the floor, closed his eyes, and let go. Instantly, his soul rose into the astral realm —a space of glowing light and quiet stillness. Gentle streams of silver and blue drifted through the air like rivers of energy. Everything shimmered, pulsing with a strange, ancient rhythm. Here, time felt distant, and thoughts moved faster than words. He waited, calm and open, for his Teacher to arrive.

A warm presence entered the space. Ari felt love radiating from this magnificent being, lifting his spirit in a way nothing in the physical world could.

The Teacher said softly, "You left yourself vulnerable and allowed a negative entity to take you. Who or what were you thinking about when this happened?"

"It was her—the one who has held my heart for centuries. I was shocked when I stumbled upon her soul in that small Kansas town after more than a century had passed. She had no recollection of our past together."

"Although you haven't engaged with her directly, your

human emotions still linger, trapping both you and her in Yesod, the astral realm. The lesson here is learning to release and allow things to unfold naturally."

"I have done my best to resist these strong emotions. When our souls connect in the physical realm, my heart aches with love, and I struggle with the longing to be close to her. I have made numerous attempts, but nothing has ever worked. I understand now that one of my spiritual lessons is learning how to release thoughts and feelings that disrupt my energetic balance."

"You know the answer."

"Let her go."

"And the emotions that you have attached to her."

"I'm addicted to her," Ari admitted, his voice low. "The more time I spend in human form, the harder it is to let go. She draws me in without even trying. It's as if her presence is stitched into my very being."

The Teacher remained silent for a moment, letting the truth hang between them.

Then, gently, he replied, "You already know what to do."

"But I worry," Ari said. "Her innocence in this timeline makes her vulnerable. If I let go, who will protect her?"

"That is your illusion," the Teacher said. "You have mistaken your attachment for guidance, your desire for love. She's not yours to protect, and her soul is not as fragile as you think."

Ari looked down, ashamed.

"True love does not bind," the Teacher continued. "It liberates. If you truly love her, let her grow—let her remember who she is, without your influence clouding her path."

Ari nodded slowly, the truth sinking into his bones. He had been trying to shield her, but in doing so, he had created invisible cords, tying them both to a cycle neither could escape.

The Teacher's words echoed through him long after he had gone. Ari sat motionless, letting the sensation of his physical shell settle around him. A swell of mixed emotions churned within him as his mentor's words sank in—regret for paths not taken, piercing nostalgia for his days with September, and a sharp sting of isolation in his current predicament. These feelings tangled with a reluctant acceptance of his mentor's wisdom, creating a complex tapestry of sorrow and resignation that weighed heavily on his soul.

The experience left him shaken. Yet, in its aftermath, a truth began to form. This was more than a rescue. It was a wake-up call. Ari realized that his mission went beyond assisting others. He needed to strengthen his soul—to sharpen his awareness, his boundaries, and his gifts. Nephilimbug's takeover had exposed a weakness, but it had also lit a fire. He would not let it happen again.

Chapter 39
Seekers

Tiff closed the door to her room and leaned against it, letting out a long breath. The quiet was welcome after everything that had happened in the woods. She still felt the warmth of Ari's presence, the way he'd made her feel seen. Safe.

But something inside her wasn't settled.

She reached into her backpack and pulled out the cube. The moment her fingers touched it, a soft pulse of light shimmered across its surface, casting intricate patterns on the walls. For a heartbeat, she saw Ari's face—not as it had been in the woods, but colder, more hollow. The image vanished as quickly as it had come.

Tiff blinked, shaken. "What was that?"

She stared at the cube, but it had gone dim again.

She tucked it into her purse and slid it behind the small dresser, close but hidden. Whatever that flash had been, she couldn't ignore the unease that followed it. Still, she told herself, maybe she was tired.

She shook her head to clear her thoughts and headed for the shower.

The hot water soothed her nerves. She took her time, letting the floral soap and shampoo rinse away the tension that had built up since arriving. When she stepped out, she felt lighter, as if some of the weight had washed away with the steam.

Tiff eyed the white dress hanging on the back of the door. It was simple yet elegant. She slid it on and brushed her short brown hair into soft waves. A touch of lip gloss was all the makeup she needed.

As she finished, the bells rang out, echoing through the halls. Tiff followed the sound of soft chatter down the corridor to a set of ornate wooden doors. Taking one last calming breath, she turned the handle and stepped inside.

The dining hall was even more magnificent than she had imagined. A long table draped in cream linen stretched down the room, set for ten. Crimson roses and white lilies sat in a lush centerpiece, their scent mingling with the smoky perfume of flickering candles.

Her gaze swept over the table. Her eyes landed on a name card.

Tiffany Lotterland.

She frowned. She didn't remember giving anyone her full name. How did they know? A small knot of unease twisted in her stomach, but she shook it off.

Tiff made her way to the chair and sat down. The fire crackling in the hearth reminded her of home. She exhaled slowly, allowing the moment to calm her. Whatever was happening, at least for now, she was safe.

Paul sat at the head of the table, his salt-and-pepper hair neatly combed. Mary took her place at the opposite end, offering a gentle smile that helped ease Tiff's lingering tension. She was surprised to see Officer Porter seated nearby. He gave her a nod—brief, unreadable—then turned his attention to Paul.

"Welcome, all," Paul said, his voice warm and resonant. "Shall we take a moment to get acquainted?"

He gestured to the older woman to his left. "Why don't you start us off?"

The woman wrapped her shawl around her shoulders. "My name is Juliette Trudeau. I'm originally from France, but I have always felt drawn to your beautiful country, especially Mount Shasta. I'm hoping this visit will provide enlightenment."

As the introductions continued, Tiff listened closely, feeling a strange connection to the guests. Maybe they were part of whatever journey she was on, even if she didn't yet understand what that was.

The guest beside her drew her attention. His name card read Brady Fortune. She recognized him but couldn't quite place where from.

"My name is Zara Pratt," said a woman with a calm, velvety voice. Her serene presence immediately drew Tiff in. "I'm visiting from Washington, D.C. I travel to places of spiritual power. It helps center me... helps me manage my anxiety and depression."

Tiff's eyes widened. She hadn't expected such honesty from a stranger. But she could relate. Ever since her mother disappeared, her own emotions had been on a rollercoaster.

"I was at Joshua Tree on retreat," Zara continued. "Then I felt drawn here. The energy of this mountain is unlike anything else. I'm hoping for clarity. And healing."

Tiff admired her certainty. This woman clearly knew what had brought her to this place. Maybe there was hope for Tiff to find some answers, too.

"And our next guest is Jeremy Johnson," Paul said, gesturing across the table.

"Thanks for having me," said a middle-aged man in a

gravelly New York accent. "I've been burnt out. Work, family, life—you know?"

He paused. "Then I started having these intense dreams. They told me I had to come here."

Tiff leaned in, intrigued.

"Since I arrived, the dreams have only intensified. But they've helped me start facing things I've avoided for years. I don't know why, but I feel like I'm meant to be here."

Her heart quickened. She wasn't the only one who had been called.

When her time came, Tiff wasn't sure what she would say. The others seemed confident and wise. Compared to them, she felt like a girl caught in a whirlwind.

Or maybe, she thought, this was exactly where she was supposed to be.

Her thoughts were interrupted as the next guest began to speak.

"Hi, everyone, I'm Emma Madden," said a petite girl with a chestnut bob. "I'm a psych major at Monmouth University. I came here during my summer break after... well, after some hard stuff."

She hesitated, then continued. "My dad was on a special assignment for his job in Peru. He went missing. Some bodies from his team were found, but not his. It's been hard on us. I started having dreams about my dad, and he kept showing me this place."

Tiff's breath caught. Another dream.

"I didn't even think it was real," Emma said, "but I found it online. In the dream, he always tried to tell me something important, but I never heard the full message."

"What part did you hear?" Zara asked gently.

Emma's eyes filled with tears. "Don't fall to the dark," she whispered. "Then I'd always wake up."

Tiff felt an unexpected surge of empathy. She wanted to reach out and tell Emma that she understood.

Before she could, Officer Porter shook his head politely, declining to share his story.

Paul nodded toward the guest beside Emma.

"Hi, I'm Brady Fortune," the young man said without looking up. "You might've heard of my band, Fate and Fortune."

Tiff and Emma exchanged glances. They both smiled, but Brady didn't return it.

"I can't sleep anymore. I keep dreaming about this place like it's calling me. My therapist told me to come, so here I am."

And then all eyes turned to Tiff.

She swallowed and spoke. "I'm Tiffany... Lotterland. Everyone calls me Tiff. I'm from a small town in Kansas—Wheatfield. My friends went on an adventure yesterday, and I got separated from them. Officer Porter found me and brought me here."

She glanced at him, but his face revealed nothing.

"Mary and Paul offered me a room. I'll probably head back to the car tomorrow, or my friends will come here. I left a note for them."

Her voice sounded steadier than she felt. She bit her lower lip, hoping she hadn't said too much. The guests nodded politely. A servant appeared with the first course.

Despite her nerves, the food's colors and aromas captivated her. She took a cautious sip of wine and let its fruity smoothness calm her pulse.

Later, as Mary brought out a chocolate raspberry tart, Tiff finally felt herself relax. The meal had been delicious. The company, warm.

As everyone finished, Mary clapped her hands with a cheerful smile.

"Now for the fun part—a tour of our facilities! Let's split into two groups."

Tiff glanced around the table, wondering if any of them understood what this place truly was—or why they'd all been drawn to it.

Chapter 40
Seven

Tiff traced her fingers along the dark wood walls, the hallway lit only by flickering candle sconces. Shadows danced across the portraits lining the walls—all women. Tiff and Emma read the names under two of the faces: Helena Blavatsky and Rachel Colman Smith. Tiff paused, recognizing the names as two mystical women from her mother's old books.

"Isis, Ishtar, Hecate, the Lady of the Lake," Mary murmured, naming the mysterious women as they passed their portraits. "Come along, ladies," Mary called.

Tiff glanced at Emma and Zara, their faces illuminated by the candlelight. Were they as uneasy as she was, or was she alone in feeling the weight of the place?

They rounded a corner, and Tiff's breath caught in her throat. A large wooden door loomed ahead, the words KNOW THYSELF blazed across its surface in an archaic script. The letters shimmered as if alive, vibrating with hidden knowledge. Tiff blinked hard.

Mary pushed open the door to reveal a spacious room, a fire crackling in a grand stone hearth. Tiff's shoulders relaxed slightly—it was cozy, welcoming. "Have a seat anywhere," Mary said, sinking gracefully onto a plush velvet cushion.

Tiff chose a worn leather armchair near the fire. As she settled in, she saw Zara eyeing her apprehensively. "You okay?" Zara mouthed. Tiff nodded, trying to appear steadier than she felt.

Tiff glanced around the room, taking in all the details. Candles of all shapes and sizes covered every surface, bathing the space in a warm, flickering glow. Intricate tapestries depicting mystical symbols lined the walls. Even as she admired it, something about the room unsettled her. Despite the comfort, Tiff couldn't shake the feeling that the room was watching her. She fidgeted in her seat, attempting to find a more comfortable position.

Mary leaned forward, resting her hands together. "I know you all have many questions. I brought you here so we could discuss them openly and honestly."

"I'll start," Emma said, sitting up straighter. "What is this place exactly? Some secret society?"

Mary smiled. "You could call it that. It's a safe space for souls to learn about themselves and their capabilities. We explore the mystical arts—things beyond the realm of the mundane day-to-day."

"What kind of capabilities?" Tiff asked, unable to hide her eagerness.

Mary turned her piercing blue eyes on Tiff. "Inner strengths and intuitive powers. Gifts passed down through generations if one knows how to access them."

Tiff's mind raced. Could this be the place her mother disappeared into that night? Had she come here, hidden deep in the red fir trees of Mt. Shasta?

A knot formed in her chest, heavy and rising. She wanted to scream out, *Teach me. I want to develop whatever abil-*

ities I have. I need to understand who I am and where I come from. But she also knew she wasn't here only for herself. *I have to find and help my friends*, she spoke out aloud, forgetting where she was.

Mary quickly responded, "The decisions we make are not easy ones, child. But the rewards of discovering who you are, and your capabilities are great for those willing to endure the journey."

Mary closed the door behind the group and led them into the meditation room.

The room was lit with candles. Thick pillows and mats covered the floor. Tiff was surprised to see water trickling from a fountain in the corner, the gentle sound of flowing water mixing with the flicker of the candle flames.

This place was unlike anywhere she'd ever been. Every detail seemed designed to hush the mind. Tiff could feel a sense of calm wash over her as she entered. The ladies spread out, finding places to sit or lie down. Tiff chose a cushion near the fountain, closed her eyes, and focused on slowing her breathing.

After a few minutes, Mary's melodic voice broke the silence. "Let the worries of the day fade away. Release all tension from your body and mind. Become aware of the present moment."

Tiff allowed her body to relax into the cushion. The scent of sandalwood filled the air. Her mind emptied of all thoughts and concerns. There was only the here and now.

"Send loving energy to yourself," Mary continued. "You are safe and at peace." A warmth spread through Tiff's chest as if her heart were being bathed in light. She had never felt so content and free.

After a moment that was both fleeting and endless, Mary softly summoned the group to return. Tiff opened her eyes, feeling refreshed in a way she never had before.

The other ladies had serene smiles as they stood and gathered their belongings.

"Amazing what even a short meditation can do," Emma said, her voice calm.

Mary nodded. "Come, let's continue our journey." She led them to the sound chamber.

Tiff glanced at the door and noticed some numbers etched into the frame: 2, 5, 8, 11. They rearranged into 26 for a split second before returning to their original order.

Her breath caught. Was this a message meant for her?

Tiff blinked hard. Was she imagining things, or was this place trying to speak to her in its cryptic language?

Once inside the chamber, Tiff's senses were heightened, and the music that greeted them vibrated through her whole body.

The ladies fanned out, lying on the floor or leaning against the walls. Tiff chose a spot near a speaker, letting the melodies wash over her. Her fingertips tingled, as if tiny bubbles were popping along her skin. She could pick out notes of piano, strings, and harp, all weaving together in a celestial chorus. The music seeped into her pores and flowed through her veins, attuning her to each delicate frequency.

As her eyes drifted shut once more, Tiff wondered if this was anything like how her mother may have felt during her spiritual awakening. She clung to that hope like a fragile thread.

Tiff's eyes fluttered open as the music faded out. She felt calm, centered, and ready for whatever came next.

Mary led them onward to a third room. Tiff heard running water even before they went inside. Determined to look for more clues, she inspected the door. This time, instead of words or numbers, two interlocking triangles were engraved into the wood, glowing.

Tiff's breath caught in her throat. It was the first symbol she recognized from her mother's old books and drawings.

Mary paused next to her and said, "These symbols represent duality and balance—the physical and spiritual, the known and the unknown. Here, you might find the balance you've been seeking," she explained, her eyes hinting at deeper secrets within as she moved forward before Tiff could respond.

Upon entering the space, Tiff's gaze was captivated by a towering crystal fountain at the heart of the room. Its structure, an upright triangle, commanded attention, while the colors cascading from it boasted shades so vibrant they surpassed anything Tiff had ever seen.

Mary began chanting, "Rota–Taro–Orat–Tora–Ator," over and over.

They all soon joined in, the words flowing from their mouths. As the chanting reached a crescendo, the fountain began glowing even brighter. Tiff was mesmerized by the pulsating lights. She could feel waves of energy washing over her, as if she might dissolve into the current.

Suddenly, Mary stopped. The fountain's glow faded back to normal.

"Come," Mary said. "It's time to move forward."

The next room offered a dramatic shift in mood. Where the fountain room had been serene and mystical, this space pulsed with dynamic energy.

Tiff inspected the door first. This time, a bar of black and a bar of white light were etched into the wood. She hesitated, sensing the contrast of opposites—something more than merely a design.

Inside, the room was pitch black. Suddenly, a monitor descended from the ceiling, and the space was flooded with red light. Mary began speaking words that Tiff could not comprehend. The color red shifted to green, then to blue, and finally to yellow. With each change, Mary spoke new, unintelligible words. The lights pulsed like a code. The language wrapped around her senses, bypassing her mind.

Tiff tried to keep up but soon felt overwhelmed by the constant stimulation bombarding her senses. It was too much.

She was relieved when they finally exited into the next space. While mystifying, Tiff found its relentless intensity a little exhausting. Her thoughts were scrambled. She longed for stillness and silence to gather herself again. But the journey was far from over, and Mary urged them onward.

Etched on the fifth door were the words *I AM THE WAY.* Inside, a lush garden bloomed with vibrant flowers. As they walked further in, the scenery shifted to a dense forest and then gave way to a towering mountain land-scape. Tiff recognized the mountain peak from her earlier vision in the car. But rather than cold and foreboding, this realm held a whimsical, fantasy quality. The mountain called to something deep in her spirit, as if it remembered her before she remembered herself.

After reveling in the mountain's liberating energy, the group moved on again. The sixth room's door was etched with an eight-pointed star that glowed and pulsed. When Mary opened the door, absolute darkness greeted them. But as they stepped inside, the blackness dissolved into an endless sea of stars and galaxies—the Milky Way coming alive before their eyes.

The women lay back on cushions, staring upward in awe. The hypnotic beauty held them transfixed until Mary gently told them it was time to continue. Tiff remained still for a heartbeat longer, wishing she could float there forever.

As intriguing as the journey had been, Tiff sensed they

were only scratching the surface of something much more profound. A nervous anticipation tingled through her.

When they came to the seventh door, Mary stopped. "This is the vault. Only those who know who they are and understand their powers may enter," she said, her voice taking on a solemn tone.

Tiff peered at the door, goosebumps rising on her arms. Carved across the vault door was the tarot card *DEATH*, with the word *GATEWAY* under it.

Mary said, "We once had a young seeker visit here. She was already highly evolved, but her path brought her here. She entered the vault only to face its consequences."

Tiff's mind spun. Her heartbeat quickened as an unspoken fear rose. She wondered who Mary was talking about. Was it Sarah? But Mary's next response shocked her.

"She was seeking information about her sister's disappearance and needed to know how to travel between timelines and other dimensions."

Tiff gasped and mumbled, "It was Rachel." She didn't think anyone had heard her. Her knees weakened beneath the weight of realization.

Emma continued her questioning. "What happened to her? Did she learn how to do it?"

Mary's eyes bored into Tiff's. "As I said, she was highly evolved. She stayed with us for a long time. Then, one day, she entered the vault to transcend the gateways."

Emma gasped. "Did she die?"

Tiff turned away, her throat tightening. She already knew.

Knowing the answer, Tiff turned away from the group for a moment as Mary warned them once again not to enter the vault.

The day's events weighed heavily on her mind as she

collapsed into bed, wrestling with all that had happened. Sleep would not come easily—not with Rachel's memory and the vault's warning lingering like smoke in her thoughts.

After the gathering, Mary retreated to her room, a nightly ritual where she admired her reflection while brushing her long, thick white tresses, one of her favorite physical forms. Despite the beauty, she remained inwardly detached. It was a lesson learned early in her initiation: do not cling to anything on the physical plane.

Her routine halted abruptly when a unique buzzing, akin to a dolphin's call, echoed in her inner ear. It was a high-frequency signal indicating energetic stress. Swiftly, she encircled herself with a luminous shield for protection and projected her consciousness beyond the physical.

Paul was in his study, poring over a book on quantum mechanics. To him, the concepts were elementary. Earth-based science was primitive compared to the under-standing held by more advanced civilizations across the solar system and beyond. Both he and Mary hailed from Sirius, where the revered teachers dwelled. Upon receiving a similar signal, Paul conjured a protective circle of light around his physical form as his light body hovered over it for a few seconds.

Officer Porter felt a surge of tension upon receiving the summons, a signal to abandon his post, issued only in times of dire need. "Oh my," he murmured, recognizing the urgency. He swiftly joined the others, having already been ensconced in his astral body.

Ari, the originator of the signal, awaited them in the high-frequency light chamber of Briah Lodge. Here, in their light forms, they communicated through telepathy, pure thought beyond language.

Mary initiated the discourse. "What has transpired, Ari, to prompt such a distress signal?"

"Dark forces have compromised us," Ari reported, his tone laced with urgency. "An agent seized control of my physical form and attempted to cast my consciousness into oblivion. I managed to stay aware on the physical plane until our Teacher intervened."

Paul's expression hardened. "You've been frequenting those low-frequency nightclubs again. Haven't you learned? Such places can diminish your vibrational state."

"My current form still struggles with generational imprints. It hasn't overcome its tendencies toward alcohol and... love," Ari confessed.

"You mean lust," Paul corrected sharply.

"Enough," Mary said firmly. "Let's stay focused. We need to address the dark forces. Anything else, Ari?"

"He interfered with Tiff in her dream state," Ari added.

"The day I escorted Tiff here, I saw a crow several times along the route and again near one of the outer barriers," Officer Porter shared, concern sharpening his voice.

"Let us be vigilant in determining the extent of this infiltration," Mary decided. "It's possible that one or more guests are agents. We'll continue offering basic teachings to everyone, but advanced instruction will be reserved for Tiff alone. Her mission is critical. If she doesn't grasp these lessons now, her soul may wait many lifetimes before receiving this chance again. Remember, our purpose is to prepare her to lead and to find Sarah, who will command our forces."

Mary turned to Ari. "You will partner with her and stay alert to the approach of dark agents."

"From my many lifetimes of dealing with them, know this. They are cunning and treacherous, and though they lack patience, they know how to strike when least expected," Paul warned.

Mary's final thought resonated with each of them.

"Be vigilant."

Chapter 41
The Vault

As Tiff drifted off to sleep, a soft knock at her door pulled her from her thoughts. The door creaked open, and Emma slipped inside, her flashlight beam dancing across the walls. She nearly dropped the light as she entered.

"Please help me," Emma begged.

Tiff studied Emma's face in the dim glow. Her eyes were wide, and her movements were jittery. Something had her spooked.

"What's going on?" Tiff asked.

"I have to get into the vault."

"The vault?" Tiff's eyebrows shot up. "Are you crazy? You heard what Mary said."

Emma chewed her lip. "I heard a voice. It told me to go there and said it would tell me the rest of my father's message. About what happened to him. He may not be dead."

Tiff's brow creased in concern. The talk of voices, vaults, and fathers was veering into odd territory. Yet the fear flickering in Emma's eyes couldn't be dismissed. Tiff knew what it felt like to chase whispers in the dark. Rachel had entered the vault and survived. Maybe Emma needed the same chance.

"Okay," Tiff said reluctantly. "I'll help you get inside, but we should be careful."

Emma nodded, a rush of relief softening her face. "I knew you'd understand."

Tiff gave her a small, uncertain smile.

They crept down the hallway, flashlight beams skimming along the walls. Past all the rooms they had visited earlier. Everything was still. Hopefully, the others were fast asleep.

At the end of the hall was the door to the Vault room. As they approached the entrance to the last room, the door with the DUALITY symbol opened. Ari stood framed in the doorway, with one eyebrow raised and arms crossed.

"Where are you two sneaking off to?" he asked.

Tiff introduced Emma. "She needs to enter the vault. I told her I would help her."

Ari's eyes narrowed. "The vault? That's restricted. And dangerous."

"I know, but..." Tiff lowered her voice. "She said a voice told her to go there. It would tell her about her dad. And I was thinking, whoever this presence is, maybe they know something about my mom, too."

Ari glanced between them, thinking. Then he sighed. "Well, I can't let you go alone. Not down there." He stepped into the hall. "I'll come with you. But stay close. I've heard this place can get strange."

Tiff exhaled in relief. With Ari's help, they might have a chance.

The trio made their way through the inky darkness of the stairwell. Ancient stone steps spiraled down into the earth. Shadows danced across the walls, cast by their bobbing flashlight beams. The air grew dank and cold.

At the bottom lay a long, narrow tunnel. They walked single file, their soft footfalls echoing through the stillness. The darkness pressed in around them.

Unbeknownst to Tiff and Emma, Ari glanced down at his pendant as they descended deeper into the earth. With a subtle flick of his fingers, the upright pentagram shifted, rotating until it hung inverted. The adjustment was not for show. He had learned long ago that some beings of shadow only acknowledged inverted symbols as signs of neutral passage, not allegiance. Ari muttered a quiet invocation under his breath, sealing in the magic for now.

Tiff shivered. What dangers lie ahead? But she kept moving. She had to see this through.

They came to an iron gate blocking the path. Behind it stood a shadowy figure.

"State your business," it rasped.

Ari stepped forward into the lantern's faint glow. He pulled a pendant from beneath his shirt and whispered something Tiff couldn't make out.

The gatekeeper studied the pendant and gave a slow nod. With a screech of rusty hinges, the gate swung open.

They entered a passageway that twisted and turned, sloping ever downward. Strange sounds echoed through the dark—whispers, wails, and inhuman cries. Tiff's skin crawled.

"Don't listen," Ari said. "Think only of our goal."

At the next gate, the ritual was repeated. The keeper inspected Ari's pendant and stepped aside.

The air grew heavier. Water trickled down the walls, pooling beneath their feet. Tiff felt something skitter across her shoe and clenched her jaw to keep from screaming.

"Let's turn back," Emma whispered, voice shaking. "This is madness. I've changed my mind."

"What about your father?" Tiff asked, her voice low.

At the third gate, Ari presented the pendant again. As they passed through, the tunnel opened into an immense cavern. Tiff's light could not reach the far walls.

Then the shadows stirred.

Dark shapes swirled before them, nightmarish images flashing in and out of view. The trio huddled together, trying to resist the illusions that were being cast over them.

"Have courage," Ari called over the rising whispers.

Tiff blinked, forcing her eyes to adjust. Wisps of shadow danced across the walls. She could hear Emma's breathing, fast and unsteady, and felt her tight grip on her arm.

"It's tricks and illusions," Ari said. "They cannot harm us."

Tiff flinched as ghostly faces suddenly leered out of the dark. Grotesque forms twisted past, warping her vision. She fixed her gaze on Ari and followed his steps.

At the fourth gate, the process repeated. The gatekeeper's eyes glowed red. He examined the pendant, then let them through.

The path narrowed. The stone beneath them turned to packed dirt. Tiff strained her senses, searching for danger.

This time, when the shadows moved, creatures emerged. Fanged beasts with glowing eyes and jagged claws.

Emma screamed.

Tiff yanked her back as claws slashed through the air where she had stood. Ari raised his lantern and shouted a phrase in a language she didn't recognize.

The creature shrieked and recoiled, dissolving into a cloud of smoke.

"Hurry!" Ari shouted.

They ran, monstrous shapes bursting from the walls and chasing them through the tunnel.

Finally, they stumbled into a small chamber. Tiff leaned against the wall, breath coming in gasps. "We can't keep this up. We'll never make it."

Ari's face was pale and tense. "The final gate lies ahead. We can do this."

Tiff helped Emma to her feet. The girl's face was ashen, her eyes wide and wet with fear.

"Let's go," Tiff said.

They pressed forward. Ari took the lead. The last tunnel was the darkest yet.

Whispers wormed their way into Tiff's mind, hissing lies and doubts.

You're not strong enough.

You don't belong here.

Give up.

She gritted her teeth. Grotesque shapes flew at them from the shadows. She swatted them away, eyes stinging with tears.

When she thought she couldn't go another step, they emerged into a massive cavern.

Tiff lifted her flashlight. In the center of the space, three shadowy figures sat on thrones. Their eyes glowed red.

Tiff sensed another presence—something she couldn't see—but it pressed against her awareness like a cold wind. The figures on the thrones reminded her of Nephilimbug. A surge of anger rose in her. She wanted to shout, *Come out, you coward.*

But suddenly, Emma darted forward. "Where is my father?" she cried. "You promised to release him if I brought her here!" She pointed at Tiff.

Tiff reeled, stunned. Her heart dropped. *It can't be*, she thought.

The shadow figures laughed—a bone-chilling sound that echoed off the walls.

"Foolish girl," one rasped. "You have served your purpose."

Ari pulled Tiff close as the shadows began to move.

"Courage," he said quietly. "We will find a way."

Tiff trembled but lifted her chin. She would not break. No matter what. She stepped forward to meet her fate.

Emma stood frozen, her eyes wide with dawning horror as the weight of her mistake crashed over her.

"What do you want with me?" Tiff demanded, keeping her voice steady.

The most prominent shadow figure rose above her, tendrils of darkness curling around its form.

"The cube and your soul," it stammered. "You will bow down to us and do our bidding."

"No," Ari declared, stepping in front of Tiff and Emma.

The shadow creature laughed, a grating, bone-chilling sound. "And who will stop us?"

It lunged toward them. Ari made a sign with his fingers that Tiff didn't understand. A blast of golden light erupted from his palm, slamming into the creature. It recoiled with an unearthly shriek.

Hope flared within Tiff. If Ari had such power, they could defeat these monsters after all.

She closed her eyes and focused inward, seeking that warm glow inside her.

Light, give me strength, she thought. Help me protect my friends.

Warmth flooded her body. When she opened her eyes,

a pale golden light emanated from her skin. The creatures cringed at it.

"Together," Ari said. "Now."

Their combined light blazed forth, driving back the shadows. The creatures wailed, thrashing as the glow seared them. With a final piercing shriek, they dissolved into wisps of black vapor.

The light faded. Tiff and Ari stood panting.

"You did it," Emma shouted. "You saved us."

Tiff managed a shaky smile. "For now. But I have a feeling this is only the beginning."

Tiff took a deep breath, steadying herself after the rush of magic and adrenaline. There would be time later to process what had happened and how she and Ari had conjured light and power to drive back the shadow creatures. They had to keep going.

"Come on. We should keep going while we have the chance."

He nodded, face still flushed from exertion. "You're right. We don't know if those things will come back."

Emma shifted nervously, peering into the darkness. "Can't we go back the way we came?"

"No, we move forward. I don't want to face those creatures again. Do you?"

"No," Emma mumbled.

"Those voices you heard were a sinister plot by the dark forces to lure us here against Mary's order. We messed up," Tiff growled.

They walked in tense silence, ears straining, bodies primed for danger. Anything could lurk, waiting for them to let their guard down again. The air felt heavier here, thick with a strange energy that raised the hair on her arms. The passage sloped downward, and the chill deepened. Tiff shivered, wishing she'd brought a warmer jacket.

Ari moved closer until their arms brushed against each other. "You okay?" he asked.

"Yeah. It's cold." She flashed him a grateful smile.

Emma trailed behind them. "Tiff, I'm sorry. Please forgive me. I didn't want anything bad to happen to you. I wanted to find out about my father," she said, crying.

"I know, Emma."

The air grew dank, the stone underfoot slick with moisture. Tiff swept her light along the walls, revealing patches of dark green growth. Those three grotesque figures were only a warning of what was to come.

"Do you know where we're going?" Emma asked, a quiver in her voice. "Or are we wandering deeper for nothing?"

"I'm following my instincts," Tiff said. "I can't explain it, but something is pulling me forward. We're on the right path. I'm sure of it."

She quickened her pace, eager to discover what lay ahead. Ari and Emma hurried to match her stride. The tunnel leveled out and then opened into a high-ceilinged cavern. Tiff lifted her flashlight, illuminating massive stone columns, glittering with crystal veins, and, at the far end, the heart of the maze. The air shimmered around them.

Apprehension and excitement warred within Tiff. Whatever answers awaited her, she had to see this through.

She stepped toward the gate, magic thrumming in her blood. "Let's go," she said.

Tiff approached the imposing gate, her footsteps echoing in the vast chamber. Strange symbols were carved into the stone archway, glinting in the beam of her flashlight. She reached out to touch them, but Ari caught her hand.

"Wait," he said. "Only those who know the magic words may pass."

As if on cue, a shadowy figure materialized before the gate. "Speak the sacred words if you dare," it rasped.

Ari stepped forward, shoulders back. He lifted the pendant from around his neck, the metal flashing, now showing the sign of an inverted pentagram.

He remembered his Teacher once saying, "These pendants are recognized across many realms as neutral tokens. They grant safe passage between dimensions."

"I call upon the ancient powers to grant us passage," he proclaimed.

"No. What are the magic words?"

Shocked, Ari showed the figure his pendant and voiced the password. "Ophiuchus."

"No," the figure repeated, lifting its sword.

Tiff thought about the cube. She didn't have it with her, but she had something as commanding. Tiff had noticed a small black rectangle on the first gate, but this one bore a faint white triangle near the top—something about it stirred a knowing she couldn't explain, as if the answer had presented itself without thought. She stepped forward, showed the gatekeeper her L.V.X. pendant, and said the Latin word for light.

"Lux."

Tiff watched, wide-eyed, as the figure inclined its head and faded away. With a groan of stone on stone, the gates slowly swung open.

They climbed a few white stone steps into the open air of the forest. The sun rose in the distance. The lodge stood not far away.

Tiff turned back. As the steps disappeared, a lily bloomed in their place.

Emma hugged them both, apologized again to Tiff,

and then ran toward the lodge. They heard a rustle in a bush as Mary stepped out from behind a tree.

"Thank you, Ari. You may now return to the lodge. I think we have our answer," she said.

Then, turning to Tiff, "Walk with me."

That was all she said.

Tiff trailed quietly behind, following a path that led to a secluded pond. Officer Porter, never letting them out of his sight, stayed a few feet behind them.

"You disobeyed and entered the vault," Mary said, her tone cool.

"I'm sorry."

"Are you reckless, rebellious, and stubborn like your mother and aunt?"

Shocked by Mary's words, Tiff didn't know how to respond. Then, like lightning striking her chest, she stopped and said, "Paul and you are the Teachers?"

"Well, you decided to wake up. We've been waiting for you, Tiff."

They left the pond, and Mary led her to a fork in the road.

"You have a choice. Stay here and train to learn your full potential, or Officer Porter will escort you back to your car."

Tiff's nervousness about breaking the rules faded as a sense of calm washed over her. Mary's tone held no judgment, only deep understanding earned through countless lifetimes.

It didn't take her long to respond.

"I'm staying. Even though I'm worried about my friends."

"Don't worry, Tiff, I'll keep an eye out for them," Officer Porter said.

"Tiff, have you heard the expression, 'Know thyself?"

Tiff blinked. The words echoed in her mind.

"Yes... I saw them carved on a door when we toured the lodge."

She paused, realizing something.

"Aren't those words from an ancient Greek temple?"

Mary nodded, the corner of her mouth lifting.

"The Temple of Apollo at Delphi. A message passed through the ages. And now, it's calling you."

"That's where we're going to start. I want you to stay a while in the forest and contemplate who you are."

"Alone?" Tiff thought about the vault and what she'd experienced.

"Oh, you won't be alone. The trees, the rocks, and the animals will keep you company."

Chapter 42
Programming

The moonlight filtered through the blinds, casting striped shadows across Tiff's face. She jolted awake, her heart pounding as she scanned the unfamiliar room. A slip of paper lay on the floor inside her door. Tiff crept over and lifted it with trembling fingers.

"Report at 4:44 a.m. to the meditation room."

She glanced at the digital clock. It read 2:07 a.m. She had over two hours to decide whether to follow the message or flee into the night to search for her friends.

Her backpack sat packed and ready beside the bed. All she had to do was grab it and go. But she remembered the impenetrable darkness of the vault and shuddered. Out there, she was powerless. At least here, she might learn something to help her find her mother and friends.

She turned onto her side, away from the mirror, holding the cube close against her chest, letting its quiet energy steady her while her thoughts spun between running and staying.

BRRRRRRRRING! Tiff jolted awake again as bells rang from every direction. It was exactly 4:44 a.m. Her

244

heart racing, she jumped out of bed and threw on the first clothes she could find: a hoodie and jeans. After a quick brush of her teeth and hair, she rushed into the hallway.

The meditation room door stood propped open. Tiff slowed and crept inside. Cushions lined the floor, most of them empty. In the far corner, Emma sat with her legs folded beneath her. She met Tiff's gaze and waved her over.

Tiff scanned the room, hoping Ari would be there. There was no sign of him.

She made her way to Emma and sat down on a cushion beside her. She might as well try to make amends, even if part of her still wanted to avoid the girl who had dragged her into so much chaos.

"Hey," Emma greeted. "Wild night, huh?"

Tiff only nodded, her eyes drifting to the others entering the room. She recognized some from the day before, which now felt like a lifetime ago. Everyone moved quickly to claim a cushion, each person sitting near their group.

A hush fell over the room as the lights dimmed, leaving only a soft glow. Gentle, meditative music flowed from hidden speakers. Tiff's shoulders relaxed instinctively.

Then, a soothing male voice spoke over the music, welcoming them. Tiff's eyelids grew heavy. The voice guided them into a deep meditation.

Before she knew it, her surroundings shifted. She was no longer in the room but sitting with the others in a serene forest valley. Birdsong and rustling leaves replaced the music.

At the front stood Mary and Paul. Paul began lecturing about their training here in what he called the Hall of Learning.

"Each morning, we'll gather here to expand your

minds and spirits," he said. "Today's lesson is about understanding yourselves as conscious, multidimensional beings."

Tiff listened as Mary described the nature of reality and the powers hidden within.

Paul added, "We must know ourselves before we can progress further. Meditate on your true essence."

As his voice faded, a sense of tranquility surged through her, erasing all worries and fears. Her inner self expanded into radiant light, no longer confined by the laws of the physical world.

Tiff had a million questions, but the vision ended. She sat up, stunned. She was back in the meditation room. Someone was snoring.

She spotted Jeremy, the banker, his head bobbing forward and backward. His mouth hung open, and his eyes were shut. Porter used a long stick to tap him on the shoulder. Jeremy awoke with a jolt as the others stirred.

The meditation room had returned. Tiff blinked, struggling to hold on to the serenity she had felt. There was so much more to learn. This was why she had come: to gain knowledge and skills to fight back against the darkness.

Each student received a note detailing the day ahead. They would reconvene later for dinner and evening meditation.

Tiff read her note carefully. She was to help clean the kitchen after breakfast and then meet her partner in the Crystal Room. She hoped it wouldn't be Emma.

Hours later, she hurried to the Crystal Room and stood before the large crystal, staring at the circulating water. It was hypnotic.

"It's very calming, isn't it?" said a voice behind her.

Tiff turned to see Ari, his deep black eyes meeting hers. Her heart skipped a beat. She wanted to hug him.

"You decided to stay," he said with a smile.

"Yes, but I'm worried about Coop and the others." She repeated her concerns about finding her mom.

"It's only natural," he said. "This is all still so new. But the answers you seek are here. I believe they will help you on your quest."

Tiff nodded, but anxiety still clutched her chest.

"I wish I could let them know I'm all right," she said. "Especially Coop. We've been through so much together."

"Have faith," he told her. "Trust the journey. Try sending them a message using telepathy. Close your eyes and place your focus on the third eye, also known as the pineal gland, and picture the person. Then concentrate on what you want to say and send it."

Tiff followed Ari's instructions. She closed her eyes and focused—not on Coop—but on Rachel.

I'm at the lodge.

"Thank you," she said, managing a small smile.

Ari smiled back. "Anytime."

He guided her to sit beside him at the fountain's edge, where the crystal's glow surrounded them. Tiff listened as Ari explained the three steps on the Path of Initiation.

"Depending on your past lives, you return here as a sleeper, unaware of who you are. When you begin to question reality, you become a seeker. And once you pass through that stage, you become an initiate," Ari said gently, careful not to overwhelm her awakening process.

"Well, then I'm a sleeper."

"Are you sure about that?"

"You said a sleeper doesn't know about any of this. That sounds like me."

Ari wanted to tell her more, but he heard his teacher's voice in his mind: *Be careful.*

"Do you have any questions?"

"Yes. What comes after the initiate?"

"The Teacher level."

"Oh. Are you at that level? And what's your story anyway? I thought you were going back to your university."

"I was supposed to. But the night before my flight, something happened. I was sitting at the airport reading a book, and suddenly, the words changed. They told me to come here."

"You're sure you saw them change?"

"Yes. When I looked again, the regular text was back."

Tiff's eyes widened. "So, you think there's a reason you were sent here?"

"I believe so," Ari said, gazing at her.

Tiff blushed under his intense stare.

"I want you to relax, look into the pool, and tell me what you see."

Tiff leaned forward. "My reflection. I see myself."

"Ask yourself, who are you, really?"

"Um... Tiff. I mean, I'm a conscious multidimensional being."

"What does that mean to you, and how do you feel about it?" he asked with a smile.

His hand brushed against hers, sending a flutter through her stomach. She gently pulled her hand away to focus.

"I'm not religious. This is all so new."

"Take your time. But remember, this isn't about religion. Like Paul said this morning, everything is One. You're made of layers: the superconscious, the subconscious mind, and the self-conscious mind."

"I'm more than my physical body. It's my vehicle for this dimension."

"Yes. And it's not only about knowing that. You need to believe it, feel it, and live it. That belief will guide you through dimensions and help you find your mother."

Tiff stared into the pool again. This time, her reflection faded. Other faces appeared, dozens of them, followed by a beam of white light. She felt free, as if she had become one with the water.

"After the vault experience, I decided to stay. Mary told me to spend some time alone in the forest. When I finally calmed my mind, the trees started to speak to me."

"What did they say?"

"They told me that everything is connected. That a unity consciousness holds us together. One tree said I could restore my energy by leaning against its bark. A stone told me to stand atop it to heal my pain. The waters said to sing, and blessings would come. Then I saw faces—past versions of me—and I think... I think one of them was you."

"What do you mean?"

"I felt your presence."

"Tell me more," Ari said, intrigued.

"That's all. It ended quickly."

The bells rang, signaling it was time for the next activity. Reluctantly, they stood.

"We'll talk later," Ari said as he helped her to her feet. Their hands lingered for a moment before they turned to rejoin the others.

As they entered, the savory smell of roasted vegetables and fresh bread wafted over them. Tiff's mouth watered as she realized how hungry she was. They got their food and joined the others at the table. After a few bites, Mary asked, "Tell me, how are you finding the training so far?"

Silence followed; no one offered to speak.

"Come on, this is the time to share," she urged.

"By sharing your story, others will learn," Paul added.

Zara, the woman from D.C., spoke up. "I've been working with Tarot cards for years, but what I experienced with them today was unbelievable. I recognize that in this esoteric system, I'm more of a novice than an experienced reader. I was in the room with all the symbols. It had changed into a cube—and I was inside it."

Tiff stopped eating, focusing all her attention on Zara.

"The symbols we saw last night were gone. In their place were four large Major Arcana cards hanging in strategic positions within the cube."

"How were they positioned?" Tiff asked, unable to contain her excitement.

"Above me was the Fool. The Teacher said it represented a soul entering a physical vehicle and beginning the journey into the material world. At the very center of the cube was the World. That's where the soul steps onto the Path of Initiation."

Tiff glanced at Ari, who gave her a slight smile but kept his attention on Zara.

"It was the Hanged Man card that made me question everything. In this Hermetic interpretation, he's the love child of the Lovers."

"Did your Teacher explain why?" Mary asked.

"Yes. It has to do with the Hebrew letter for this card —*Mem*—which means 'water.' You don't see water depicted on the card, but symbolically, it connects to a fetus in the mother's womb. The mother is the Empress."

Zara paused and continued eating.

"What else? You can't stop there!" Tiff blurted. The others nodded, urging her to continue.

"That's as far as the Teacher took me."

Mary tapped her glass. The guests turned to her.

"Each of you will experience the cube. To prepare you, I've left a book in your room: *The Book of Formation*, or *Sepher Yetzirah*. That's your reading for tonight."

Tiff swallowed a bite of bread and leaned toward Ari. "It's... a lot to take in. But can we go to the room with the cube for our next session? You know why I want to go there."

"Each lesson is designed for each guest by the Teachers. I have no say."

"Who was Zara's teacher? Mary or Paul?"

"Neither," Ari said. "Some Teachers show up from other realms, depending on the lesson and what a soul needs at that time. Sometimes you'll work with a group of teachers. Other times, it may be Mary, Paul, or even me."

"Then you're a teacher?"

"Let's just say you trust me. That will help your evolution progress more quickly than if you were with someone you didn't feel safe with."

Mary interjected, "We have a few more minutes. Tiff, what did you learn today?"

Tiff told them about seeing her past lives. The others listened intently, nodding along.

"There was a healer," she added quietly. "A young monk. And... someone who died too young. I didn't expect it to feel so personal."

Mary nodded. "Old souls, some might say. We return again and again, each lifetime offering new lessons—until we remember who we truly are."

Paul added, "And when that remembering begins, the

soul quickens. Your memories surface not to burden you, but to awaken the parts of you still asleep."

They ate in silence, lost in contemplation for a few moments.

As they finished their meal, Ari looked at Tiff. "I'm glad you stayed."

Her heart fluttered.

A connection was growing between them, even though part of her felt it was wrong because of Coop. They sat for a moment longer, a quiet understanding flowing between them.

The bells rang, signaling the end of the lunch hour. It was time for Tiff to do her service work and prepare for the next training session.

She rose with the others, wondering what she would discover next—about herself, this place, and the mysteries of the universe.

Chapter 43
Groundwork

Tiff stood in the center of the dimly lit room. Her eyes were closed, concentrating on the energy flowing through her. The air was charged with the scent of burning sage and the faint hum of whispered incantations. Around her, the teachers—a group of seasoned occult practitioners—watched her every move, their expressions a blend of stern concentration and cautious approval.

"Focus, Tiff. Draw upon the energy around you," instructed Matra Avalon, her voice both commanding and encouraging. She was a tall woman, her silver hair pulled back tightly, her eyes sharp and knowing.

Opening her eyes, Tiff felt the power surge within her. The runes etched into the floor beneath her glowed softly, responding to her presence. She extended her hands, palms outstretched, feeling the ancient energy of the symbols pulse against her skin. This part of her training had become her favorite—tapping into powers she once believed belonged only in fairy tales.

Her days were long and intense, filled with back-to-back sessions that pushed her physical and mental boundaries. Each morning began with meditation and lessons in harnessing her inner energy, followed by afternoons practicing hand-to-hand combat against opponents who moved with an eerie, unnatural speed.

In one morning class, Matra Avalon handed her a parchment and gestured toward the golden chalk and small box of Major Arcana cards at her side.

"You've learned the sigils of the elements and planets," she said. "Now it's time to spell something sacred—to you."

Tiff leaned over the parchment, heart quickening. She had seen others trace names in angelic scripts or code affirmations using Hebrew letters tied to specific Tarot cards, but she had never tried it herself.

She closed her eyes and whispered, "Shalom," then carefully drew each Hebrew letter—Shin, Lamed, Vav, Mem—using golden chalk within the sigil wheel Matra Avalon had taught her the day before. The runes began to pulse faintly.

"Now," Matra Avalon said, pulling three Tarot cards from the box and placing them face down, "read this message. It's for you."

Tiff flipped them over. The cards were the Magician, the Lovers, and the Star. She gasped slightly.

"The Magician is your divine potential," Matra Avalon explained. "The Lovers reveal your inner choice—to align with truth or illusion. And the Star is the promise that peace is found only after darkness."

Tiff studied the cards again, this time sensing the vibration behind their images. She began decoding the message into a phrase:

"You have the power to choose peace."

When she repeated it aloud, the sigil shimmered and

dissolved, leaving a warmth in the center of her chest. It wasn't just symbolism. It was an awakening.

Later, Matra Avalon introduced her to a different method—using numbers to encode and decode sacred messages. Each Tarot card was assigned a number. Each Hebrew letter had a numerical value. By translating words into numbers and comparing them across systems, Tiff began to see hidden patterns. A phrase like "love" might share the same numerical vibration as "truth."

"The numbers," Matra Avalon said, "are another language of light."

She learned to recognize and draw ancient sigils in the air, each stroke of her finger leaving a trail of shimmering light. These symbols could shield her or unleash energy with a force that still surprised her. Now, even words and numbers held power—when shaped through the lens of sacred geometry, vibration, and intention.

The knowledge felt like a remembering, as if each symbol was a word in a magical language her soul had always known, even if her mind had forgotten.

Despite the exhaustion that settled into her bones, the idea of quitting never lasted long. Whenever doubt crept in, whispering that she wasn't strong enough, she thought of everything at stake and pushed forward. That unfinished thread from the past gave her strength when she needed it most.

"No, I won't give up," she whispered during a particularly grueling session, weaving between phantom attackers. Her breath was ragged, her muscles burned, but her spirit held firm, anchored by determination and the unshakable sense that her purpose belonged to something greater than herself.

As the day's training ended, Tiff collapsed onto the cool stone floor, her chest rising and falling with effort.

Sweat traced the curves of her face, but her eyes gleamed with unspoken victory. Her progress was visible, and her teachers nodded in quiet recognition, their approval shining in their eyes.

Matra Avalon's words were a grounding presence. "You're getting stronger, Tiff, not only in power, but also in spirit. However, the training won't fully take hold until you believe in yourself," she said, helping her up. "It's not about facing what's out there. It's about facing what's inside you."

Tiff nodded, her fatigue giving way to a quiet sense of purpose. She was learning not only how to fight and protect herself, but also how to uncover her hidden strength.

Chapter 44
Green Eye Monster

After morning meditation, Paul announced new partners. Tiff's heart sank, dreading that her time with Ari was over. Back in her room, a note awaited: her new partner would be Teacher Mary. Tiff sighed, a mix of excitement and melancholy. Included in the note was a request for her to bring the cube. Tiff wondered how Mary knew about the cube and thought perhaps Ari had told her about it. She also wondered what else Ari had shared with the Teachers.

She stepped into the sound room, taking in the vast library—there was still time before her next lesson with Mary. Tiff wandered over to the bookshelves, trailing her fingers along the old leather spines. She had always loved how books could transport you to different worlds.

One book caught her eye – a thick, leather-bound volume titled *Book of Hermetic Tarot Keys*. She carefully slid it from the shelf and placed it on the table. The heavy book made a solid thump as she set it down.

Tiff eased open the front cover. The pages were delicate, covered in intricate illustrations of the Major Arcana.

She slowly turned each page, studying the cards with their beautiful colors. Each one was associated with a Hebrew letter tucked in the right lower corner of the card. They vibrated with an unseen force, pulling her into their depths with an irresistible allure. As she flipped through the pages, the energy of the cards pulsed stronger, enveloping her in a world contained within the illustrations and letters. It was as if the book itself was alive, whispering secrets meant only for her ears.

As Tiff scrolled through the book, the Death card caught her eye, causing her to shiver. The card's Grim Reaper wielded a scythe, standing over a fallen body and a broken crown. With a quick snap, she closed the book, her pulse racing with a mix of fear and anticipation.

Mary entered the room. "I see you've found the *Book of Hermetic Tarot Keys* already," she said smoothly. "Don't be afraid. When understood, Death is not to be feared. It's simply a transformation and a necessary part of the journey."

Again, Tiff pondered how Mary seemed to know her every move.

"You may borrow the book. Sign it out." Mary gestured to a corner desk where the book was placed.

Tiff searched the book for the author. "That's odd. It says The Adepts are the authors, but who are they?"

"Sometimes the ancient ones don't sign their names because they don't want the recognition. We have work ahead. Let's begin."

Mary gestured for Tiff to take a seat. She opened the tarot book again and turned the pages until she came to the death card.

"The cards are keys, each one a door that can be unlocked," Mary explained. "When meditated upon, the door opens and reveals inner truths."

She described how the 22 Major Arcana cards corresponded to the paths between the sephirot on the Tree of Life. Tiff listened as Mary showed how the Major Arcana tarot cards were linked to the Hebrew alphabet and the mystical teachings of the Hermetic Qabalah.

"Rachel spent many hours with these cards, using them to go deeper into her mind," Mary said. "They guided her on her inner journey."

Tiff envisioned her aunt sitting in the same spot, studying the cards and their hidden meanings. She longed to have Rachel and now Zara's skills with the tarot and the cube. "I want to understand how they connect," Tiff said eagerly. "Can we go to the room where Zara first saw the cards in the cube?" She dug into her hoodie pocket and pulled out her cube, holding it up.

"Don't try to be Rachel or Zara," Mary advised. "You must walk your path to get to where you're supposed to be."

"There's so much to learn about how the cube works."

"Well, step one is to become one with the cube, and you do this by accepting what the keys can teach you. To help you with this, I want you to visualize the west side of the cube."

Tiff asked, "What side is the west?"

"You know the answer; close your eyes and think."

Tiff thought about her cube and cards. Then, the Wheel of Fortune appeared before her. She opened her eyes and turned the cube to the side with the Wheel of Fortune.

Mary pointed two fingers at the cube. The cube rose out of Tiff's hand and stayed suspended in the air for a second before fading away.

"What happened?" She asked. "Where is the cube?" Tiff frantically scanned the room.

"I encased it in a circle of light. Use the God Code to access it and unlock its wisdom."

"What's the God Code?"

"It's a high vibratory frequency of energy. You reach that level by breath work, specifically using pranayama breathing techniques."

"Yes, Ari taught me that pranayama breathing will elevate life's energies. But how do I know when I'm at that frequency?"

"Look at it. It's brilliant and spinning, waiting to be activated by your thoughts and breathing. If I send negative thoughts and the frequency is low because of shallow breathing, nothing will happen. I deactivated it, and it's no longer protective. You have been studying the power of energy. Put a circle of energy around it," Mary instructed her.

Staring at the cube, Tiff imagined her hands filling with light energy and sent a burst of it to the cube. It lit up with brilliant colors and began to vibrate again.

"Try and activate it now."

Tiff thought about the love she felt for both her mother and father and transferred that love to the cube while focusing on her breath. She was no longer in the room with Mary but inside the cube. Tiff followed the arrow pointing to the West Below. The Devil Tarot card appeared. The Devil sat on a half-cube, and its red eyes pierced her own as images appeared. Several minutes later, she opened her eyes, and Mary asked, "What did you see?"

"I saw the Devil card."

"Did it give you a message?"

"It said to be careful because things aren't really as they seem."

"Always protect the cube and never share the God-

Code with anyone who is not of the Light force. Do you understand?"

"Yes."

Mary told Tiff to take a short break before their next session. Grateful for the pause, Tiff stepped outside to clear her mind. That's when she saw Ari walking with Emma. Her heart sank as she watched them chatting and laughing together.

She scolded herself for the pang of envy that rose inside. After all, she had Coop in her life now—someone who adored her. She should be grateful for what she had.

Still, her gaze lingered on Ari's handsome face as he smiled down at Emma. Why did the sight of the two of them make her feel so hollow? Tiff didn't understand the conflicted emotions churning inside.

She had returned to the training room with Mary, but the emotions lingered. The energy of what she had witnessed still clung to her—an uncomfortable mix of jealousy, confusion, and sadness.

The air around her shifted, and a dark form materialized before her.

"Meet your shadow side. The embodiment of your darker emotions—jealousy, anger, resentment," Mary said.

"That's not me. I would never—"

"But you would. And you have. Jealousy already has its hooks in you, child. The question now is—what will you do with this energy? Study the cards. They will teach you how to accept all of you. Negative emotions create tears in your energetic aura, allowing darkness to seep in."

Tiff turned to the table where the *Book of Hermetic Tarot*

Keys lay beside the cube. She signed the book out and picked up both before leaving.

As she walked, she thought about Nephilimbug getting into her head—and into the minds of her friends. Next time, she promised herself, she'd be ready for him.

That night, she pulled out the cards and studied their images until sleep overtook her.

She was startled by the sound of bells. Quickly showering and dressing, she hurried to the meditation hall.

Ari approached her after the session, asking if they could talk.

"Where's Emma?" Tiff asked sharply.

"Resting."

"What happened to her?"

"She's struggling to adjust here. I've been trying to help her through it." He paused and met Tiff's eyes. "But I wished I could have talked to you too. I... I've missed our time together."

Tiff's heart swelled. "Me too," she admitted.

"Mary gave strict instructions to focus on Emma," Ari said, voice lower now. "Otherwise, I would have stayed with you."

Before she could respond, Paul appeared and summoned her away.

Tiff followed him, her mind tangled with more questions than answers. She glanced back at Ari. His eyes held a sadness she hadn't noticed before—and it made her chest tighten.

Paul led her into a small meeting room.

"Have a seat," he said, gesturing to a chair.

Tiff perched on the edge, hands folded tightly in her lap. Her thoughts raced. Was she in trouble? Had Mary told Paul about her encounter with the shadow?

"You're not in my group, but I like to spend time with

each of our guests," Paul began. "How are you finding the training so far?"

Tiff relaxed a little. "It's challenging but also amazing. I'm learning so much about myself—and my abilities."

Paul nodded. "Good. That's what we aim for here. Self-discovery is the path to enlightenment."

He steepled his fingers and studied her.

"Mary tells me you've connected with the Tarot."

Pride flickered in Tiff's chest.

"The cards hold wisdom," Paul said, "if you have the right key to unlock it. Do you feel you're finding that key within yourself?"

"I'm trying. Perhaps with the cube, I won't feel so fearful," Tiff said. "Some days, that door feels so close to opening. Other times, I feel fear. Why is that?"

Paul's expression shifted, softening with understanding. "Because fear lives in the subconscious. And it doesn't go away just because you understand something logically. Fear is the echo of past pain, and unless it's faced, it keeps looping in the background like an old recording."

"I was pinned down by a creature in the wheat field and thought I was going to die," Tiff said quietly. "Then this woman floated over and saved me. But every time that creature comes around, I feel this churning in my stomach. My palms get sweaty, and I want to run and hide. He shows up in my dreams."

"And every time he does, it's another chance," Paul said. "The dark appears to be fought, but in truth, it's meant to be seen. Light and dark are the same energy, just vibrating at different speeds. You're learning to raise your vibration so fear no longer dominates the field."

Tiff blinked, absorbing his words. "So, what I feel isn't weakness?"

"No. It's feedback. You're being shown where your

power is still hidden. What you choose to feed matters. Are you feeding fear—or faith?"

The question struck her. She didn't know the answer—but she wanted it to be faith.

"Don't be discouraged," Paul added. "The process takes time, but you have great potential."

Suddenly, the bells began ringing again—this time, with urgency.

Paul's expression shifted to alarm. "Hurry to the entrance hall," he said.

Chapter 45
Disintegration

Tiff followed closely behind Paul as he and others rushed to the lodge's entrance hall. Mary and Ari stood with tense shoulders in the large open room. Mary's eyes scanned the gathering students, silently counting each one as they filed in.

Tiff's heartbeat pounded in her ears.

"Emma is missing!" she said.

Mary's eyes snapped to Tiff's. "What do you mean?"

"I haven't seen her since last night. She wasn't at breakfast or meditation this morning." Tiff's words tumbled out in a rush.

Ari stepped forward, brow furrowed. "That's not like her. She never misses morning meditation."

"Something's wrong. I can feel it."

Mary's voice remained steady, but Tiff saw a flicker of fear in her expression. "Fan out in pairs and search the grounds. Return here in one hour."

The students murmured, shuffling into search parties. Tiff grabbed Ari's hand, relieved when his warm palm squeezed hers in return.

They moved into the forest, calling Emma's name. The trees stood silent, offering no clues. Tiff shivered despite the warm sun filtering through the leaves.

Where are you, Emma?

They pressed deeper through the underbrush. No birds sang. No squirrels darted through the fallen leaves. The silence felt unnatural.

Tiff paused, skin prickling. "Do you feel that?"

Ari stopped beside her, his face grim. "Something's wrong. The energy here feels off."

Tiff rubbed her arms, trying to shake the chill. "It's like life has been sucked out of this place. Even the trees look dimmer, faded."

"I think something darker is happening."

Ari took her hand again, anchoring her. They turned back toward the lodge, moving quickly. As they neared the building, Officer Porter appeared from a side door, his face pale and his glasses slightly askew.

"What's wrong?" Tiff asked.

"Our protective energy field has been compromised," Porter said, voice unsteady. "I checked it last night, and everything was stable. Now there's a massive breach."

Ari muttered under his breath. "Just as I thought. The forest feels dead, too."

Tiff's stomach dropped. If the auric shield had failed and Emma was missing, they were all exposed to psychic interference, or worse.

"We should warn Mary. Now," she said.

The three of them rushed into the lodge. Mary stood in the center, her expression drawn tight. Relief passed across her face when she saw them.

"Any sign of Emma?"

"No, but something worse is happening," Tiff said.

"Yes, we know. Porter, where is the breach?"

He stepped forward, voice low. "It's on the west side of our energy field. The frequency around the lodge is unstable. We're losing containment."

Gasps and murmurs rippled through the students. Mary raised a hand for silence.

"Do we have time to seal it?" she asked.

Porter shook his head. "No, the damage is too extensive."

Mary's calm exterior cracked, replaced by quiet urgency. "Everyone, gather your belongings and return here within five minutes. The lodge will begin to break down quickly. Leave now."

The students scrambled. Tiff stood frozen, her thoughts racing. Were they abandoning the only safe place they had left?

Ari grasped her arm. "Tiff, let's go. It's not safe here anymore."

She nodded, letting him lead her back to her room. Her mind was foggy as she stuffed clothes and two precious items into her pack: the cube and her mother's diary.

Minutes later, they joined the others in the hall.

"Divide into your groups and follow your group leader to safety," Mary instructed. "All of you except Tiff and Ari." She waited until the others were gone before continuing.

"You'll take the vault passage." She handed Ari a large silver key. "This will unlock all the doors. Now go."

Her voice allowed no argument as she ushered them out.

Tiff looked back one last time, but Mary was already gone, dematerialized as if she had never been there.

Ari tugged her toward the vault. The memory of its

decaying walls and lurking shadows hit her like a wave. Her stomach turned.

"We can do this," Ari said. "I'll be right there with you."

Chapter 46
Gone Rogue

Tiff steeled herself and entered the vault behind Ari, praying they'd make it through to the other side unscathed. The ground rumbled beneath her feet as she hurried to keep up. Dust and grit fell from the vaulted stone ceiling, and she could feel the ancient magic protecting this place beginning to unravel.

Near the first gate, the tunnel lurched violently. Tiff slammed into the wall, and Ari barely kept his footing. Darkness swallowed them.

Fumbling with the flashlight clipped to her backpack strap, Tiff switched it on with trembling fingers. The pale beam landed on Ari's tense face as he helped her up.

"What was that?" she asked.

"I'm not sure, but it can't be good. The best possible route is to get through the gates as fast as possible." Ari's tone was grim.

They pressed forward, Tiff's breath loud in her ears. Ancient carvings glared from the walls as they passed. At the first gate, Ari unlocked it with the silver key.

Beyond, faint rustling and skittering echoed from the

dark—the vault's unnatural inhabitants. Tiff's skin prickled as she swept her flashlight across the shadows.

They reached the second gate quickly. The tunnel groaned, showering them with fine dust and loose stone. At the third gate, Ari struggled with the lock, his usual calm slipping.

"Hurry!" Tiff urged.

The lock clicked open. They bolted through as a sharp crack split the air. Tiff glanced back. A fissure raced across the ceiling toward them.

"Run!" Ari shouted.

They sprinted. The crack widened above, and a chunk of stone crashed down, narrowly missing Tiff. Her heart pounded as she pushed herself faster.

The fourth gate loomed. Ari yanked it open and shoved her through, diving in behind her. He slammed it shut just as the tunnel collapsed in a roar of stone and dust.

Breathless, they stared at each other. The path behind them was gone. The only way left was forward.

"We have to keep moving," Ari said. "Come on."

Tiff set her jaw and followed. She forced herself not to think about what waited at the seventh gate. Focus. Get through this.

Eventually, the faint outline of the fifth gate emerged from the shadows. Ari hurried ahead, unlocking it. The gate creaked open. Beyond it, hulking shapes slept in the dark.

Tiff held her breath as they tiptoed past the beasts. One massive eye cracked open, glowing faintly. She froze, heart pounding. The creature huffed once, then closed its eye again.

They slipped into a hollow chamber, heading toward the narrow doorway of the sixth gate. Tiff looked back.

The beasts were only shadowy mounds now, their snores rumbling through the darkness.

She exhaled a shaky breath as Ari opened the sixth gate. Only one remained.

"Hey," Ari said gently. He squeezed her hand. "We're going to make it."

Tiff held onto his hand. She had to believe it.

With a steadying breath, she followed him through. The final stretch of tunnel awaited. The end was close, for better or worse. Tiff managed to grip his hand. She had to believe that.

Squaring her shoulders, she followed him through the gate. The final stretch of the tunnel awaited. The end was in sight, for better or worse. She whispered a silent prayer as they plunged deeper into the darkness of the vaulted underworld.

The tunnel twisted sharply, forcing Tiff and Ari to duck under jagged outcroppings and leap over deep cracks. The air turned colder, laced with the scent of damp stone and something fouler beneath.

Without a word, Ari slipped off his flannel overshirt and draped it around her shoulders. She clutched it tight, not for warmth, but to calm the rising dread in her chest.

"Thanks," she murmured, eyes scanning ahead.

They pressed on. The only sound was the distant drip of water—and the faint, wrong kind of echo that made Tiff's skin crawl. The passage leveled out ahead, opening into a vast cavern. Tiff tensed. The seventh gate lay somewhere in the shadows. She peered into the gloom, searching for movement. Everything was still. Too still.

"Ari, wait," she said, halting. "I think something's in there."

He paused, listening. "Get down!"

He shoved her to the ground as a dark shape burst from the shadows with a piercing shriek. Tiff hit the stone hard, and the breath knocked from her lungs. Ari shielded her as leathery wings flapped overhead. She caught a flash of glowing red eyes and jagged fangs before the creature veered upward and vanished into the dark.

"What was that?" she gasped.

"Trouble," Ari said, scanning the cavern.

An ominous clicking rose from the depths. The sound crawled up Tiff's spine. She pressed closer to him.

"Move," he said. "Now."

They ran. The clicking followed, louder and faster. Tiff's heart pounded as they sprinted across the cavern floor. Ahead, she glimpsed a stone archway carved with ancient symbols. The seventh gate.

They were almost there when her foot caught on a rock. She stumbled with a cry, hitting the ground hard. The impact knocked the cube from her pack, sending it skidding across the stone.

"No!" she cried, scrambling after it on hands and knees. Behind her, the creature shrieked again. She heard the slap of wings and claws against the floor.

With a desperate lunge, Tiff grabbed the cube. At that moment, Ari wrapped an arm around her waist and yanked her back. His hand came down over hers, steadying her grip on the cube.

Wings battered the air above them. Claws raked the spot where they'd been. The creature shrieked in frustration as Ari dragged her into a small recess beside the seventh gate. They collapsed inside, gasping for breath.

For now, they were safe, but the danger hadn't passed. Freedom was beyond the gate.

Before Tiff could move, Ari pulled her back into the crawlspace. His face was grim in the cube's faint glow.

"Tiff," he said, his voice low. "There's something you should know. Emma caused all this. She sabotaged the lodge's defenses. That's how the dark creatures got in."

Her eyes widened. "Why would Emma betray us?"

"She's not who you think. She's a dark agent working with Nephilimbug. She led you to the vault on purpose. She didn't count on me being with you."

"So, the story about the missing father?"

"There's a real Emma. She was waylaid on the road. The agent took over her body to gain entry to the lodge and reach you. The real Emma will wake up in the forest with no memory. Officer Porter will make sure she's safe."

Tiff stared at him, stunned. The girl she had pitied, defended, maybe even envied, was a lie.

What else do you know about this agent?

"Mary had me work with her to contain the threat and uncover any other dark operatives. But the agent figured out what I was doing. She vanished after breaching the barrier."

The ground trembled. Dust and pebbles rained from the ceiling. Time was running out.

Ari moved to the vault door. He pulled the key from around his neck and pressed it into Tiff's hand.

"If we get separated, use this," he said.

Tiff's throat tightened. Her earlier questions faded under the weight of his words.

"What do you mean? You said we'd get through this together. I can't do this alone."

"You can," he said firmly.

He pulled her into a sudden embrace. She froze, startled, then felt his lips brush hers—brief, gentle, real.

Before she could react, he stepped back.

"Have faith in yourself. One day, you'll wake up. Now come on."

He grabbed her hand, and they ran. Her thoughts swirled with the kiss, the betrayal, his strange words. But those questions would have to wait. Right now, survival comes first.

Tiff followed Ari through the crumbling corridor, dodging debris and me over cracks in the stone. She stayed close to him, the key gripped tight in her hand.

Ari's focus never wavered. Watching him, Tiff felt strangely grounded. The strength in his grip reminded her she wasn't alone.

She had thought Ari was a student. But Mary's trust in him, his knowledge, his calm—it pointed to something deeper.

"Stay with me, Tiff. We're almost there."

She nodded, shoving down her doubts. The answers could come later. For now, they had to move.

They advanced through the maze of tunnels. Tiff's hand was slick with sweat around the key. She didn't let go of it, not with Ari beside her. As long as he was there, she could keep going.

Her breath caught as the final stretch came into view. They had encountered danger near every gate. She braced herself for the same here.

Beside her, Ari drew his blade. His eyes scanned the gloom. "Stay close."

The seventh gate loomed ahead. Beyond it, a staircase led upward. Tiff steadied herself and slipped the key into the lock.

It jammed.

She jiggled it once, then again, her heart sinking.

"No," she murmured. "It's not working."

They stepped back together, scanning every shadow, a creeping unease threading through the silence.

A dark figure peeled away from the wall.

Nephilimbug.

Tiff gasped and stumbled back. Ari surged forward, sword raised.

Nephilimbug screeched, crouching low. Tiff's heart pounded. This was it. Their moment to stop him. She planted her feet, heart hammering, and summoned her sword.

She called on the cube, focusing all her will to form a shield of light.

Nephilimbug circled, slow and predatory.

"Give me the cube," he hissed, "and I'll let you both live."

"Never," Tiff snapped. She could tell he didn't know the cube's secret.

Ari feinted left, then right, trying to draw him away. Nephilimbug dodged the attacks and lunged for Tiff. She twisted out of reach, striking back with sword and foot. Her kick connected with his chest.

He snarled and struck again. Tiff ducked, narrowly avoiding his claws. Ari swept his blade toward Nephilimbug's back, but the creature's armor deflected it.

They fought with everything they had. But Nephilimbug matched them at every turn. Tiff could feel her strength waning.

Ari sensed her fatigue. "Get to the opening! I'll hold him off!"

Tiff hesitated, not wanting to leave him behind. But

she knew he was right. With a final burst of effort, she sprinted toward the exit.

Behind her, the clash of combat rang out. Tiff choked back a sob. "Please let him make it," she whispered. If something were to happen to Ari, she would never forgive herself.

Her heart pounded as she ran. She glanced back. Ari and Nephilimbug were no longer in sight.

The light was just ahead. The final steps stretched before her.

Tiff stopped, wavering. She couldn't go on alone. Should she turn back? What if Ari needed her?

Before she could decide, something slammed into her back. She cried out as she was hurled forward, face-first onto the stone floor. Dazed, she tried to rise, but a crushing weight pinned her down.

Hot breath stirred her hair.

"You didn't think you could escape me, did you, my love?" Nephilimbug sneered.

He flipped her onto her back, eyes burning into hers. She writhed, trying to resist, but his grip was too strong.

"Give me the cube, and I'll give you anything you desire. You'll be my queen."

Tiff's stomach turned. The words made no sense. He was delusional—and dangerous. With a growl, she shoved against him. "Get off me, you slimy creep."

The air around him stank of sulfur and decay. The stench clung to her skin, thick and oppressive. His voice dropped, cold and commanding.

"Hand over the cube, little girl, and I'll spare you… and that pathetic creature over there."

She didn't answer.

Nephilimbug tightened his grip, forcing the air from

her lungs. It became nearly impossible to move, to breathe. Panic surged.

She tasted blood from her split lip. The sharp tang mingled with the smell of fear and sweat.

Her vision darkened.

Then she heard it—Ari calling her name.

The weight lifted.

Tiff rolled to her side and gasped for air. She pushed herself up, dizzy, and saw Ari battling Nephilimbug once more.

He fought hard, but Nephilimbug struck with a vicious kick. Ari crumpled, clutching his ribs.

Tiff's heart clenched. She had to stop this.

Ignoring her injuries, she staggered forward and placed herself between Ari and Nephilimbug.

"I won't let you hurt him," she said, barely able to stand. Her hands lifted, hoping the sword would return. Nothing came.

Still, she faced him, furious, defiant. If this was her final moment, she was ready.

Nephilimbug hesitated, startled by her courage.

Then he turned on Ari.

With inhuman speed, he seized Ari and hurled him through the air. Ari hit the ground hard, letting out an unearthly cry.

"No!" Tiff screamed.

She lunged at Nephilimbug, striking him with everything she had.

But he was too strong.

He caught her, lifting her off the ground with ease. She struggled, but his grip was unbreakable. Her backpack slipped from her shoulders and hit the stone floor.

Darkness closed in as she lost consciousness.

Nephilimbug's gaze flicked to the fallen bag and the silver cube glinting beside it. He bent down and scooped it up, and its light died.

He left the pack where it lay, next to Ari's motionless body.

Chapter 47
Integration

Nephilimbug combed through the vault, intent on finding Ari and making him pay for sabotaging his plans at the lodge with Tiff. Though his search proved fruitless, his disappointment faded quickly—he had the cube and the girl.

But there was a problem.

The cube wouldn't respond. He had tried every method known to the Order, but the device remained inert. The girl was the key, and he would break her.

Nephilimbug grudgingly acknowledged that he had never encountered someone with such a strong will. Her aura pulsed with an intense light that could overwhelm him if she ever learned to fully harness it. She was, without question, the perfect weapon to overthrow the Order. But for now, he had to keep playing their deceitful game.

She slept, which worked in his favor. The Leader of the Order of the Black Shadow had summoned him for a council session. Ignoring the call would be seen as rebellion. Reprimand or even banishment from their universe might follow.

When Nephilimbug entered the vast chamber, the twelve leaders were already seated in a half-circle. Their expressions were unreadable, their presence heavy with judgment. He knelt before them and remained bowed until Ute, the presiding leader, gestured for him to rise.

"Nephilimbug, the crossbreed son of our mighty slain god Nunanki," Ute announced. "Stand and report on your mission with the Earthlings."

"My lord," Nephilimbug said, rising to his feet. "I have acquired the cube. And the girl who wields its power."

A moment of silence stretched across the chamber, then erupted into cheers and guttural roars of approval. Ute raised a hand, commanding silence.

"Show us the cube and the girl."

Nephilimbug stepped forward and offered the cube with careful hands. Ute hesitated before taking it, then passed it around the circle. One by one, each leader prodded, shook, and inspected the object. The cube remained still, as Nephilimbug knew it would.

"My lords," he said evenly, "the cube cannot be activated without its rightful bearer. The girl."

"Then where is she? Bring her here to activate it."

Nephilimbug bowed his head. "If we bring her here, she will destroy everything. Her power, once awakened, will not distinguish friend from foe."

"Explain this claim," Ute said.

"We cannot allow her to activate the cube while in our presence. The risk is too great. Instead, we'll persuade her to reveal the code she uses. Only then can we control the artifact."

"And how do you propose we do that?"

"I'm studying her nature, searching for weaknesses we can exploit. In time, she will trust me. When she does, she will divulge the secret and become our most powerful weapon."

He raised one hand, summoning a flickering screen into existence. Tiff appeared on it, curled in a corner, trembling.

"She appears harmless. Like her mother."

A low murmur moved through the room.

"Her mother?" Nephilimbug's voice sharpened.

"Yes," Ute answered. "After she killed your father, we captured her. We believed she possessed the cube, but she did not. She resisted conversion to our way of life. Useless to us, we cast her into a place of eternal uncertainty. But somehow, she escaped into a new timeline. Only recently did we learn her location. She will be captured again and obliterated this time."

"And the daughter?" one of the council members asked. "Are you sure she holds the power?"

"Yes, my lord. She is the one."

"With our latest Visio-technology, we can access her mind directly. Bring her here. Let us extract what we want."

Nephilimbug's brow furrowed. "Visio-technology could damage her mind beyond repair. I ask for time to train her myself. I swear on my father's life that I will complete this mission."

The chamber fell silent. Whispers rippled between the council members until Ute raised his hand again.

"The council has reached a decision. You will be granted this opportunity. But if you fail, you return the girl to us and forfeit your new rank. Today, however, you will be honored for your success. You are now promoted to level four."

A fresh wave of cheers erupted. Nephilimbug bowed low.

The celebration that followed was a haze of intoxicated laughter and indulgence. Once the others were asleep or too drunk to notice, Nephilimbug slipped away to the archive room. His new rank granted him access to higher-level documents, and he scanned them with cold precision. But even as he worked, his mind drifted to Tiff.

Clutching the newly retrieved files, he retreated to the deepest shadows of the vault, already forming the next phase of his plan.

Chapter 48
Bait

Tiff slowly regained consciousness, aware of a soft surface beneath her. Upon opening her eyes, she found herself in a bedroom adorned with ornate decorations. Gone were her jeans and T-shirt, replaced by a flowing white satin dress and matching slippers.

She sat up carefully, wincing at the ache in her body. The beating she had endured left its mark. Gingerly, she reached for her pendant. It was gone. A hollow ache spread through her. The pendant had been more than a keepsake—it was a tether to her mother, her past, and the power she'd only begun to understand.

Swinging her legs over the side of the massive bed, Tiff stood on unsteady feet. She made her way to the door and tried the handle. Locked. She looked around for windows, but there weren't any. Tiff searched the room from top to bottom, looking for anything she could use to escape or defend herself. The ornate furniture offered no help.

She hammered at the unyielding walls in desperation. In a fit of frustration, she seized a golden candlestick and hurled it at the door. The candlestick warped upon impact, yet the stubborn door stood unmoved. She had to find a way out. Tiff refused to give up after coming so far. She would keep fighting, no matter what the cost.

A meal had been left on a dresser—bread, roast chicken, potatoes, and greens. After days of sparse vegetarian fare at the lodge, it was tempting. But Tiff ignored the plate of food, unwilling to accept anything from her captor.

Exhausted, Tiff sank onto the lush carpet. "Let me out of here!" she said repeatedly until her voice grew hoarse.

Not sure if it was night or day, an icy knot of fear settled in her stomach. As the candles burned down, she had never felt more alone and afraid. But she refused to give in to despair. The light continued to dim, only making her feel more desolated. She had no idea how long she had been there.

Tiff's thoughts turned to Ari. Had he managed to escape when she was captured? Was he out there somewhere, trying to find and rescue her? She hoped with all her heart that he was safe. Tiff clung to the belief that Ari was plotting her deliverance at this very moment. He wouldn't abandon her to this fate. She had to endure a little longer.

The room grew steadily darker as the candles burned down. Soon, Tiff could barely see her own hands in front of her face. She strained her ears for any sound—footsteps in the hall, voices, anything—but she was enveloped in silence.

Time itself stood still. Seconds stretched into minutes, which in turn stretched into hours. The blackness was absolute. Tiff had no way to gauge the passage of time.

Tiff's body curled up on the floor. She fought against the panic rising within her. She focused on her breathing, picturing a bright light surrounding her. She would not give in to fear. Finally, Tiff drifted into an exhausted, troubled sleep.

Nephilimbug's voice boomed through the darkness and abruptly jolted Tiff from her fitful sleep. "Let me show you what you could have if you joined my Order."

With a sudden jolt, Tiff gasped and was back in the suffocating dark, her body curled on the cold floor. She blinked, disoriented, then felt herself rising again—not physically, but as if being pulled into a dream. Before Tiff could react, she felt herself floating up, right through the ceiling of the room.

Blinking in the sudden light, she found herself face to face with Nephilimbug. He was dressed in an elegant 18th-century suit as if they were about to attend a grand ball. The gown she wore was a deep emerald green, with intricate beading and jeweled embellishments adorning every inch of fabric. It hugged her figure perfectly, reflecting the flickering candlelight with each movement.

They found themselves in an opulent palace hall, where elegantly attired lords and ladies were dancing to the strains of classical music. It dawned on Tiff that they were in 18th-century Paris.

She had no time to take it in before Nephilimbug swept her into the dance, twirling her around the floor. His drab, ominous features had transformed into those of a handsome prince.

The scene shifted, and Tiff became the wife of a wealthy oil baron in 19th-century Texas, dripping in diamonds and silk. Nephilimbug grinned at her side, playing the dutiful husband.

The transitions continued. Each era more extravagant. Suddenly, she found herself back at Wheatfield High, perched at the cafeteria table designated for the in-crowd. Her appearance was startling to her: sleek, straight hair, artful makeup, oversized hoop earrings, and a heart tattoo peeking above her chest emblazoned with 'Coop.' She was clad in designer denim, a stylish top, and a chic purse.

Everyone was hanging on to every word she uttered. Others ran to get anything she wanted. The scene rapidly changed to her driving the jeep she always wanted and arriving at the farm. The house no longer looked old and worn. It was renovated to be more exquisite. She watched as her father issued orders to several workers. Tiff wanted to call out to her father. Chip stopped and cocked his head, looking into space.

"Chip, Chip," she called out. He started barking.

She yearned to be home so badly. But something inside her recoiled. It was all too perfect. Too staged. With a flash, she was back in the dark room where her ordeal began.

"You can have all of this. It's yours. Look how happy and prosperous your father looks. Are you going to deny him this after he has worked so long and hard for you? Don't be selfish."

Tiff cried. She wanted so much to help her father live a better life. Her mind raced with thoughts of giving in to his wishes and escaping jail. But would he let her go? Could she trust him? Then she remembered he wanted her to be his bride. Revulsion steadied her. Tiff began to wake up, breaking through the deception.

Nephilimbug's charming facade melted away, leaving his true, sinister face leering down at her.

"All this and more could be yours," he scoffed, "if you join the dark forces and tell me how to activate the cube. What has the Light done for you? Nothing."

Tiff trembled but stood firm. "Never," she declared. "I will never join you."

Tiff's head spun as she tried to process everything she

had experienced. The opulent scenes Nephilimbug had shown her were tempting but hollow. She thought of her faithful friends—her mom and dad, Coop, and Ari. They were what mattered.

Bracing herself, she glared at Nephilimbug. "No! Let me go."

She tried to summon her light weapon, focusing all her energy. But nothing happened. Why wouldn't her powers work?

Nephilimbug laughed. "There will be no escape. Maybe a companion would lift your spirits."

Titanu, in Emma's body, entered the room. The sparkle and innocence in her eyes were gone.

"Please, Tiff, tell him, or he's going to hurt or even kill both of us," she pleaded.

Tiff shook her head. "Cut the act; you aren't Emma. Who are you?"

Shocked, Titanu changed into her Japanese form.

"Let's not play around anymore; tell me the code or?"

"Or what?"

Tiff and Titanu glared at each other, waiting for the other to make a move.

"I should have let them destroy you in the vault. But Nephilimbug forbade it," Titanu hissed. Jealousy twisted her expression. Her body coiled to strike.

Titanu snarled and lunged forward, striking first. Tiff reacted swiftly, pivoting just in time to avoid the blow and drive a solid punch to Titanu's chest. The impact surged through Tiff's arm, her energies igniting with adrenaline. Titanu's foul breath washed over her, and sharp nails grazed her skin as she recoiled.

As Titanu prepared to strike again, Nephilimbug stepped between them and shoved her back.

"Enough. The mission comes first," he said, his voice cold and commanding.

Titanu hesitated, fury burning in her eyes. But something deeper flickered—a flash of fear or bruised pride. Under Nephilimbug's withering gaze, she turned and swept out of the room in a storm of rage and frustration.

Chapter 49
Threats

Tiff tried to slip out the door with Titanu, but it slammed shut in her face. Sliding down the wall to the floor, she felt a swell of panic. She had to get out of there. "Where are you, Ari?" she called out silently.

Instead, Nephilimbug reappeared. He had the physical body of an extremely handsome young man and said, "I have an offer for you."

"I don't want anything from you."

"I think you might change your mind when you hear—or I should say see—what I have to offer you."

"What do you want in return?" Tiff sneered at him.

"I want you to show me how to activate the cube, then destroy the Order of the Black Shadow."

"You want to kill your people?"

"I'm half Earthling and want to find my mother's people and live with them."

"I don't believe you. Do you think I'm stupid?"

"No. I think you're brilliant—and ambitious. Once you and I destroy the Order by banishing them to the outer edges of the Cosmos, your people will hail you as the greatest warrior ever. The Light will rule on Earth."

"And you'll be King, I guess?"

"King of the Universe, why not? All I desire is a Queen worthy of standing beside me."

"Emma is available. Besides, I prefer a partner whose behavior and presence are consistent, not someone who hijacks a body and shuts down a mind."

"As I told you, I'm part Earthling. I took after my mother, and for that reason, the Order has always disliked me because I have something most of them want: a human body to live in the third dimension. I can switch between the two bodies or, for a short time, become a walk-in."

"What is a walk-in?"

"I take over the consciousness of a human being."

"Where does their consciousness go?"

"It's still there, but it's mostly trying to push me out, sort of like your friend Ari tried to do."

"What do you mean?"

"It was me you were talking to in the forest when you were going to run away from the lodge. Ari was hovering above us, but there was nothing he could do."

Tiff jumped up and attacked Nephilimbug, screaming, "What did you do to Ari?"

Nephilimbug felt the blow. "Chill, he managed to knock me out of his physical vehicle and lock me out for good. Watch this." He flicked his wrist, and an image appeared before them.

The woman and man sat at a polished wooden table surrounded by large windows that displayed the tropical landscape outside. The vibrant green plants and bright flowers added a splash of color to the otherwise modern and sleek interior of their home. The man's dark hair was perfectly styled, and the woman's brown curls cascaded down her shoulders. They were a picture-perfect couple. Tiff didn't recognize them.

Ava Pepper was renowned for her achievements as an astronaut and astrophysicist. Tiff was confused as to why Nephilimbug had shown her these individuals. "That wasn't enough for you?" Nephilimbug snapped his fingers again, and the screen shimmered, now revealing an archive window filled with rotating glyphs. However, her question was answered when she found herself face-to-face with Ava, sitting across from her. Though Ava and her husband couldn't see Tiff, she could both see and hear them perfectly.

"I know it's uncomfortable for you when I bring this up, but it happens all the time." Ava glanced at her husband, hoping he would understand the gravity of the situation.

"I don't want to keep you from sharing these moments with me. I want to make sure that you understand their reality. Remember, after your last trip to space, the doctors gave you a perfect score on all of your psychological and physical exams."

"Why do I have this feeling that someone is watching me and trying to reach out to me in my dreams, and when I'm awake? I can sense a presence with me." Tiff's eyes widened, and she let out an audible gasp. "Did you hear that?" She covered her ears with her hands. Her husband got up from his seat and wrapped his arms around her in a comforting gesture.

"You should rest, Ava."

She replied with equal fear, "But I'm scared."

"I insist. Get some rest. Sometimes, you even talk in your sleep."

"What do I say?"

"One night, you sat up and whispered, 'Mommy's

pretty baby girl.' You called her by a name. I think it began with a T—Tiny, Tammy, no wait, Tisa."

Tiff screamed, desperately yelling to breach the barrier that stood between her and Ava. But Nephilimbug intervened and shut down the screen.

Tiff paced back and forth in the room, glaring at Nephilimbug as she said in frustration, "How do I even know if any of this is real? It could be another one of your illusions."

"You wanted to find your mother. There she is, trying to make sense of the dilemma she's in. You can free her consciousness from that earthly being and come back to be your mom. I'll help you."

"I don't believe you."

Nephilimbug prayed that he wouldn't have to resort to what was about to come. He had already disobeyed multiple laws of the Order, but a few more wouldn't make much difference at this point. He flicked his wrist, and the screen displayed an archive file filled with symbols that told the story of Sarah's journey.

"I don't understand these symbols," Tiff said, frustration rising with each moment.

Tiff's eyes followed the symbols until they transformed into recognizable English words. As she read, tears streamed down her cheeks.

The entity known as Sarah Lotterland has been under our observation for countless lifetimes. She has risen to become a devoted member of the Order of L.V.X., and we have learned that, with guidance from her mentors, she has created a version of the ancient cosmology cube using magic.

Our strategy to entice the luminous entity into the crop circle gateway proved successful on numerous occasions.

She possessed an insatiable curiosity about the universe, portals, and the inner workings of things.

However, she did not possess the cube and fought fiercely, even managing to kill one of the highest gods, Ninantu. As punishment, she was banished to the far corners of the universe. She escaped to a different timeline, where she now lives under the veil of forgetfulness. However, due to a strange concept called love, her daughter's constant yearning for her has begun to stir her awakening. When she fully wakes and emerges from that timeline, we'll have our chance to complete what we started.

"No," Tiff screamed. "What timeline is she in?" She turned to Nephilimbug, desperation in her eyes.

"Tell me how to activate the cube, and then I will tell you what you want to know," he said, his voice dripping with a sinister promise.

"At least tell me how your Order captured her?"

"She decided she couldn't resist one last trip through the crop circle portal before it closed for good. It was there that my father and his soldiers encountered her, and she killed them all. The Order sent many troops to capture her as she traveled through the universe. They did, and you read what happened. I will give you time to consider my proposal: join me or face the consequences of the Order. They can't destroy your consciousness, but they will fry your brain—the mechanism Earthlings use for consciousness to function."

Tiff clenched her fists. Her head throbbed, but not from fear—from fury. If they wanted her to break, it would take more than threats.

Chapter 50
Life IS But A Dream

Closing her eyes, Tiff breathed deeply, seeking inner peace. She reflected on her training with Mary. *Keep your frequency high, and the darkness cannot touch you.* She had attempted several times to do exactly that, but nothing happened. Tiff continued to tell herself to go within, go within; after several minutes, she heard a soft but distinct voice say, "You can do it."

She pictured herself enveloped in pure white light. Warmth flowed through her, driving back the oppressive gloom. Tiff centered herself in the light.

A glow flickered in the distance, small at first, then growing stronger. Tiff recognized it as the luminous being who had saved her when a creature attacked her in the wheat field. The gentle luminescence filled the space, casting a warm, ethereal glow. Its light was a beacon to her. She fought with all her willpower not to surrender to sleep by focusing on the many ways the Being had appeared to her, sometimes as a child, a woman, or even an animal.

Nephilimbug's visage still appeared, lurking in the

shadows, trying to unsettle her. But the light always prevailed, dissolving his specter into smoke.

Through a slow shimmer of golden light, a figure materialized, serene and radiant. Tiff blinked several times as she beheld the being before her, robed in iridescent garments that shimmered with a light that seemed to come from within. As an ancient connection stirred within her soul, she recognized the timeless companion who had journeyed beside her through countless lifetimes.

"Peace be upon you, Tiff," the Being said, the voice a harmonious blend of kindness and authority, one that she recognized—the Teacher, whom she affectionately called Papa.

Overwhelmed by a mixture of reverence and profound recognition, Tiff's voice trembled with emotion as she managed to speak.

"The dark force holds me captive, demanding the cube's code, and refuses to reveal where my mother's consciousness in this lifetime resides in this timeline."

"Go within; your soul knows who you are and what to do," the Teacher gently advised.

Tiff nodded, tears of relief and understanding brimming in her eyes. "But can't you guide me more directly?" she implored.

"You possess free will. I cannot interfere with your choices," the Teacher reminded her. "Doubt and uncertainty are fertile ground for profound growth. Embrace them."

Tiff's voice edged with desperation. "If you can't help me, I fear I may succumb to the darkness."

"Remember, your journey is yours. Each challenge, each moment of enlightenment or confusion, weaves the rich tapestry of your soul's evolution. Your soul chose your struggles to unlock its full potential," the Teacher explained, his presence enveloping Tiff in a calming aura.

Their exchange unfolded like a sacred river, flowing through truths of existence, divine nature, and the interconnectedness of all life. Her heart expanded, and her spirit opened to the wisdom being revealed.

With those final words, the Teacher vanished, leaving behind a lingering presence that filled Tiff with a newfound sense of purpose and peace. She knew that her journey was far from over, but with the Teacher's visit, she felt equipped to face the winding road ahead with courage and hope.

In a meditative position, Tiff considered her life and how similar it was to her mother's. She thought about what her mother had done and knew what she had to do now.

For a second, she forgot where she was. Tiff sat in the dark until she heard Nephilimbug's hissing. He was back. She ignored him, sinking deeper into meditation.

"It's time. Tell me how to activate the cube, or both you and your friend will suffer." Nephilimbug held up the cube. "Then, I will pursue your mother and personally return her to the Order. I will make sure you stay around long enough to meet her before expulsion."

Ignoring Nephilim, Tiff focused inward, visualizing a cocoon of white light surrounding her. The light emanated from deep within, flowing through every cell of her body. She repeated the mantra, "I'm one with the light. The light protects me."

Tiff stared at the cube in Nephilimbug's hand. At that instant, it flew to her, and as she grasped it, a memory stirred — not from this life, but from countless others. An ageless knowing rose within her, clear and undeniable. *"Yet I carry the darkness too, not to destroy it, but to bring it into harmony with the light."*

Nephilimbug's taunts and threats seemed distant. She was untouched in her sanctuary. The light continued to grow, expanding outward and mingling with the shadows until they curved around the cube, like yin and yang. Tiff stared at its harmonizing field, alive with energy.

Nephilimbug shrieked as the cube vibrated, shooting off red-hot energy. What he feared had come true. She had awakened to her powers. Nephilimbug tried to flee but was halted by an invisible barrier that penetrated his mind, searching for Sarah's whereabouts. "No!" he cried.

Tiff allowed the light to flow freely, keeping her strong and steady. She imagined it filling the room, leaving no space for darkness to reign alone. Nephilimbug writhed in agony, still thrashing to escape her grasp. He weakly cried out for help.

Emma appeared but quickly vanished, as the light was too intense for her to bear. She hurried to inform the Order of what was happening.

Courage filled Tiff as she visualized the light breaking down the barriers that had kept her trapped. Then came a tremor, a distant rumbling. The walls shook around her.

With a brilliant flash of harmonic light emanating from her, the dark chamber trembled. Tiff's body radiated a blinding light that filled the room, driving back the shadows and causing the structure around her to shudder and crack. Nephilimbug, overwhelmed by the intensity of her power, staggered back, his form dissolving into the encroaching brightness.

The rumbling grew louder and closer. Dust and debris sprinkled down from the ceiling. Tiff stood poised. With a loud crash, the door blasted outward. Tiff shielded her face from the splintered wood. Squinting through the dust, she saw a familiar form silhouetted in the doorway.

"Tiff," Ari yelled as he rushed into the now crumbling

vault, his voice filled with awe and relief at the sight of her glowing figure. Thunder clapped again, and more debris fell, and both jumped.

"Yes, let's get out of here," Tiff responded, her voice steady and commanding. Her light was still flaring around her as the walls began to collapse.

"We don't have much time," Ari said, recognizing the danger as the vault's structure gave way under the force of Tiff's unleashed power. Together, they raced through the disintegrating tunnel, dodging falling debris—an escape made possible by Tiff's monumental release of energy.

As they emerged into the open air, the vault behind them collapsed, leaving no trace of the dark hold it once had. Tiff, looking back at the rubble, felt a profound sense of closure and freedom, knowing it was her inner light that had led them to safety.

"I was so worried about you. Where were you?" she asked.

"I was trying to find you, but I had to shut down my light body so that Nephilimbug couldn't detect me with his Visioscope goggles. I hid in the shadows, like he would have done," he said, handing the backpack to her.

Tiff looked in and saw her mom's diary. She added the cube to it. "Thank you."

They looked into each other's eyes as eons passed before them.

"It's you," she said.

"Until our souls meet again."

"Your friends are waiting for you," a voice behind her said. Tiff turned and looked into Officer Porter's smiling face.

She turned to get Ari's reaction, and he was gone, like everything else.

Tiff heard her name being called, and it got louder and louder. She ran toward the sound.

Tiff halted in a small opening amidst the trees. Coop, Rachel, and Harvey stood there, their eyes fixed on her. She raced towards them and into Coop's waiting arms.

"I'm relieved nothing happened to you and that you're safe," she expressed as she squeezed him, her lips grazing his in a brief kiss. *This is how it's supposed to be on this timeline,* she thought.

Coop's furrowed brow and intense gaze questioned her, his concern evident. "The portal opened again, and we got out to get you. But you were gone. Where were you?"

"Didn't you see the map with the note on it?"

"What map?"

"I—I," Tiff couldn't answer.

As several crows flew towards them, Tiff closed her eyes and focused on the fire inside her. She directed the flames toward the crows. She then summoned her sword, which instantly appeared in her hand, and used it to defeat the one circling her. Tiff didn't see this as showing off or being prideful. She was saving her friends.

Unable to contain himself, Coop said, "Cool, that's my girl."

Rachel looked at Harvey and said, "I knew it. She is the one."

Harvey asked, "The One?"

"Yeah, the enlightened one, to lead the young souls who are waking up. The dark forces will come after them to stop their ascension. A war is coming."

"What about me and the rest of us, old souls?"

"That's what you have me for."

"You think she will find Sarah?"

"She already has."

They all heard and saw it at the same time. A portal

opened up. Tiff grabbed Coop's hand and motioned for the others to follow as she leaped through the gateway, singing:

Row, row, row your boat, gently down the stream.
Merrily, merrily, merrily, life is but a dream.

Nephilimbug lay on the ground, unable to open his eyes. He saw Earthlings moving about a bonfire and then heard Ute's voice.

"Did you think you could deceive us, Crossbreed? We knew all along your love for the Earthlings and desire to find your Earth family. Titanu was assigned not only to help you on your mission, but also to keep us informed of your activities."

"No, you don't understand."

"Oh, but we do. Because you have lost the cube and the girl, you have been demoted and exiled to Earth, where you will no longer be an immortal being with powers. Instead, we will allow you to remember who you once were while you listen to the constant babble of the consciousness you replaced in that feeble body. However, prove to us that you can be an asset in the coming war, and we will consider restoring your powers and rank."

"Don't discard me!"

But all he heard was a voice—not his own—screaming from inside of him, *help.*

Nephilimbug saw a woman walking towards him and heard her call out to him, "L.R., what are you doing all alone out here? Come and join the group," Maddie demanded.

Nephilimbug gazed at his new body and joined the voice inside of him, hollering, "Help."

Book Review

Did the cube speak to you?
If you felt the magic, mystery, or meaning in these pages, I'd be honored if you shared your experience. Leaving a review is like weaving a thread into the tapestry of this story—and lighting a beacon for fellow seekers who are searching for their own path.
You can share your thoughts on:

• amazon.com/jjmichaelauthor
• goodreads.com/jjmichaelauthor
• instagram.com/jjmichael
• X (formerly Twitter) - twitter.com/June Michael
• facebook.com/jjmichael.author

Even a few words can ripple through the ether and make a difference.
Thank you for being part of the journey.
Stay curious. Stay luminous.

About the Author

J.J. Michael writes stories that pull back the veil on reality. She weaves together storytelling and spiritual reflection to illuminate the hidden forces shaping our lives. Her visionary fiction invites readers to awaken their inner light and explore the deeper mysteries of consciousness. At the same time, her nonfiction offers practical tools for unlocking personal power and navigating life's path with intention.

Based in Washington, D.C., J.J. is an intuitive numerologist, tarot reader, blogger, and Chios Master Healer. She's also an ordained priestess of the Order of Melchizedek and the CEO of Path to Truth Press, a publishing house dedicated to spiritual awakening and self-discovery. With a background in library science and research, she blends ancient wisdom with grounded knowledge to guide seekers toward clarity and transformation.

A proud member of International Thriller Writers and the Builders of the Adytum, her work continues to inspire readers across generations and belief systems.

Books by J.J. Michael

Life is Never as It Seems

It's Not Over Yet

Five Days of Darkness

Secrets and Serpents

Awakening the Spirit

Awakening the Spirit Journal: 31 Days to Inner Peace and Growth

Connect with J.J. Michael:

twitter.com/June Michael
facebook.com/jjmichael.author
LinkedIn.com/in/jjmichael
www.pathtotruth.com
www.jjmichael.com
instagram.com/jjmichael